W9-DCZ-027

Also by Robert Rosenberg

Avram Cohen Mysteries

HOUSE OF GUILT
THE CUTTING ROOM
CRIMES OF THE CITY

Nonfiction

SECRET SOLDIER

AN ACCIDENTAL MURDER

■ ■ ■

An Avram Cohen Mystery

ROBERT ROSENBERG

HIGHLAND PARK PUBLIC LIBRARY

SCRIBNER

SCRIBNER
Rockefeller Center
1230 Avenue of the Americas
New York, NY 10020

This book is a work of fiction. Names, characters, places, and incidents either are products of the author's imagination or are used fictitiously. Any resemblance to actual events or locales or person, living or dead, is entirely coincidental.

Copyright © 1999 by Robert Rosenberg
All rights reserved,
including the right of reproduction
in whole of in part in any form.

SCRIBNER and design are trademarks of Macmillan Library Research USA, Inc. under license by Simon & Schuster, the publisher of this work.

Designed by Erich Hobbing
Set in Garamond

Manufactured in the United States of America

10 9 8 7 6 5 4 3 2 1

Library of Congress Cataloging-In-Publication Data is available

ISBN: 0-7432-4416-8

For information regarding the special discounts for bulk purchases, please contact Simon Schuster Special Sales at 1-800-456-6798 or business@simonandschuster.com

For all my friends and family,
but mostly for Silvia and Amber.
By keeping faith with me
they kept the faith with Cohen.

Cast of Characters

(In order of appearance)

Benny Lassman—journalist turned author, he translated Avram Cohen's book

Tina Andrews—Cohen's literary agent

Carey McClosky—Cohen's editor at TMC Publications

Ahuva Meyerson—Cohen's lover

Herman Broder—Cohen's friend from Dachau

Ephraim Laskoff—Cohen's banker

Herbert Wang—CEO of TMC publishing

Mr. Smitbauer—CEO of Koethe, Cohen's German publisher

Kristina Scheller—Cohen's editor at Koethe

Frank Kaplan—veteran best-selling author and supporter of right-wing causes in Israel

Francine—Kaplan's nurse/escort

Marina Berendisi—a chambermaid in the hotel

Mathis—security officer at Frankfurt hotel

Helmut Leterhaus—Frankfurt police officer

Leon Hadani and Avi Hakatan—Jerusalem underworld figures

Shimmy Rozen and Vered Rozen—Jerusalem underworld figures

Nissim Levy—Southern District Police Command Intelligence commander, a former assistant to Cohen in the Israeli police

Hagit Levy—Nissim's wife

Michael "Misha" Shvilli—a former assistant to Cohen in the Israeli police

District Commander Ya'acov Bendor—Southern District commander, Israeli police

Yoheved "Jacki" Ginsburg—assistant to Nissim Levy

Phillipe "The Beast" Bensione—news photographer

Rafi Uzan—mayor of Yeroham, a desert town

Shula—school principal in Yeroham, Hagit Levy's boss

Boris Yuhewitz—Russian mobster

Shuki Caspi—senior officer in the Southern District police command

Kobi Alper—Israeli gangster

Nahum Nahmani and Buki Abutbul—not-so-innocent victims of Kobi Alper

Yvgeny Yudelstein—Russian mobster judge

Alex Wikoff—Russian mobster

Raoul Kochinski—Israeli police pathologist

Rose—Ephraim Laskoff's secretary

Pinhas "Pinny" Shimoni—Eilat hotel security guard

Meshulam Yaffe—Special assistant to the police minister

Shaul Machnes—member of Knesset

Yossi—a Tel Aviv pimp

Sonia—a Tel Aviv madame in a bordello

Haim—a Tel Aviv pimp

Andrei—muscle at the bordello

Vlad Zagorsky/Lev Lerner—pseudonyms for Russian mobster

CAST OF CHARACTERS

Masha and Yevet Karlinsky—Russian-Jewish dissident couple of the 1970s

Shmulik—senior Shabak (security services) officer, now retired

Maya Bernstein—daughter of a Jerusalem rape victim

Itzik Alper—Kobi Alper's brother

Rafi Peri—Jerusalem hotel security officer

Yosef and Gregory—Russian mob muscle

AN
ACCIDENTAL
MURDER

■ ■ ■

· 1 ·

Of all his many regrets, it was his decision to write his memoirs that Avram Cohen now regretted the most because for the first time in a long time, there was someone he would have liked to have killed.

Actually, a whole group of people. Agents. Publishers. Journalists. Especially journalists. Particularly Benny Lassman. Many others might have agreed with Cohen. Cohen blamed himself, of course. He never should have given the manuscript to Lassman.

When he began, the writing had been an experiment, just a way of learning how a computer worked, specifically the word processor that came with the machine. It all began as an exercise. He had written a few paragraphs, which became a few more pages, and then as his fingers learned to fly faster over the keyboard and he had begun to hear his own voice telling the story, the writing had become cathartic, almost visceral, the release of something long denied. So by the time he had reached the telling of his years in Jerusalem as chief of criminal investigations, he had decided that he *was* trying to write a book. Or was it a book—of that he wasn't sure.

Over the years he had met several of Jerusalem's most famous authors, under circumstances that included returning stolen property to a longtime contender for the Nobel Prize, breaking up fistfights between a pair of best-selling authors in a rivalry that had its origins in the different undergrounds they had joined as teenagers during the British mandate in Palestine, and once, under orders, letting a magazine writer spend a week as Cohen's shadow for a profile of "the top detective in Jerusalem."

None of the authors had really trusted Cohen—he was, after all, a policeman, who observed too much. "Nice, nice," they had all said, each in his own way, when Cohen had taken his manuscript around to ask their opinion. "But it needs work." And none had volunteered to help.

The poet had been impressed with the quantity of words; the historian had said it was anecdotal, though it did show the connection between Cohen's life and the larger forces of the times he saw. The novelist had suggested there were copy editors who could help him with the grammar, "and add some color, some spice."

Nonetheless, by the time he had called Lassman he had decided that if Benny didn't offer help, he'd shelve the whole project. Of all the journalists in Jerusalem, Benny Lassman was the one he came closest to trusting, certainly the one whose articles best reflected Cohen's work as CID chief. Now Lassman was writing books himself. His book on the effects of the Intifada on the Israeli military had won him more foreign acclaim than local, but that was a result of the politics of envy. Cohen liked Lassman's book because it was nearer to the truth than the reports in the newspapers.

Lassman had been surprised by the call from Cohen, who was famous for keeping to himself, especially after an inheritance that overnight had made him wealthy. But when Cohen had explained what he wanted, Lassman had been both flattered and curious. No problem, he promised. He didn't say that if he liked the manuscript, he'd translate a few chapters and send them to his agent,

Tina Andrews. Cohen didn't ask for that. But that's what happened.

She had called late one summer night to tell Cohen that TMC Publications, a media giant that bought and sold books, movies, records, TV shows, and multimedia CD-ROMs, was offering a million dollars for the North American rights.

"I've got Carey McCloskey on the other line. What should I tell him?"

"Who?"

"He's the editor at TMC."

"Will he help make the book better?" Cohen had wanted to know.

"Of course," she had promised. "But maybe I can get more. I'm still waiting to hear from . . ."

Cohen had interrupted. "Will he help make the book better?"

"He's very ambitious. And young. He'll work around the clock for the book if he thinks it can be big. And he does."

"If he'll help make the book better, that's all I care about," Cohen had said.

"Then we have a deal. Great."

A few minutes later, they had all been back on the phone together in a conference call. It had begun with a young man's voice saying, "I loved it. Loved it. Despite everything, your struggle with your own conscience even in the face of pure evil comes through as authentic."

"I am not really a writer," said Cohen.

"Well, I understand that you did get some help from . . ." McCloskey paused, not remembering the name. Cohen meanwhile was having a difficult time with the pronunciation of McCloskey.

"Benny Lassman," said Tina.

"Right," said the editor. "Lassman. Yes, well, it needs

17

work. More color, perhaps, fix the rhythm with some careful cuts, and I think," the editor paused for effect, "we'll have a big book."

At the time, Cohen had thought the editor meant a physically oversize coffee table–type book, and was worried that he meant pictures. He did not like to be photographed, and kept no personal albums of photos. Of course, the veteran wire services working Jerusalem and local newspaper archives had his picture. But other than the mug shots, "killer photos" in local slang, which appeared on his various identity cards, he owned only two photographs that he cherished. One was the black-and-white wedding picture from 1968, when his hair was still black and his equally young bride's face optimistic. Four months later, she was dead. He visited her grave once a year on their anniversary. But every time he opened his desktop drawer, he saw that photo. The other showed him with Ahuva Meyerson, the woman who had been a special part of his life since her first week as the youngest judge in Israel. She was a legal prodigy who had given up an academic career for the bench. Both had felt the attraction from that first time they had set eyes on each other, and within a few weeks Cohen had found plenty of reasons to go by the courthouse to observe a proceeding or testify in a case, and, of course, to guarantee they'd meet again, and again.

They kept the relationship secret for nearly ten years, and even after he was forced to retire, they kept it discreet. By the time the gossip columnists figured out what was going on, observing Cohen and Ahuva appearing together in public on rare but significant occasions, Cohen was rich and Ahuva, twenty years Cohen's junior, was deputy president of the Tel Aviv District Court, on her way to the Supreme Court.

His picture of him and Ahuva was recent, taken on a trip to a tiny Greek island where they had spent a month that summer, the first vacation Cohen had ever enjoyed. The Greek housekeeper who took care of the little house they rented took the picture of them on the patio. The happy couple, against the blue backgrounds of sky and sea, stood smiling in the wooden frame on his desk.

So Cohen had protested, "no, no pictures," when McCloskey explained, but Tina told Cohen that whenever possible, autobiographies should include photographs.

"We'll need some publicity shots," said McCloskey, "and maybe we'll get someone to shoot some video we can use for a commercial and to pitch you to TV shows in the U.S. Then when you're here, we'll have some more taken . . ."

"Can't the book speak for me?" Cohen asked. For that was what he believed a book should do, especially an auto-biography, a memoir, written to pass on a lesson. If the book worked, it was self-explanatory, he figured. "Why interviews? And why do I have to go to America? Why can't the book speak for me?" he repeated.

"Avram?" asked McCloskey, "I can call you Avram?" Despite the combination of the phone speaker and long-distance connection disembodying the voice, McCloskey's voice suddenly seemed cooler, just a notch or two, but enough for the old detective's trained ear to catch the patronizing tone.

"Cohen is okay," he said.

"To make your book famous, we have to make you famous, Avram."

"That's the way it works," Tina confirmed.

"The way things work," McCloskey repeated.

Thus it began. The Americans commissioned Lassman, who had done the translation and initial editing before sending the manuscript to Tina, to research the archives. Lassman's ten percent of royalties grew to twelve and a half, so he didn't mind searching for photos of the retired detective. He found more than forty, mostly in newspaper archives, going all the way back to the passport-size official police portrait taken when Cohen was appointed to deputy CID chief. But the Americans wanted more. Reluctantly, Cohen found himself in the studio of a Jerusalem photographer he once used as a witness in a drug case. But the portraits were not good enough for Carey McCloskey.

A New York photographer so famous even Cohen had heard of her was dispatched to Jerusalem. She insisted on spending from morning to night with the old detective, wanting him to take her around the city to favorite haunts and scenes of crimes he wrote about in his book. Cohen demurred at that. In tiny Jerusalem word traveled fast, and Cohen preferred that, at least until it was published, the book remain a secret. The last thing he needed was word going out that he was getting his portrait taken. It would start the gossip. "Just in case," Cohen told McCloskey, who called annoyed at Cohen's lack of cooperation, "I want to keep the book secret until it's out."

"In case of what?"

"Who knows? Maybe you will change your mind."

"Nonsense," said the editor. "I've got sales excited about this project. No way this is going to coitus interruptus."

"I'd just prefer it remain secret until it's done," Cohen said. "Printed. In my hand."

McCloskey's enthusiasm for the project cooled another five degrees. The situation that puzzled everyone in publishing was that Cohen wasn't interested in money. He would cooperate with McCloskey to improve the writing, the story, the telling, the explanation. But Cohen showed no interest in the marketing. "You do what you have to do," he told Tina, "and I'll do what I can."

When Tina began pitching the book to German publishers, she suggested—with Lassman stuck in the middle, understanding Cohen's sensitivities, appreciating the PR value of Tina's idea—that Cohen might want to look up his birthplace in Berlin, or even travel to Munich for a memorial visit to Dachau, and add a chapter.

Cohen didn't get angry. He just said softly, "It's as if you didn't even read my book," and from then on, Tina was much more careful about what she suggested to him, while Cohen realized that Lassman, for all his work as a translator, editor, and intermediary between Cohen's semihermitage in Jerusalem's German colony and the strange and different world Tina and McCloskey and the photographer represented, didn't really understand.

Tina tried not to worry. "The fact TMC paid a million made it a lot easier to bring the Germans on board. And with them, we can get the Japanese and the English and probably the French . . ." And Cohen, who had been enjoying a certain euphoria since the day Lassman had called excitedly to say that Tina Andrews loved his chapters, finally began to realize that he was in over his head.

· 2 ·

"This is not about state secrets or personal secrets," the book began. "It is about what I saw and what I did, what I thought and what I felt, during the last half of the twentieth century."

He wrote about the camps and about vengeance, about personal survival and Jerusalem's survival. But he glared down those few questioners who managed to break through the perimeters of his solitude—including the video crew Carey McCloskey sent, as promised—who dared ask about Cohen's love life, or whether the book's sale had changed his lifestyle. And just like the inheritance, which despite all his efforts was changing him, so did the book make him change. He would not go to America but he would go to Frankfurt, after all.

Ahuva thought he should go. She lived now in Tel Aviv, after being appointed deputy to the president of the Tel Aviv District Court, a promotion that put her on course for a seat on the Supreme Court.

"You made the bed, you've got to sleep in it," she pointed out, when he said that he was having second thoughts about the whole project. "It's too late now to change your mind. You wrote the book. You let the agent sell it. You signed the contracts."

"They pressured me," he complained.

She scoffed at him, but lovingly, without any condescension. "No, they flattered you. You never do what you don't want to do."

He had paused, held his hand to his forehead, thinking. They were on the beach at dusk, across the street from her apartment house, on an evening stroll before the dinner he planned to cook for them. The surf washed up over his bare feet, dampening his trouser cuffs. "You know," he finally admitted to her, and himself, "when the editor called and spoke so respectfully, I really began to realize that maybe I had done something even better than I thought. I wrote the book because I had something to say."

He was facing the horizon, the clouds on the horizon a deep purple, the setting sun turning red as it neared the water's edge. Now he turned and looked into her eyes. "Now they want me to do a second one."

"Congratulations," she said, genuinely pleased for him.

"I don't think I should agree," he answered.

He had kept the writing of the first book secret from her—indeed, only gave her a copy of the manuscript after Lassman told him that it was good. So, confessing that he had been asked to write another one was a big step, a presentation of unexpected testimony.

"Why not?" she asked.

"I'm not sure I have anything more to say," he told her.

"I see," she said after the long pause. "But perhaps you will find something to say, if you work at it."

"I am not a writer," he said. "It is not my work. You know what my work is."

"No. I don't. You're not a policeman anymore. You're retired. Enjoy it. Do what you can do, and stop thinking about what you would be doing if you were still on the force."

She at least understood enough to know why he didn't want to do a sequel. Counting on the expected success from the book, Lassman, Tina, and McCloskey were already taking for granted there would be a sequel. And when he agreed to go to Frankfurt at the end of the American author's tour they were convinced it was proof of his flexibility. It only made it all the more shocking to all involved that he cancelled his American tour planned by TMC.

Ever since he had found himself heir to a fortune, as a result of a private case, Cohen had been trying to buy the downstairs apartment in the former British Officer's Club in the German colony, where he had been living since the Six Day War. He would then own the entire property.

Cohen bought the upstairs two-room apartment when he and his bride had found the flat in Jerusalem a month before their January 1968 wedding. One hundred days later, Cohen was a widower, losing both his wife and their unborn child in a car bombing in downtown Jerusalem. He stayed in the apartment, owned by the estate of a tribal patriarch who made millions by bringing the first industrial bakery to Jerusalem, selling bread first to the Turkish army, then the British (who leased the house from him for their officer's club) and finally the Israelis. Bequeathed to members of his tribe, whose own fortunes ranged from huge to nothing, the property was a subject of dispute by the heirs.

By the late eighties, when all the grandchildren and cousins were counted, twenty-eight signatures were required for the property to be sold. Some were old enough to remember the house as their grandfather's home; others believed it was worth far more than the offers that came in through the law firm that handled all the real estate they owned in the city. So, the downstairs flat had remained closed and empty ever since Cohen's elderly neighbor passed away in the late seventies. But six weeks before Frankfurt, a week before his planned departure for the

American author's tour, the long-standing offer Cohen had made to acquire the entire building, including his own key-money flat, won the twenty-fifth of the twenty-eight signatures needed. That set into motion a series of meetings between Cohen and Ephraim Laskoff, his banker, with the last three signatories.

It was a difficult time for Cohen—and one that he needed to see through to its end. He originally made the offer soon after the inheritance came through, but during the lengthy process of collecting signatures from all the heirs—and their heirs—doubt began to grow in his mind about the wisdom of the purchase. The last three great-grandchildren of the original patriarch did not need the money and didn't care about the property. But they hated each other enough to use Cohen's offer as a battleground.

Each conditioned his negotiations on the others getting less for their signatures. Cohen had already crossed the Rubicon of one million dollars, and was well on his way to two, purchase price by the time the negotiations reached the final three heirs.

Along the way he saw his own efforts twisted by the heirs' greed, he saw Jerusalem itself changing in ways that made him wonder why he wanted to stay. No family held him down there, no job demanded his effort.

The more he heard people laying exclusive claim to the city the more it sounded to him like his own original obsession to own the whole house. Just as he had seen the insanity of the family quarrel holding up the purchase, so he could see how belief in the city's holiness was being twisted by greed into most unholy acts.

Laskoff partly prodded him on, saying it would be a wise business deal, for the demand for housing in Jerusalem was predicted to be on a constant rise toward the year 2000. "For the millennium," Laskoff would say, pointing out that the combination of the Russian immigration, the fundamentalist birth-rate, and even the limping peace process guaranteed that demand for housing in Jerusalem would remain on a constant rise for the coming years. "It's a good investment," said the banker. "Real estate is always a good investment in a tiny country. Even if you don't do anything with it," Laskoff said enthusiastically.

That's not why Cohen wanted it. He wanted it because he could imagine having it. Yes, he had ideas. Maybe he'd open a school. Maybe a restaurant. But those were fantasies that had more to do with his self-inspection, with his wondering about how his life had forced him to be guarded with others, rather than any entrepreneurial instinct. Buying the house was crazy from the start, he began to think. Ahuva and he would not have children. What did he need with such a large place? It was greedy of him, he thought.

Over the years, he began giving the money away. Trust funds to pay for university for the children—and a few grandchildren—of needy former colleagues, mostly subordinates from the past, and some struggling families of victims of crimes that Cohen felt guilty about because of his own failures.

And during those weeks when he should have been in America, he came face-to-face with his feelings. As the delicate game of three-way talks ensued, he would leave the meetings, sometimes with Laskoff on his heels asking whether he really wanted to go through with it, after all. "You talked about a school, you talked about a restaurant, you talked about a library just for your friends. You've had so many different plans for the house, Avram, that I don't know anymore if you want the house or something else. You have to answer that question." But the closer they got to a deal, the more doubt crept into his mind. It prolonged the negotiation enough to miss the author's tour.

Carey was patient the first time, understanding that Cohen had important personal business that came up unexpectedly. But the second time Cohen called to report he'd missed the Washington to Los Angeles leg of the trip, Carey was not so calm. He pleaded, he begged, and finally he said that Cohen would be to blame if he lost his job. If anything, it was proof that McCloskey had done his job. Hadn't Cohen himself described how he had often bent over backward to protect those who had been innocent, yet affected by the decisions Cohen made?

Tina was very worried. She worked hard to patch things up all around. Not only did Cohen's canceled author's trip hurt his deal, it also soured Carey to Lassman, which meant that she was having a difficult time selling TMC the writer's new idea for a book about the white slavery traffic from Eastern Europe.

"I've got to tell you, Avram, you are not Carey's favorite author right now. The book's doing okay. But not great. Far from great, as a matter of fact. If at least you could have come up with a better excuse for missing the trip. If at least you had told them from the start that you wouldn't make it. But you led them on. And we were going to use L.A. to seal a movie option," Tina complained in a long phone call one night in early September. "Hollywood, Avram. And right now, it looks like you blew it."

It made him nauseous to think about it. Not "blowing" Hollywood, but the idea his book—his life, he now realized—would be handled by that monster. Cohen had been to Hollywood once before, right after his unhappy retirement. It was supposed to be a reunion, with Herman Broder, the man who had saved his life, the man who taught him to take lives, the friend who tried to liberate Cohen but instead burdened him with wealth. The trip had turned into a nightmare about his past.

So, the crisis over the missed author's trip didn't go away, even if Cohen tried to pretend that it did. Nonetheless, he did give in to the pressures. Which is why, a month later, he was in a burgundy Mercedes heading to downtown Frankfurt, to attend the world's largest book fair. "If at least you gave that *People* interviewer what she wanted . . ." Tina was saying as the car sent by his German publisher, Koethe, rolled out of the Frankfurt airport, heading to the city.

She had met Lassman and Cohen at the airport, to take them directly to the Koethe pavilion at the fair. "But you obviously didn't give her what she wanted, because she never ran the story." The *People* writer wanted Cohen to talk about Broder and the money. "Believe me," Tina added, "a story in *People* would have been far more important than the *New York Times* review." Cohen didn't know whether to laugh or cry when he read the review, which called his book "a revelation." Just a year earlier, the Jerusalem novelist who wrote the review had not offered to help with "adding some color."

"So, please, be friendly and cooperative when we meet Carey and Herb," Tina said as the driver sped past mist-covered green woods between the airport and the rainy city.

Cohen was in the front seat beside the driver, Tina and Lassman in the back. He blinked at the forest, hardly listening to her. The green was a color he had forgotten since childhood. "Avram," Lassman piped up from the backseat. "Herb is Herbert Wang, Carey's boss. President of TMC."

From the start, he was confused by the various names of the editors and agents and publishing houses, because he only worked vis-à-vis Carey and Tina, with Lassman's help. The American version of the book would be the final version from which all other editions would be made in translation.

But he was able to remember the name of his German publisher, Koethe. It was a name he knew from childhood.

Indeed, if there was a reason why his writing a book was so important to him it was precisely for the same reason he knew the name Koethe.

Cohen's grandfather was a publisher, and so was his father. None of the vengeance, none of the work he did in the fifties, nothing he had ever done about his survival of the Holocaust meant as much to him as the fact that despite everything, he was able to continue the family tradition, by dedicating the book to the memory of the family he lost to the Nazis.

He remembered the name Koethe because it was often mentioned by his grandfather and father when they sat together at home talking business after dinner; Cohen, the boy, the heir, at their knees playing with his toys, but nonetheless hearing everything they talked about. The memory had come back to Cohen the moment Tina reported that Koethe had signed on for a hundred thousand marks.

For his grandfather, Koethe was the house to match. For his father, Cohen remembered, Koethe was the house to beat. But, by Kristallnacht, Koethe had stopped publishing Jewish authors, and a few weeks later, Cohen's family press was closed.

Writing a book had served many purposes in Cohen's life. Cathartic as an emotional release, it was an achievement he never expected of himself. But most of all, his book was his best revenge of all, and in the end, that formed the rationalization for his trip to Frankfurt. It was, after all, Koethe's invitation.

· 3 ·

"Look, Avram," Lassman said excitedly when the driver from Cohen's German publisher, Koethe, pulled into a VIP parking spot inside the fairgrounds. "There you are." Twice as tall as a man, a poster displayed Cohen's book cover in a billboard advertisement—Koethe was simply calling it *Jerusalem Policeman*—hung high over the plaza, one of six Koethe advertisements for their authors that year.

Cohen glanced up at the poster, raising an eyebrow at his own image staring out at the German city. A light rain made the plastic frame glitter, making the monochrome portrait more colorful than it really was. He turned down Lassman's request for a picture, Tina shook her head at him, and the driver led the way to Koethe's pavilion.

Mr. Smitbauer, president of Koethe, greeted Cohen warmly. But the publisher was clearly distracted and nervous. The chancellor's presence on the floor amidst all the pavilions was signaled by the bright lights of the TV cameras following him on the traditional opening day tour of the most prestigious of Germany's trade fairs, in the city famed for being Europe's longest-running market. Smitbauer was waiting for the chancellor to come by the Koethe pavilion. Lassman went straight for the mini-bar with sharp beer on tap that provided refreshment for the Koethe staff and guests, then immediately began flirting with one of the pretty assistants helping out at the pavilion. "The third-largest in the German hall," Smitbauer proudly told the chancellor, who arrived barely five minutes after Cohen and Lassman.

Not wanting to meet the politician—and wanting to get as far away as he could from another wall-high poster of the cover of his book, his face alone almost as tall as he was—Cohen tried to find an unobtrusive space from which to watch.

He found himself up against a display case of his books, and realized too late his position put him in the background of most of the photographs that would show the Koethe president with the German politician. While the politician and publisher—apparently old friends—chatted in front of the cameras, Cohen stupidly faced a hundred copies of the German edition of his book, beside a woman in her forties, cigarette dangling from her lower lip, her honey blonde hair already half white.

"Shalom," she said to Cohen.

"Shalom," said Cohen, slightly surprised.

"That's all the Hebrew I know," the woman said in badly accented English, taking the cigarette out of her mouth and dumping it in her empty beer glass.

Cohen, as he had vowed to himself so many years before, chose to answer in English. "That's all right."

"My English is bad. Very bad."

"That's all right, you can speak German. I understand the language. I just don't speak it."

"I know," said the woman. "I brought your book to Smitbauer. I am the editor. Kristina. Kristina Scheller." She offered her hand.

Embarrassed that he didn't even know her name, Cohen shook her hand warmly, smiling a half grin and explaining that he had only worked on the American edition, and was surprised when Tina said the book sold in Germany. He made the decision not to interfere with the Koethe edition, not even reading the translation until it was in galleys, and even then, just skimming through it, not enjoying the German, but not finding anything to complain about. "The translator did a good job," Cohen admitted.

"I wish you had written it in German," said the woman.

Cohen said nothing to her.

"I understand," she said. "I think it's why I decided to publish the book." She smiled and they stood in silence for a minute. "You don't want to meet the chancellor?" she asked.

Cohen shook his head.

From a pocket in her skirt, she pulled out a packet of cigarettes, offering him one. He shook his head, but took out one of his own cheap Noblesses from his shirt pocket packet. He was rationing them to himself, and was calculating how many he had left until the evening when she interrupted him. "Well, it looks like you might have to."

"What?"

"Meet the chancellor. They're coming this way."

And so, despite his efforts to keep a low profile, the shot of the smiling chancellor shaking hands with a dour-looking Cohen was taken by at least a dozen cameras both still and video.

"So you are the one who says Israel sent us criminals in the seventies," the chancellor said softly enough for only Cohen, and Smitbauer, who was looking on proudly, to hear.

"Witnesses," Cohen corrected the politician. "Informants."

"Well, you did good work against the fascists," the chancellor said.

"Nazis," Cohen corrected him.

Smitbauer's smile was fading rapidly.

"Yes, yes," the politician said, still holding Cohen's hand, not hearing.

His voice suddenly rose, and speaking for the microphones pointing at them, he said, "I will be visiting your country next month. Your city, Jerusalem, is a favorite of mine."

"Good luck," said Cohen. On his forearm, between his wrist and his elbow, he felt the itch of the eczema above the tattooed number the Nazis had given him when he was fourteen.

Finally, the chancellor dropped his hand, and Cohen fought the impulse to scratch until the big man was gone, and the TV camera crews and still photographers, the aides and the hangers-on and the handlers from the fair and the politician's office had all moved away.

For the next six hours, Cohen stayed at Koethe's pavilion, as journalists came by every half hour to interview him. Lassman disappeared from the scene when he sadly realized that none of the journalists were interested in him.

Cohen, surrounded by people, felt alone. He answered the questions succinctly but politely, except when he realized the journalist had not read his book. In those cases, he scolded them and found an ally in Kristina Scheller. She had a beer for every two sips of cognac Cohen pulled from his flask.

By seven, he was exhausted, with a thick headache. But at eight-thirty, he was due at a banquet thrown by Koethe in honor of their authors that year. He wanted a shower and a nap.

Lassman had disappeared hours before. "He said he was going to find the Israeli pavilion," one of the assistants told Cohen.

"If he looks for me, tell him I went to the hotel," Cohen said.

"Do you know where to find it?" Kristina asked, coming up behind him.

"The driver pointed it out to us as we went by. It's almost directly across the street, no?"

"We have a little bus to take us all at seven-thirty," she promised Cohen.

"I don't mind walking."

"It's raining out."

"It hasn't rained in Israel since March. I miss it. Maybe it will help clear my headache."

"I have some pills," she offered.

"Mine are at the hotel," he said. It was a lie. He had already eaten three aspirins laced with a touch of codeine, sold over the counter in Israel, and had the rest of the packet in his pocket. But he still had a headache. "I haven't had any real exercise all day." At home he tried to walk at least a kilometer a day.

"You want to be alone," Kristina decided. He nodded. "Well, you'd better take my umbrella," she suggested, going to the little closet behind the reception desk of the pavilion. On her face as she handed it over was a look of disappointment. "I'll take the van back to the hotel," she said.

As he expected, the walk in the rain pleased him, making his headache go away. From outside, the hotel was aglow. Through broad windows that showed off almost the entire first floor, Cohen could see a lobby that seemed to have been taken over by a cocktail party. He again experienced the nervous numbness he had felt earlier that day when he signed what seemed to him the hundredth copy of his book for yet another stranger who had looked at Cohen with an indefinable longing that the old investigator couldn't interpret. "What do they want?" Cohen had asked Kristina at the fair, and she had said, "You are now a celebrity, yes?" making him blurt out, "No, no thank you."

The doorman shook his head at the white-haired man coming out of the dark park, cutting across traffic where no traffic lights gave pedestrians permission to cross, his trouser shins wet, his shoes soaking. Cohen ignored the uniformed doorman's looks. At the entrance to the hotel, up six red-carpeted stairs beneath a canopy, he had to tell the concierge that he was a guest at the hotel.

At reception there was a wait of five minutes before he could catch the attention of a clerk behind the counter. He identified himself. Once the clerk behind the desk realized it was Mr. Cohen from Koethe's reservations, things moved quickly. He sent a bellboy to get Cohen's suitcase, which the driver delivered earlier.

"Has Mr. Lassman checked in yet?" Cohen asked. It took the clerk a couple of minutes to find Lassman's name on the reservation list. He had a room on the floor below Cohen.

"Yes, he has been in since four o'clock," said the receptionist.

"And Miss Andrews? Tina Andrews?"

"Oh, no, not yet," said the clerk, not even having to look to see if Tina's key was in her mailbox, let alone look up the agent's name. "She will be here at seven forty-five. Can I take a message for her?"

"No, nothing," said Cohen. What he was thinking of saying would best be said face-to-face. "Please have me woken in an hour," he requested. That would leave him half an hour to get ready for the Koethe banquet.

"No problem," the receptionist promised.

The bellboy led him, skirting the crowded lobby, which indeed felt more like a party than a waiting room, to the elevator doors. On the sixth floor, he confused the bellboy by tipping the young man as soon as the suitcase was on the luggage rack at the end of the bed, refusing a tour of the room.

The bed and bathroom both seemed oversized, the furnishings combined both ultramodern fixtures such as the bathroom faucets and the telephone with baroque decorations, like the tapestrylike curtain covering the window view to the street below, the park, and the convention center across the street. As much as the hotel seemed aglow as he approached, the fairgrounds across the street now seemed ablaze with lights. He opened the window.

He sat down on the edge of the bed, kicking off the wet shoes he had bought for the trip, then testing the mattress. The bed had too much of a bounce, making him scowl. But he lay down and soon was dozing, vaguely aware that by the time he fell asleep, the phone would ring him awake. That awareness stayed in the back of his mind so that he didn't actually reach deep sleep, just touching the edges of where he could hear his breathing become rhythmic. Sure enough, just reaching that sweet slide to sleep, the phone rang with his wake-up call and he was back on his feet, in the shower, shaving, and finally dressing for the banquet.

He decided to leave the blue necktie Ahuva packed for another time, and wearing a clean white shirt, gray twill trousers, and the still-damp loafers, he headed down the long corridor from his room overlooking the park and the convention center beyond.

The elevator doors opened to an old man sitting in a wheelchair, while in the corner, her back to the elevator doors, a tall brunette, her hair in a large bun, peered at the mirror, checking her makeup.

The lift was slow enough for Cohen to realize the man in the wheelchair was staring at him.

"You're that Cohen fellow," the elderly man said with a voice as hoarse as tearing cloth.

Cohen nodded. The woman turned away from the mirror.

"Frank," said the man in the wheelchair, ignoring her.

"Frank Kaplan," the man repeated, watching Cohen's face for a reaction, curious to see if Cohen recognized the name. When there was no response, the older man looked down at his blanket-covered lap and shook his head, then snorted a laugh. "If I were fifteen years younger," he finally said, "I'd beat the shit out of you."

The comment stunned Cohen. "Pardon me?" he said, "I do not know what you are talking about . . ."

"He thinks you wrote about him in your book," the woman tried explaining to Cohen, grabbing the handles of the wheelchair as if trying to take control over the elderly man.

"And it's a good book," the old man added, suddenly cheerful, almost friendly, instead of resentful. "I've got to admit. It's a very good book."

"Where? When?" Cohen asked, not worried but curious. He had no memory of writing about anyone named Frank Kaplan.

"You didn't mention my name. Just called me and some friends of mine, crazy. Fanatics. Terrorists."

Cohen racked his brain.

"This elevator moves faster than you think," Kaplan mocked him.

"It wasn't just you," Cohen said, finally remembering. "There were many of you. A fund-raising banquet in New York for people with fantasies about religious war in Jerusalem." Cohen didn't know all the names of the contributors at the banquet, but he knew how much money was raised and what bank accounts it went through to reach causes that wanted an ideological offensive up to the destruction of the Moslem mosques on the Temple Mount, to make way for the Third Temple.

"No," Kaplan protested, "people standing up for the rights of the Jews."

Cohen shook his head and would have argued that in the sovereign state of Israel, the law, as promulgated by the Knesset, determined the rights of the citizenry. But just then, the elevator came abruptly to a stop at the first floor. The woman turned Kaplan's chair abruptly to face the doors.

"Jesus, Francine," Kaplan moaned. "Not so fast."

As the elevator doors slid open, and Francine moved the chair forward, Cohen added, "And you're not even religious," feeling foolish immediately afterward, sounding to himself like a kid calling someone a name, not even sure Kaplan heard. Worse, the remark seemed to cut the commotion in the lobby, which dropped a beat in deference to the man in the wheelchair's arrival.

A few eyes fell on Cohen, still standing in the elevator as a circle quickly closed around Kaplan in the wheelchair. Cohen didn't like the feeling of being watched, and for a moment considered hitting the elevator button again.

Instead, he slipped through a clearing that bypassed Kaplan at the center of attention in the lobby, and went into the banquet hall, where Koethe's festive dinner for five hundred valued guests was taking shape.

He spotted Lassman leaning close to a brunette at a table at the far end of the hall. Cohen found his name tag at the head of a table at which he was flanked on one side by a man who introduced himself as the owner of the largest bookstore in Switzerland, and on the other by an author who specialized in counterespionage.

Tina came by his table before the speeches that preceded the dinner, to whisper to Cohen that she was making progress with a French publisher and hoped to have good news by the end of the fair. "But I'm still worried about TMC," she said. "Maybe it will help that you're on CNN."

"What?!" Cohen exclaimed.

"Their item on the fair. The chancellor shook your hand."

"They couldn't find anything else to use?"

His question and its tone made Tina sigh. "I'll never understand you," she said. "I know authors who would cut off their right arms for a chance to be seen on CNN. Your friend Benny would, easy. Anyway, I'm hoping Herb Wang sees that, and realizes that you plan to be cooperative now. We're seeing him tomorrow at five o'clock." She paused, before adding, "You are, aren't you?"

"What?"

"Going to cooperate?" she asked.

"I'm trying," he said half-heartedly, giving her a smile that calmed her enough to continue her table-hopping onward.

But very quickly it became apparent that the Swiss bookstore owner wanted to talk about money and the German author wanted to talk about the Mossad. Cohen wanted to sleep, and excused himself after the soup, shocking the Swiss bookstore owner—though making his wife smile—and leaving the espionage expert convinced that Cohen indeed was an agent for the Israeli secret service.

· 4 ·

"You missed an amazing night," Lassman bragged the next morning when, bleary-eyed, the translator showed up at the Koethe pavilion. "After dinner we went to a discotheque, and then back to another hotel. Amazing scene. Agents, publishers, editors. Everyone getting drunk. And," he paused for effect. "I got lucky."

"Good for you," Cohen said, not meaning it.

He had slept badly through most of the night, only finding sleep with a final cognac alone in his room near dawn, and then needing the wake-up call at nine in the morning. He spent the morning wandering around the fair on his own.

Occasionally, he'd be stopped by a stranger, and asked for an autograph. Twice, a small crowd grew around him, strangers all, smiling, eager, wanting. It frightened him each time a little more. In Jerusalem, even the strangers were familiar to Cohen, who knew every alleyway and courtyard in the heart of the city, both east and west. For the first time in a long time, he felt himself fighting the feeling of being lost.

He was twenty minutes late for the Koethe luncheon, arriving at their pavilion only to find a nervous Kristina Scheller waiting for him.

"You are late," she complained.

"I'm sorry, I got lost."

She shook her head, as disappointed as the day before,

40

when he turned down her advances. "Well, we can go join them, or go have lunch on our own," she suggested.

"I'm not very hungry," he admitted. It was only partly true. He had fallen to the temptation of two different sausages sold at two different refreshment stands between the halls. And with each sausage and sauerkraut, he had a tall beer. He was full, for now, and secretly glad he had missed another heavy luncheon.

"Well, what would you like to do?" she asked.

"I like cookbooks," he admitted.

She beamed at him, and took his arm. For the rest of the afternoon, she led him from one pavilion to another, as he looked through the newest cookbooks the worldwide book industry had to offer that year. But at five, he was back at his hotel, waiting in the lobby for Tina and Lassman, Carey McCloskey and Herbert Wang, the president of TMC. He was finally going to meet the voice from the other end of the planet.

Around him now in the hotel lobby, men and women air-kissed and embraced, shook hands and stood in small circles, briefcases and handbags in hand, talking. A few held drinks— wineglasses or whiskey glasses. Behind the reception desk, four uniformed clerks overseen by a worsted-suited manager were handling a crush of guests.

Through the plateglass window to the street, Cohen could see the busy traffic of a boulevard divided by a large park. A waitress walked by carrying a tray of drinks. He stopped and pointed to one of the tall glasses with white wine. She smiled at him. He took a glass, and then, before she could move on, he took another glass. He drained one, turning slowly as he drank, looking for Tina.

"Avram?" said a voice behind him. The voice was familiar. He turned.

"Avram Cohen?" asked the young man in the blue suit

41

with a yellow and red polka-dotted bow tie hanging under a sharp Adam's apple. His pinched features included a narrow nose, squinty eyes, and an almost lipless mouth.

"Carey?" Cohen guessed.

"You're just what I thought you would be," the editor exclaimed, grabbing Cohen's arms with both hands and pulling him forward to air-kiss. With a glass in each hand, Cohen took the embrace passively, careful not to spill the full, second glass he had taken from the waitress.

McCloskey backed away from Cohen as if to inspect him, and then clucked his tongue and shook his head. "You're gorgeous. Just what I expected. Fantastic." Suddenly, his tone changed to disappointment,

"If only you had agreed to go on tour," he said. "We would have had a hit, a real hit on our hands. Now we have to play catch up."

"Now Carey," Tina's buzz saw voice interrupted, coming from behind Cohen, "don't get bitchy."

She was not a pretty or even handsome woman. But she carried herself with a low-key but constant sexual energy that Cohen figured probably played a part in her success as an agent—though with McCloskey, Cohen suspected, the voice was more persuasive than a peek at her cleavage.

"What's done is done. We're here to fix things, aren't we, Avram?" she said.

"Tina, darling," said Carey, welcoming her effusively with the same air-kissing with which he greeted Cohen. "I'm so glad to hear that." He suddenly smiled to someone beyond the circle and waved a few fingers, not far from Cohen's face. The detective noticed a large gold ring, inscribed with a florid script and studded with a dark stone. Then just as suddenly, Carey was smiling at Cohen. "Good," the editor continued. "Can I be frank?" he suddenly asked, lowering his voice.

"Please," said Tina, icily.

"The truth is," Carey said, "Mr. Wang is not very happy, and asked me to find out just what's going on before he meets with you, Avram. So, shall we go find a quiet corner?" he suggested. "And find out?"

"What about Benny?" Cohen asked.

Carey looked at Tina. "Do we need him, you think?" She shrugged.

"I'd prefer to wait for him," said Cohen. "After all, if not for him, there would be no book."

"Yes, yes," Carey relented, making no effort to hide his impatience, "you're right." He pursed his lips for a moment, thinking, and then excused himself to say hello to a friend. "You know, I'll be right back," he promised, "or you come get me when Benny shows up," he offered, and without waiting for a response, joined a short fat man in a tailored suit. Arm and arm, the two went off to huddle in a corner, the little fat man looking over his shoulder once at Cohen and then laughing at something Carey said.

"You are, you know," Tina said when they were gone.

"What?" he asked.

"Well, maybe not gorgeous," she admitted, "but definitely attractive."

"I'm an old man," he protested, not wanting to explain Ahuva.

"I'm sorry you think so," she shot back. "How's the wine?" she asked, reaching for the full glass he was still holding. While she sipped, she scanned the crowd.

He answered her anyway. "A Riesling," he said. "Too sweet for my taste. Keep it."

"Ah, yes, you prefer cognac."

Across the lobby, Cohen watched the elevator doors open and close twice. Still no sign of Lassman. But Carey came back. "No Benny?" he asked impatiently.

Cohen shook his head. Carey checked his watch. So did Tina.

"Avram," she said first, "we really have to be at Koethe on time. And Carey's probably . . ."

"I've got to be at the Intercontinental . . ." Carey said.

"I'll call up to him," suggested Cohen.

"Avram, really, I'm sure he can find us," Tina promised.

"Of course," said Carey, putting his hand on Cohen's broad back and steering him through the crowd to an alcove where a corner of red leather chairs around a low coffee table covered with leftover cups of coffee and pastry, liquor glasses, and cigarettes, was being vacated by a party of six.

Carey took the seat Cohen would have preferred—facing the lobby—and Tina sat on a sofa between the two men who were in chairs at opposite ends of the coffee table.

Cohen had a view of the glass entrance to the hotel, but the weather had changed from a misty drizzle to a more intense rain that created trails of windblown water on the window. The wet glass refracted the lights of the traffic outdoors, both the cars passing the hotel and those pulling into the driveway to disgorge or collect passengers.

"Now Avram," Carey began, leaning forward in his chair. "As you know, we are not happy about you missing the tour. Sales are far from what we expected."

"I know."

"But it's nothing that can't be fixed," Tina jumped in, with a nervous smile at the editor and a slightly pleading look when she turned to Cohen. "He'll do a tour, of course. He knows what it says in his contract."

Carey smiled at the Jerusalemite. "I'm sure he does," he said. "We put a lot of money into this book," he added.

"I'll pay it back," Cohen said softly.

Neither the agent nor the editor heard him. He repeated himself.

Tina looked at him with shock. Carey was curious.

"What do you mean, you'll pay it back?" Carey said.

"Just what I said," said Cohen. He gestured over his shoulder with a wave of his hand toward the crowded lobby, then pointed out the window toward the misty glimmer of the fair building. "I don't belong here. I don't. This really was a mistake. Maybe the book was a mistake."

"Now Avram, you don't mean that. The book's wonderful," Tina exclaimed, so shocked her voice rose loud enough to make the nearest clutch of people break off their own discussion. She smiled uncomfortably at them and then back at Cohen. "And you'll be wonderful on tour." One last time she turned to Carey as she tried to convince both men that everything was under control.

Carey ignored her, instead squinting at Cohen as if he were a particularly interesting item on display. Only a flash going off somewhere behind Cohen in the lobby made McCloskey blink. "Let's hope," he said, softly, almost too softly for Cohen too hear, "that they want your picture, as well."

"What do you mean by that?" Tina demanded, but it seemed as if she knew the answer. Cohen didn't.

"Sorry I'm late," Benny interrupted as he entered the alcove. "Frank Kaplan's here," he said with an exaggerated nonchalance, sitting down next to Tina, who had to pull at her briefcase to give him space, distracting her from her concentration on Carey.

"Tell me about him," Cohen asked, directing the question to all three of the literary professionals, surprising them all with his sudden curiosity.

"You know him?" Tina asked.

"Sort of," Cohen said.

"He practically invented the disaster genre," Benny said enviously, reaching for a menu beneath a tea cup and saucer. "He's sold millions of books, literally millions. . . . God, the service here is bad," he added, almost knocking over a half-drunk bottle of beer left in the remains of the last party that had used the table. "Anyway, Kaplan is . . ."

But Carey wasn't interested in Kaplan. "Benny," he said in a casual tone, "Avram says he's ready to drop the whole thing. Pay TMC back, and, and, and, I don't know what. What, Avram?"

"Oh, no, please, no," Lassman moaned, slumping back in the sofa as if suddenly defeated. "Not after everything we've been through. Not now."

Tina, too, was shocked, but with Carey's tone of voice. Her mouth seemed to drop open, but she, too, turned to Cohen, wondering the same thing as the editor.

Carey ignored Lassman's moaning and Tina's gaping, facing Cohen. "What *do* you want, Avram? To pull the book off the market? Buy back all the copies? Make it go away? It's too late for all that, Avram. It's out there," Carey pointed out, and then his sarcasm gave way to frustration. "Jesus, Avram, what *is* your problem?"

Maybe my problem is that from the start I let you all call me Avram, he thought, almost saying it aloud. It wasn't that he felt superior. It was that he felt threatened by the intimacy it included in its use. He learned that while he was writing the book. But that didn't make it any easier for him. For years, people called him Deputy Commander Cohen, and or just plain Cohen. Behind his back, he was sometimes known as *HaCohen HaGadol*, the High Priest, but that was only used by his loyalists, and never to his face. Avram was for very few. And now, even Lassman was calling him Avram.

But that wasn't really the problem, he knew, once again realizing that as much as writing the book had liberated him from his past, its physical existence as an object, printed in tens of thousands of copies, had taken over his life in ways he never expected, never wanted, never needed. The book was supposed to answer questions—about the Holocaust, about Israel, about Jerusalem. He didn't want to have to explain it—or himself. And as far as he was concerned, that was the publisher's problem, not his.

"Avram," Carey suddenly said, thinking he might have understood. "Are you afraid? Is that it?"

"Don't be ridiculous," Lassman jumped in to defend Cohen. "Cohen? Afraid?"

Cohen snapped his fingers at his translator, silencing him. "Of what?" he asked Carey, challenging the editor.

Carey shrugged. "I don't know. Cameras? Microphones? Fame? I mean, are you the same Avram Cohen who wrote 'Fear can be, must be conquered by willpower'?"

"Carey!" Tina exclaimed, offended for Cohen's sake.

"It's all right, Tina," Cohen said softly, keeping his eyes on the editor.

Carey had learned a lot about Cohen during the months they worked on the manuscript. They had never met face-to-face, but as Cohen thought back on the time since they had first met on the phone, him stumbling over the name McCloskey, and Carey laughing and saying "just call me Carey, and I'll call you Avram," Cohen realized that Carey knew a lot more about him than he did about the young American. Maybe Carey's right, he thought. Maybe. He might have admitted it, if Frank Kaplan had not at that moment been pushed into the alcove by the same little fat man Carey had gone off with while they waited for Lassman.

Kaplan loudly gave an order to park him facing Cohen. The little fat man quickly abandoned the wheelchair and stood beside Carey, who could do nothing to hide the expression of amazement on his face as the old author growled at Cohen, "I owe you an apology. Let me buy you a drink."

Before he could answer, a photographer following Kaplan into the alcove flashed a snap in his eyes, unexpectedly blinding Cohen for a second. He naturally shaded his eyes with his hand. "Of course, you owe me one, too," Kaplan added with a wry smile.

Cohen dropped his hand. A moment before, while Kaplan maneuvered into position beside Cohen, Tina had been grinning—nervously—from ear to ear. Suddenly, she looked worried.

Carey leaned back in his chair, arms crossed against his chest, studying Kaplan, who was patting Cohen on the shoulder as if they were old friends. The photographer remained poised, waiting for action to capture.

Cohen sighed. "You don't owe me an apology."

"I'm glad to hear that," Kaplan said.

"You owe Israel an apology," Cohen said softly.

Lassman covered his eyes and Tina's expression changed to fear.

Carey kept his poker face.

"For what?" Kaplan demanded.

"For helping to pay for a campaign that ended with the assassination of our prime minister," said Cohen. "As I wrote in my book."

"What are you talking about?" Tina exclaimed. "Avram?"

"In the chapter about how the undergrounds are financed by American contributors," Lassman reminded her.

"You didn't mention Mr. Kaplan. Believe me, I would have caught that," she said, then turned to the author in the wheelchair. "I'm so sorry, Mr. Kaplan. I'm Tina Andrews, Avram's agent. And I've been a huge fan of yours since I was a little girl . . ."

Kaplan gave her a practiced grin. But he was concentrating on Cohen. "It's too bad, really. I don't want to have to sue you for libel and slander."

"Oh, shit," Carey moaned. Kaplan's narrow eyes shifted to gaze at him.

"Carey McCloskey," the editor offered, rising out of his chair to extend his hand. "TMC."

"Yeah, I've heard of you. The golden boy. A real smart-ass, I hear."

McCloskey could only smile weakly.

"Don't worry, smart-ass," Kaplan said, suddenly changing tone. "I'm not going to sue. Unlike him," Kaplan added, pointing a thumb at Cohen, "I believe in free speech."

Cohen scowled, working to hold his temper. But the dam broke. "Mr. Kaplan, we were in a meeting here," he tried, wanting the old man to go away and leave him alone. "Until you interrupted us rudely." He was tired of fighting. The book was supposed to do the fighting for him. Tina was appalled, Carey amused, and Lassman was watching both Kaplan and Cohen like a fan suddenly allowed into the dressing room to meet the boxers before the fight.

Kaplan easily ignored Cohen's request; as one of the ten best-selling novelists worldwide for more than three decades, he could set rules of behavior. And he set a new one on the spot, suddenly turning on Tina to ask if she was Jewish.

"Like Charlie Chaplin said," she answered, almost automatically, as if she had used the line many times before, "I'm afraid I don't have that honor."

"And I know *you* aren't, McCloskey," Kaplan added. "So neither of you really have any idea of what Cohen's book is about. What it's *really* about."

He paused to create a sense of mystery, but lost his advantage when Lassman interrupted.

"It's about how 'reason, not religion; faith, not fanaticism, must prevail,' " Lassman quoted from memory.

"So he's ready to sell out to the Arabs," the old author

hissed. He turned to Cohen. "Who's he?" he asked referring to Lassman.

"My name's Benjamin Lassman. I translated Avram's book, and my own book, about..."

But Kaplan wasn't interested. "Bernie?" he asked the little fat man, "can you see Francine? She's supposed to be bringing some champagne."

Cohen shifted in his seat, but said nothing.

"Avram, what *is* he talking about?" Tina asked.

"Jewish wars," Lassman explained. "It's what brought down the commonwealths in the past. The stronger we get, the more we argue among ourselves about whether we're really strong—and if God has anything to do with it."

"Jews didn't used to argue about God having something to do with it." Kaplan sneered.

"I leave discussions of God to religious people," Cohen finally interrupted. "I am not religious, Mr. Kaplan, and as I told you before at the elevator, as far as I can tell, neither are you. Which is why I am not interested in arguing with you, sir. At least not on this issue. I can say I am surprised that a man like you, traveling the world, making movies, able to write stories that interest hundreds of millions of people, is nonetheless more interested in finding excuses in the past than solutions for the future."

He spoke as politely as possible, making sure to control his temper.

"Bravo!" Tina exclaimed.

"You're right, Carey," the little fat man suddenly squealed, "he sounds just like Kissinger."

"Sounds like a dreamer to me," Kaplan said.

Cohen hated being discussed in the third person in his presence. It came with the uniform, but it was never the uniform that Cohen loved about being a cop. He scowled at the little fat man, who, conscious of it or not, backed up a step away from Cohen's expression.

"Please, Bernie," McCloskey said in an annoyed tone, and surprised everyone by keeping his eyes on Cohen. "I'm trying to understand what they're arguing about." He looked at Cohen. "It's not just politics, is it?"

"No," said Cohen. "It's not."

· 5 ·

Yes, Cohen knew how to fight, but if he had to point his finger at the single reason for his survival in a world he regarded with much suspicion, it was that he had learned to dodge and hide, as well as hunt, and if need be, to kill. Was he afraid? He didn't know anymore. Of what? Death?

His heart was still strong, despite the incident, as his doctor called it. He cut back his smoking and felt the difference. He drank and it made him feel either more alive or sleepy, and he knew how much he required for each need.

He did not take any pills stronger than an over-the-counter codeine-laced aspirin. He generally ate only food he or a cook he knew prepared. His eyes were not as good as they used to be, forcing him to carry a pair of half-rim spectacles for reading fine print. Alcohol was his own painkiller, and he had plenty to kill. Writing the book had also been a painkiller of sorts, looking into his memories, looking into his soul. Publishing was the mistake. The book was supposed to carry on his fight. Writing it had convinced him he was past fighting.

Carey was right: Cohen was afraid. He was afraid of the trap he had laid for himself. Once his fingers learned their way around the keyboard, the first draft poured out of him. He had never told the story before, not from start to finish, and by doing so it cleared passages clogged by guilt, wiped clear windows clouded by shame. There were moments he had found himself crying as he typed. He wrote to reveal his thoughts, but the writing had freed his emotions.

He wrote *Twentieth-Century Cop* by accident. Trying to learn one thing, he learned another, so what had begun as one story turned into two. It wasn't a religious book, of course. But because so much of it was about what it meant to be a Jew in Nazi Germany, and then later a cop in modern Jerusalem—a city of flesh and blood that could be spilled in the name of religion—his book was a text that spoke to longings both political and spiritual.

For some Jewish reviewers much more moderate than Kaplan, perhaps, but no less jealous about their idea of Jewish survival, Cohen's book was indeed only one step shy of heresy, controversial precisely because it differentiated between the idea of a united Jerusalem and the reality of its internal divisions. While the politicians in Israel said they'd never let Jerusalem be divided, he described in anecdotes and stories how the division ran deeper than ever because of political obsessions that regarded the symbol of Jerusalem as more important than the safety of its people, no matter what their religion.

Nobody could question Cohen's defense of the Jewish people, nor his work on behalf of the safety of Jerusalem. Yet it was precisely his profound distrust of ideology and fanaticism that made him so suspicious to so many in the city. Ultraorthodox teenagers rioting over Sabbath desecration, hurling rocks and bottles at cops and citizens trying to get home by car, called him a Nazi; as an Israeli cop, he was known as fair by Palestinians in the city but was never fully trusted, for as much as he put the law above ideology, he was a Jew. The powerful of Jerusalem respected him but treated him warily, fearing his knowledge of what they knew of him, knowing his integrity was not for sale.

Among the dishonest, he was considered honest. That's why he was retired earlier than he wanted to leave the force. And why now, he wanted a drink. But definitely not Frank Kaplan's champagne.

"You'll have to excuse me," he said, standing up, startling them all except the photographer, still lurking in the corner, waiting for his shot. Again, a flash blinded Cohen momentarily, forcing him to rub his eyes.

"What's the matter, Cohen?" Kaplan asked in a suddenly concerned tone. "Don't go now, Francine should be here with the champagne soon."

Cohen ignored him. "We have to be at Koethe's reception at seven?" he asked Tina.

She could only gape and nod.

"Where are you going?" Carey asked.

"I'm going for a walk before the reception."

"It's pouring out there," Tina pointed out.

"I like the rain," Cohen said.

"We still have business to discuss," the TMC editor reminded him.

"I know," Cohen said wearily. "Tell Mr. Wang I keep my contracts," he added and left them in the alcove, heading toward the elevator back to his room to fetch the raincoat.

The bustle of the lobby had only intensified since his arrival. An outsider, he felt that everyone knew everyone, except him. But he was aware of sideways glances at him as he tried to find a path through the crowd to the elevators.

At a narrow entrance under a sign promising a bar the crowd was thickest, which explained why there had been no service to the alcove. Two waiters were trying to get through, but they were outnumbered five to one by young men and old men, young women and old women, all apparently in a high state of excitement, trying either to get into or out of the bar.

Winding through the crowd, he found himself face-to-face with Francine. She was carrying a bottle of champagne and a cluster of upside-down glasses, their stems under the palm of her hand.

"Where's Frank?" she asked. "He said he'd be with you."

"Back there," Cohen indicated with his thumb, the expression on his face saying all that he felt about Kaplan.

She leaned toward him to whisper in his ear. "He's a little crazy, you know. You shouldn't take him so seriously."

"That's very loyal of you," Cohen said.

"Loyal?" she scoffed. "He's crazy. He's paying me three thousand a day plus all expenses—including appropriate wardrobe—for the week. Now that's crazy. He needs a servant, not an escort. And if it keeps up like this, I'm not sure I'm sticking around the full week."

"You knew he didn't like my book," Cohen asked, by stating the fact, telling himself he just wanted that one contradiction cleared away and he'd put Kaplan out of his mind.

"If you ask me," she said, "he envies you."

Cohen found that hard to believe.

"It's true. He was so mad to see you on CNN with the chancellor last night."

Cohen scowled.

"You know, he hates his own books. It was practically the first thing he told me when I took the job. I even went out and bought a copy of *The Hurricane* for him to autograph. I asked him to sign and while he's doing it, he says, 'It's all the same shit.' Can you believe it? About his own books. Maybe he doesn't like what you wrote—don't ask me, I'm not Jewish, I don't know anything about Israel or anything. But he told me and he told you himself, he thought it was a good book. I think that's what makes him so mad."

"Excuse me," blurted a gray-haired woman, clutching a stack of folders to her chest, blocked by the crowd, and trying to get past Francine, who stepped aside toward the alcove, away from Cohen.

"I've got to go," Francine said. "It's too bad you didn't stay for the champagne. See you," she added and was on her way, adding over her shoulder, "I bought your book."

"Handsome woman," a man beside him said with an English accent. "Last year he brought an Asian. He's famous for it. Every year, a different one."

"Sad," Cohen said softly.

"He doesn't think so," the Englishman said.

"For the girls," Cohen said.

"They seem pretty happy about it," said the man. He offered his hand to shake Cohen's. "Jeremy Roth," he introduced himself. "Just out of curiosity, is Tina using Diane to handle U.K. rights for you?" he asked, and out of his sports jacket pocket, a business card appeared in his hand.

"You'll have to find out from her," Cohen said. He had never heard about any Diane from Tina.

"Because I am a Jew, Mr. Cohen, I would like to help your book in the U.K. market," the British agent said.

"Really, you'll have to ask her."

"So you didn't meet Diane?"

Cohen snorted a little laugh. "In the last two days I met what feels like several hundred people, Mr. Roth. Swiss bookstore owners and Berlin publishers, specialists in Hindu philosophy and a woman who I understand is my competitor in the autobiography market this year, only her book is all about the men she slept with until she became a lesbian."

Roth laughed.

"Believe me, Mr. Roth . . ."

"Jeremy, please."

"I have lost all interest in this business of being a writer. It was a mistake. If Tina hasn't sold the rights yet in the U.K., I probably will ask her not to do so."

"What?" Roth asked, astonished.

But just then Lassman interrupted, yanking at Cohen's jacket, curtly said "excuse me" to the Englishman, and turned to Cohen. "I need to talk with you," he said in Hebrew. Cohen nodded farewell to the Englishman, hesitated for a second, and then took the business card Roth had been offering since he began talking with Cohen.

Cohen told Lassman to accompany him to the elevator. "I want to pick up my raincoat." It was a trench coat Ahuva bought him for his birthday last year.

"Kaplan was trying to pick a fight with you and at the same time," Lassman tried to explain, "he was trying to make friends."

"I'm not interested in him," Cohen said. "I'm not even sure I want to stay. I'm thinking about going home. This really was a mistake."

"What are you talking about? We're halfway through it. You said you were ready to do the American tour. This is a piece of cake compared to a tour."

The elevator doors opened. Cohen took a step forward. Lassman grabbed his arm. "Please, Avram, don't screw this up," he begged. "You know how much I've been counting on this."

Some Japanese businessmen were holding the elevator door, all four looking at Cohen with expectation in their eyes. He signaled to them that they should go up, and turned to Lassman.

"Look, Benny. This isn't for me. Dinners, banquets, luncheons, receptions. Interviews, speeches. It's not for me. I don't know how to be polite to people—and that's what people want. I'm tired of smiling at people I don't know and listening to people like Kaplan. This is not for me."

Lassman lowered his voice and pointed Cohen to a set of stairs that led into a huge banquet hall, draped with tapestries of hunting scenes, courtrooms, and at the far end, largest of all, a crucifixion. They were alone, except for a pair of women setting a distant table.

"Avram, I know you're paying for this trip for me. I appreciate it."

"The money's not important," Cohen said.

"For you. But for me it is. Very important. I'm counting on this book's success. They've spent a lot. They want to make it back. If they do, the success rubs off on me, too. After all, as far as they're concerned, I discovered you." He paused, realized what was wrong with what he said, and added "in the literary sense."

"So you can stay. I told them you can speak for me."

"They don't want me to speak for you. *I* don't want to speak for you. I wanted this trip to try to sell my books, as well as yours. But I'm also here with you. If you walk out, it looks bad for me. They'll wonder if they can trust me not to back out of a contract. I didn't want to say this, but remember, Avram, we have a contract, too."

"You'd sue me, as well?" Cohen asked.

"If you pull out now, we're both facing a huge lawsuit," Lassman tried. "You and me."

"Both of us?" Cohen asked.

"Well, I'm liable, too. And for me, it's a lot of money—especially considering the book was expected to do well, very well. If you made the public appearances. I helped you get this book published, Avram. I shouldn't be punished because you suddenly aren't happy with it."

The money wasn't the problem. It was Lassman's emotional blackmail, even if so poorly presented, that made Cohen wince. It was an old story in Cohen's life, an Achilles' heel made even more vulnerable by the knowledge that money couldn't solve every problem. Lassman's career was on the line. And even if the book was a mistake, when Cohen needed help on it he *had* asked Lassman.

"I was serious," Cohen said. "I'll pay them back the money, if that's what they want. They have the book. And I'll make sure you don't lose. It's enough. I'm not made for speeches. For politics."

"Come on, Avram, you were great back there," Lassman insisted. "Carey loved it—except for when you walked off. He wanted more. Kaplan did you a favor. He made you look good. Poor Tina. She's devastated. She's been a fan of his for years. But forget Kaplan, he's crazy." Lassman smiled at the irony. "You said so yourself."

"Everybody seems to think so," Cohen said, remembering Francine. "But it's not Kaplan. It's the whole business. I didn't know it would be like this. I didn't know," he repeated.

"We still have that dinner tonight," Lassman said, with hope in his voice that maybe Cohen's talk about leaving was just that—talk.

Cohen nodded, almost sadly. "As long as I'm here, I must. I signed the contract—and I don't have a lawyer here to get me out of it."

"I'll go with you."

"Thanks, Benny," Cohen said. "But no need. I want to be on my own for a little while. I'm just going upstairs to get a raincoat and then I'll go out for a while."

· 6 ·

He rode the elevator alone to the sixth floor, going back to the room he had left that morning. Turning into the corridor heading to his room at the end of the hall, he nearly fell over a chambermaid's cleaning cart, startling the woman pushing it down the hall.

"Sorry, sorry," the tall young woman muttered in German in a very low voice, but Cohen barely noticed, glancing at her profile as she kept her face lowered, stepping aside as she moved on toward the service elevator he had noticed at the far end of the corridor.

He watched her receding figure for a second, before turning up the corridor to his door. The chambermaid had piled his laundry in a corner, for the third evening in a row leaving a printed flyer from the hotel management saying that they had a laundry service—all he had to do was fill the folded bag that lay on top of the pile; she had made a stack of the magazines he had bought for the plane trip and didn't read because he had used two double cognacs to get to sleep for the five-hour flight. His single suitcase was closed, on the low bench at the foot of the bed. She deserves a tip, he said to himself as he headed to the bathroom, picking up one of the magazines he had bought in the airport for the flight.

It was a computer magazine. Cohen's original sin in writing the manuscript had begun with the acquisition of a personal computer. By the time the book was done, he was facile enough on the machine to database his record collection and recipes. In the months he waited for the final proofs, he learned how to make images with software, and lately he had been trying to create slide shows that went with specific recordings.

So he sat on the toilet, reading *Wired,* waiting for his bowels to move. Nothing happened, and once again he regretted the way all the carefully nurtured routines of his life had broken down as a result of the book.

Sighing, he dropped the magazine on the floor in front of the toilet seat, pulled up his pants, and stood in front of the mirror over the sink, looking into his own eyes, asking himself what to do.

Go? Stay? None of the lines of his face, none of the flecks in his silver-gray eyes, nothing told him what to do. His mind said he should stay. His heart told him to leave. He was known for following his instincts, for an intuition that was right more often than not. Cohen's method was always to look for what was wrong in the picture, even if it was sometimes a picture that only he could see.

Behind him, the white plastic shower curtain was drawn closed. He had found it open, and he left it open. He had very little experience in hotels. None in German hotels. Why would the curtain be closed, he suddenly wondered. He turned around and looked at the curtain, then took two strides and yanked it to his left.

A young woman, eyes bulging, tongue protruding, naked except for a pair of white panties and Cohen's unused blue tie embedded into the skin around her neck, lay leaning into the corner of the tub, staring blindly at Cohen's own tired eyes.

Only someone who had read his book, who knew Cohen and his background, would have understood why the man didn't gasp in horror. Death was an old companion in his life.

He stood there, looking down at her for a long minute, and then used some toilet paper to pick up the phone so conveniently hanging on the wall beside the toilet. He asked the operator to send a hotel security officer to his room. The receptionist did not ask why he needed a security officer. He did not say.

He was careful not to touch anything, except the door, which he opened the same way he had picked up the phone, with two dabs of dampened toilet paper on his thumb and forefinger. But while he waited for the hotel security officer he began a thorough search of his own in the room until finally, he got down on his hands and knees and with his fingernails lifted the hem of the bed cover to look under the broad double bed.

Just then, there was a knock at the door. "Security?" Cohen shouted out, still on the floor, almost paralyzed by what he was seeing.

"Avram?" It was Lassman. "One more thing . . ."

"Benny, get away. Now."

But before Benny could say anything, another voice came from the doorway. "Herr Cohen?"

"In there," said Lassman from the door.

"Security?" Cohen called out.

"Yes. My name is Mathis," said a young man's voice coming into the room.

"Do you have any bomb disposal experience?" Cohen asked, still kneeling on the floor, still staring at the elbow-pipe bomb, its clock aimed upward so he couldn't see the timer, wires leading into the slit cut into the cloth of the box frame beneath the mattress.

"A bomb?" Mathis asked.

"A bomb?" Lassman repeated.

"You'd better call your local bomb squad," Cohen suggested, uncomfortably standing up, his knees aching from
the effort. "Don't touch that door," he commanded, as
Mathis stepped in, naturally reaching to close the door.
"And homicide," Cohen added.

A blond man in his mid-thirties with a military haircut
and posture to go with it, Mathis froze long enough for
Lassman, behind him, to exclaim "fantastic."

"In the bathroom," Cohen directed Mathis. "And you,"
he pointed to Lassman, "not a word. Silence."

Mathis went into the bathroom, and came out quickly,
swallowing hard to halt vomiting, but at the same time
pulling a small communications device out of his inside
jacket.

"Marina something," the security officer said, unable to
precisely identify the dead chambermaid. "I'm new on this
job. I really should contact my boss."

"First the bomb squad. There's a timer. But it's facing
up, so we can't see it. Take a look."

Mathis swallowed again, nodded, and then got down on
his hands and knees beside Cohen, flashing a penlight on
the object under the bed. It was a short elbow-pipe bomb.
Cohen could see the timer, but it was too murky in the pen-
lit darkness to see how long they had left before it would
explode. If that's all he had seen, he would have suggested
they lift the bed away from the bomb for a better look.

But there was something far more ominous. Three wires
ran from the device into the cut through the fabric. "Now
will you call the bomb squad?" Cohen demanded, "and
then your boss?"

Mathis obeyed. Cohen stayed a moment longer on the
floor, looking for a sign that the bed had been moved.
There was none that he could spot—no depressions in the
carpet that showed the legs had stood elsewhere. Forensics

would sweep the carpet, of course, and do much more. He sighed, knowing it wasn't his case, and knowing that by touching any of his belongings, he could harm the investigation. But all he really wanted to do was go. He sighed as he climbed back to his feet and found himself face-to-face with Lassman.

"What are you doing here? I told you to get away."

"Are you kidding?" Benny said. "Who do you think did it?" Cohen glared at him.

"C'mon," Benny begged. "You must have some ideas."

"Let me think," he snapped at Lassman and turned around and went to the window, opening it. The street was six floors below, but there were no cars parked on the three-lane road opposite the hotel. Beyond was a dark portion of the park that divided the thoroughfare. In the glitter of city lights in the rain outside his window, it was impossible to spot a lookout for the explosion. So he worked on his memory. He was certain there was a mole above the chambermaid's jawline. She had very dark eyes. Black hair. He wasn't sure how long. She wore a cap. Her nose. Maybe it had been broken in the past? When he paused to let her pass, he watched her walk—she had a narrow bottom, her shoulders much wider. Her calves were muscular, shapely. The shoes. They were black. Boots, not the uniform footwear he had seen on other hotel staff. It suddenly occurred to him that the chambermaid he saw in the corridor might have been a young man. He returned to the face in his mind, wishing he had noticed the chambermaid's hands.

"I figure Nazis—or their kids," Lassman said confidently. "Either that or someone you must have sent here for relocation after a trial."

"You came up wanting to tell me something," Cohen said, not wanting to discuss the bomb with him. Not until he knew more than what he knew.

"Yeah, thought you might want to know. Carey's not discounting the offer to repay the advance money. But he'd want damages—additional money to recoup other costs. A full two million."

When he opened the window he could hear the sirens. Now the green-and-white police cars began arriving down below. He saw the hotel general manager, to whom he had been introduced his second day there, greet the first officers to arrive outside the hotel. In another moment, Cohen realized, the organized chaos of a crime scene over which he had no control would erupt around him. If he were the lead officer on the case, would he regard the visiting author as a suspect, given what was known so far?

· 7 ·

The police wanted to evacuate the entire building and conduct a search of the hotel for another device. The hotel management didn't want that, of course. For a few minutes there was a standoff in the corridor far down the hall from the open door to Cohen's room.

The sappers noted that if the bomb went off, it would destroy the bed, but the meter-thick cement floors of the old building that had survived Allied bombing would barely be damaged.

"Maybe there will be a twenty-centimeter hole in the floor. You can fix that," the sapper told the worried hotel manager, who begged the police not to evacuate the hotel.

"There must at least be a search for other bombs," Cohen pointed out.

"Please, Mr. Cohen," said the senior officer on the scene, Helmut Leterhaus, a local State Police Criminal Investigations department commander. "Allow us to handle this."

The corridor quickly filled with plainclothesmen and uniforms. Officials—from the local branch headquarters commander of the BKA; and from the BND, the agency for the protection of the Constitution, which in the old days of the Berlin Wall conducted counterespionage against East Germany, but now focused on countering industrial espionage as well as terrorism. An officer from GSG9, the German counterterrorist unit, attending the fair on a private visit, was also alerted to the attempted bombing. And a young Israeli diplomat, assigned to the Israeli pavilion at the fair by the foreign ministry, also wanted to know if Cohen needed any help.

All he wanted was to leave. To go home. Leterhaus was right. He had no position in an investigation of the murder or the bombing attempt. Yes, it appeared aimed at him—though he was still not certain. But he had convinced himself that he was done with investigations.

Certain that whoever had planted the bomb had planned it well in advance—"The chambermaid," he told anyone who asked, "must have surprised the assassin. The murder was clearly an accident on the job."—Cohen doubted whether there would be another attempt on him in the coming days. But he was certain that he would be safer at home, where he had control over his environment.

The sappers worked on the bomb in the room and others searched the rest of the hotel. From the walkie-talkies, Cohen heard that there was a mild panic in the lobby at first, as word spread through the hotel. But the police had it under control. Within twenty minutes, the police announced no other bombs were found in the hotel.

The management heaved a sigh of relief and as a good-will gesture, offered Cohen the presidential suite a floor above, to use as his room for the duration of his stay.

"I won't be staying," he told the hotel manager.

"Excuse me?" Lassman asked.

"I'll be leaving tonight."

"I understand," said the manager. "I, too, would be afraid."

"I don't understand," said Lassman. "Don't you want to stay, find out who did it?"

But before Cohen could answer, Helmut Leterhaus was back, wanting to go over the same questions again.

"A young woman," Cohen said. "Early twenties, perhaps. Very tall. Maybe a meter seventy, black hair, dark eyes, a large mole on her cheek, here," Cohen said touching his own face just above the jawbone. "Maybe a broken nose. And black boots," he added. "And maybe a man in disguise. Maybe . . ."

But Leterhaus and the others were more interested in Cohen having enemies in Germany.

"How long have you been a homicide detective?" Cohen finally asked back.

"Fourteen years," Leterhaus said.

"And how many enemies have you made?"

Leterhaus fell silent for a moment. "Some," the German officer confessed.

"Multiply by two—that's how long I was on my force, and that's how many enemies I made."

"Here, in Germany?"

"Now, that's a good question," Cohen admitted. But he didn't have an answer that made sense.

In the late seventies and early eighties, the Israeli police had sent many an informant from the underworld into exile in Europe—often to Germany—in exchange for information that resulted in convictions. It worked as an option into the mid-eighties, but by then enough of the Israeli "exports," as they were known to the few who knew of the practice, had grown into gangs struggling for turf, and the German police caught on to the ploy. Since then, coordination, not concealment, became the byword on relations between the two forces.

Cohen ran through the names and faces in his memory. Off the top of his head he could think of at least twenty— but none of them, at least as far as he knew them in their day as state witnesses and squealers from the street, were capable let alone had reason to want to try to kill him. He could find out, perhaps, he told Leterhaus, "but only at home."

"Terrorists, perhaps," Leterhaus suggested. "An Israeli policeman. A famous Israeli policeman," he repeated. "Famous now, because of your book. You write about hunting Nazis. Perhaps someone seeks revenge for the revenge you wanted."

Cohen snorted with disbelief.

"Perhaps Arabs?" Leterhaus tried. "Maybe even fanatic Jews?"

"I am not Salman Rushdie," Cohen grumbled.

"No, you are not," said Leterhaus. "I liked yours much better. Very inspirational."

"Thank you."

A junior detective arrived, to whisper something in Leterhaus's ear.

"The dead woman is Marina Berendisi. From a Turkish family. And we found the chambermaid's cleaning cart. In a storeroom in the basement. I must ask you again, why a bomb? Why you?"

"I don't know," Cohen could only say. "But I'm sure that you and your people will find out. No?"

Cohen didn't mean it as an insult, but Leterhaus took it as such. He didn't say so, but Cohen could see it clearly in the German's eyes. Cohen had a hundred ideas in his head about who might want to kill him, but when he asked himself who would have gone to all the trouble to do it here, in Frankfurt, a city he had never visited, in a country he had left almost fifty years earlier, he had no answer.

He racked his brains for names of Israeli criminals he had sent to Germany, and Leterhaus took down the names. It was probably useless. "I have no idea what name they might be using here," he admitted.

"This is great, Avram," Tina said behind him. Somehow she managed to get past the guard at the elevators and came up behind Cohen in the corridor where he was talking with

Leterhaus. She was thrilled. "A murder, a bomb. Think of the press we can get from this. Carey's in seventh heaven."

"What are you talking about?"

"The press, the publicity, it's perfect. For sales. Forget everything he said about suing you. He loves you. You've got the perfect excuse why you can't go on tour."

"Someone is dead, Tina," Lassman reminded her.

"Of course, I know. Poor girl. But it really solves our problem, doesn't it?"

And Lassman had to agree. Meanwhile, Cohen asked Mathis to ask the hotel expert for the fastest connection from Frankfurt to Tel Aviv. Nobody tried to stop him. He wouldn't have cared if they had. He didn't care if people thought he was running into hiding.

· 8 ·

The first available flight out of Frankfurt that night was to Rome. From there, he caught a flight to Tel Aviv. He bought a first-class ticket and rode with a sleepy English rock and roll band and some bankers allowing themselves giddiness with celebration after signing a half-billion-dollar deal.

Cognac helped him sleep most of the way, but it was an uneasy race home ahead of the dawn, made uneasier when he saw the morning's tabloids at the newspaper stand at the arrivals hall at Ben-Gurion. His photo, getting into a car outside the hotel in Frankfurt, was on the front page of the morning *Ma'ariv*. He had avoided all the press in Germany—except Lassman, of course, who had stuck to him, like Tina, all the way to the airport.

But he had heard a Hebrew question among those shouted at him in the lobby when he was escorted out in a pack of security, and at the bottom of the stairs outside the hotel, where Koethe's black Mercedes S600 waited to take him to the airport, more reporters doused him with TV camera lights, flashing cameras, and questions while he, Tina, and Lassman got into the car.

The headline in *Ma'ariv* asked "Who Tried to Kill Avram Cohen in Germany?" with a subhead reminding the reader that Cohen was "the secretive millionaire detective" whose "controversial autobiography" had been published in the

United States. He didn't buy the paper. Instead he strode briskly to his car in the long-term parking lot. Dawn caught up with him on the road to Jerusalem, the white sun blaring into his bleary eyes. All he wanted was a hot shower, a drink, and his bed. Traffic was already thick coming into the city, but he caught a green wave of traffic lights from the foreign ministry all the way to Liberty Bell Park, and from there, it was only a couple of blocks home. Getting out of his car in the tin-walled shack that had long served as the garage in the corner of the property in the little side street off Emek Refa'im, he could hear the phone ringing in his upstairs apartment. He didn't rush to answer.

So he ignored the speaker playing the message on the answering machine as he came into the apartment, dropping his bag on the living room-turned-study floor, unbuttoning his shirt, kicking off his trousers, and unbuckling his belt as he headed to the bathroom.

When he came out of the shower, there was another voice, a second message. It was an American TV network "trying to reach Deputy Commander Cohen—for the second time." Cohen didn't respond. As soon as the man hung up, the phone began ringing again.

Cohen went to the machine, rubbing his hair with a towel, absentmindedly turning on the computer to collect his e-mail, as he picked up a pair of half-spectacles he had lately needed to read—because of the computer, he forlornly admitted to himself—and peered down at the answering machine. Through the little plastic window he could see the tape had come to its end. In the five years he had owned the machine, it had never done that before.

He looked at the phone for its fourth ring. At the end of the sixth, the machine would answer. He answered on the fifth.

"Hello?" he asked gingerly.

"Is this Avram Cohen?" a screechy-voiced woman asked.
"Who is this?"

"I think it's too bad they didn't get you," the voice
shrieked at him. "You should rot in hell, you Arab-lover."

He hung up, unplugged the phone, and looked at the
monitor screen.

Through the second phone line, the computer was con-
necting to his Internet provider. The two modems whis-
tled at each other and within a minute, his mail client
software was opening his mailbox.

"Downloading 1 of 173," the message bar said.

Ordinarily, he received an average of five mail messages
a day, all lists to which he subscribed, but only rarely par-
ticipated. Two were about food and recipes, one a histori-
cal discussion of the era of the Romans and the Jewish
Wars; there were occasional digests that announced new
recordings, and one in which Jews and Arabs tried at civil-
ity in a discussion of the future of Jerusalem.

He had early on signed up for several law enforcement
discussion groups, but too much conspiracy theory and
not enough intelligence showed up in them. He had
retreated from them all.

But he had conducted brief exchanges with individuals on
some of the lists, a question here, an answer there. And TMC
had a Web site, where for a few weeks during the site's
construction—without his knowledge—Cohen's e-mail
address had appeared. As soon as he found out about the
TMC site, he asked that his e-mail address be removed, and
he changed his username at his Internet service provider.

Once let loose, information is free, he knew. He clicked
at the cancel button, but the program wanted to go on, so
he flicked off the machine, cursing Lassman, and everybody else involved with the damn book, including the two
reporters and three photographers who showed up outside

his house that afternoon, woke him with knocking on his door—which he didn't answer—and then camped out in the street until he turned off the lights to go to sleep that night.

He cursed them all, but mostly himself: his vanity, his folly, his mistake.

· 9 ·

"You are a *potz*," Ahuva said softly. Cohen snorted a laugh. Her opinions from the bench were always praised by the professionals for their clarity. In Hebrew, after all, the word *mishpat* means both law and sentence. She was known for writing a judgment that both the lawyers and clients could understand. Her precedents had yet to be overruled by the Supreme Court, and she made her first new point of law as a magistrate in her first year.

Only with Cohen could she use a word like *potz*—about him or a colleague. It meant someone flaccid and pathetic. Only with her could he tell the whole truth. That was the magic of their relationship. "You are behaving like an idiot," she said. "You have money. You have freedom. You have me," she added with a slight coyness that nobody in her courtroom ever saw. "But you force yourself to be unhappy."

They were in her apartment in Tel Aviv. Just before dawn the day after he arrived home from Frankfurt, the last of the photographers gave up and left the street outside his house. A few minutes later, he slipped into his car and drove down to her place in Tel Aviv, quietly opening the door to her flat with his key.

He sat in her living room, reading the weekend press coverage of the bomb attempt and his departure from Frankfurt. The speculation in the press ranged from Nazis and neo-Nazis to terrorism. Two papers pointed out that he had made

sworn enemies of several of the most extreme of the nation-
alist rabbis, those who were known to have found halachic
rationale for the death of the prime minister. One was
quoted as saying that he wouldn't mourn if Cohen had
been killed, but of course he didn't recommend it. At least
one Islamic fundamentalist group issued a statement deny-
ing they had anything to do with the bombing attempt.

In the most serious of the Israeli press, that morning's
Ha'aretz, he found two stories. One was about the bombing attempt, the other about his book. The item about his
book mostly complained that the book came out in English and German, but had not yet appeared in Hebrew. One
publisher was quoted as saying he wanted to publish it in
Hebrew, but that Cohen was "hesitating." Cohen snorted.
The most important sentence in the report was the last
one: "Sources at the book fair told *Ha'aretz* that Cohen
was in a dispute with his American publisher about the
proper way to publicize the book. Now, with the attempt
on his life, there should be no problem in making the book
well-known around the world."

Cohen dropped the paper to the floor and pulled off his
reading glasses, rubbing his eyes. When he finished, Ahuva
was standing at the entrance to the living room. She was
wearing a bathrobe and her hair was wet.

"Where have you been? The whole world's been searching for you. People are even calling me."

"I'm here."

"Are you all right?"

He shrugged. "I needed someplace to stay. To think."

She sat down on the sofa beside him and put an arm over
his shoulder and her head on his chest. "Of course," she
said.

He stayed indoors all day. She had to go out for a meeting, but came home by two and found him in the kitchen,

preparing dinner that night. It was as if nothing had happened to change their routine.

They made love while the sun set into the sea behind a stretch of cirrus clouds, the changing colors faintly reflected on the white walls, sharply bouncing off a full-length mirror beside the bed. Then they went out to the patio in bathrobes to let the cool breeze from the north dry their sweat.

"A real *potz*," she emphasized. "You think the book was your mistake? You're wrong. The book wasn't the mistake. That wasn't your vanity. Your vanity is your attitude. All high and mighty. You're a martyr looking for a cause."

He knew she was right. But he didn't know what to do about it. He hoped she would hand down a sentence. Not a punishment or fine, but a discipline of some sort that would define his direction, free him from the ambivalence that so plagued him.

All his life, things had been clear to him. In childhood, as in all happy childhoods, everything was clear. On the run, in the camp, survival was clear. Afterward, hunting the killers was clear until it disgusted him. And even in the midst of a case, even when the only clarity was the faint sparkle of light reflecting through the fog, his questions never brought him up against the sense of paralysis that he felt crawling into his soul with the money he had inherited.

Writing the book liberated him. But the attention that came with the book's publication brought back the paralysis, the fear—yes, he admitted to her, he wasn't afraid of the bomb or the bomber. He was afraid of the way he had become part of a spectacle. So much of his survival depended on his privacy, and more, on his ability to be anonymous. Even in the streets of Jerusalem, where he knew many faces and many more knew him, he could make himself almost invisible in a crowd.

Yes, he was barrel-chested, but if he was ever seen in shorts in public it would reveal somewhat spindly legs. Of average height, his black hair had gone white over a very long period, with the last dark strands disappearing only in the last year. His skin was only dark on his face, forearm and hands, as well as a small triangle of chest where his top shirt button was usually unbuttoned. Over the years the hair in that triangle had thickened against the sun, turning into a little white forest where Ahuva's fingers now played, teasing him.

"You know what you ought to do?" she said to him suddenly, turning in her seat, holding his face with two hands, looking into his eyes.

"Please, tell me," he said. In the fading light, her red hair seemed to darken to a deeper shade, framing an oval face that was beginning to wrinkle. The difference in age had never been an issue between them their first ten years, in which secrecy ruled the relationship. The last seven, it was only a matter for gossips. But lately, she was drawing his attention to the years, the wrinkles, even asking if he thought a face-lift might one day be in order for her. The question had made him laugh. He had only discovered during that island vacation that she had been using coloring to control the whitening of her hair and keep it honey red.

"Please, tell me, what should I do?" he asked again in exasperation.

"No," she decided sadly, "you'll laugh."

"No, I promise I won't."

"Get a new wardrobe. Indulge yourself." He did have to stifle a laugh.

She hit him on the chest. "I'm serious. Get a new wardrobe and a new car, pay the extra money, whatever it takes to fix up that house—if that's what you really want to do. Build the computer system you want. Open a school or a restaurant, or any of those other ideas that you know you'll never do. Or move in with me."

He grinned again.

"No, you're right, maybe *that's* not such a good idea. I understand, you want to keep your privacy. Keep it. Spend what it takes and keep it. But stop blaming yourself. Start enjoying yourself."

"I *am* enjoying myself," he said truthfully, "with you. And right now I'm going to enjoy myself even more by basting that roast in the oven," he added, standing up. "The mushrooms this year are fantastic."

"You're not taking me seriously," she protested, reaching for him.

But he stepped out of reach and curled a finger at her, humming tunelessly the *Aranjuez,* trying to be romantic. "Oh, but I am," he said. "Come, I'll show you." And for the rest of the Shabbat weekend, they both, indeed, did enjoy.

· 10 ·

For almost two months he spoke once a week with Helmut Leterhaus in Frankfurt, asking about progress in the investigation. Leterhaus was looking for Cohen's mystery chambermaid with the mole, but also collecting data on Israeli underworld figures in Germany.

The BKA and BND meanwhile looked for references to Cohen by terrorist groups. There were none, of course, as Cohen could have pointed out. Certainly none that had appeared in German. But as Lassman—who stayed in Frankfurt—had already pointed out to Leterhaus while Cohen was in the air going home, there were groups, small perhaps but zealous of their cause, who had targeted Cohen. "I understand there were at least two leaflets that named you among the people they consider—let me get my glasses—yes, 'dangerous to national Jewish interests,' " Leterhaus had said, surprising Cohen as much as Cohen had surprised him the first time Cohen called after returning to Jerusalem.

Leterhaus, after all, had the distinct impression that Cohen didn't want to help. Cohen didn't say it was part of Ahuva's sentence. And he also had not told Leterhaus about the leaflets. Lassman did.

The BKA—specializing in counterterror—asked the Mossad for copies and translations of the leaflets found in the most radical of the settlements, as well as the short list of names of Jews around the world known for their support of violent opposition to the peace process, beginning with no regret over the assassination of Yitzhak Rabin, whom they regarded as a traitor for conceding to the Palestinians control over parts of the Land of Israel.

The Mossad complied, getting the documents through the Shabak, which since Cohen's days as chief of CID in Jerusalem had its informers and agents, unwitting or not, infiltrate the radical Jewish right wing, where vigilantes plotted provocation and retaliations against the Arabs and the terrorism that came from their own fundamentalists and militants.

For his last ten years on the police force, Cohen had spent at least half his time on the danger of civil wars. After Baruch Goldstein's Hebron massacre, which Cohen practically predicted long before it happened—while the chief of the general staff called it "a thunderbolt out of clear skies"—he hoped the system would have learned the lesson.

Many were Americans; there were a few rabbis who said that assassinating Rabin was halachically acceptable, for a Jew was forbidden, under punishment of death, of handing another Jew over to the enemy, and as far as these rabbis were concerned that's what Yitzhak Rabin had done by agreeing to make peace with the PLO. Six members of the Jewish Defense League and a few Israelis held under house arrest—mostly in the Hebron area—for a year after the Rabin assassination were also on the list. Leterhaus read the list aloud to Cohen, who recognized many of the names.

"They believe it is in the Jewish interest to remove the mosques on the Temple Mount, in order to rebuild the Temple," Cohen pointed out. He had wanted to believe that the assassination of the prime minister had entirely quenched the flames of violence that threatened civil war. He was doubtful, however, knowing how deep revenge could run a motive into darkness.

With Dachau behind him, he had seen the limitless depths of evil and ever since had that as a measuring stick for the deed itself. But he never ceased to be astonished by the thin line between good and bad, and he knew from his years in Jerusalem that religious orthodoxy was no guarantee of goodness.

But the idea that he would be targeted by the lunatic fringe, no matter how many of their plots he had foiled or friends put in jail, was absurd. When, fully serious, Leterhaus told Cohen that "Mr. Kaplan was disappointed his name wasn't on the list," Cohen lost his temper.

"Find the woman with the mole," he ordered. He spent hours working with Israel's finest portrait painter, paying several thousand dollars for a set of drawings ranging from full-figure to a close-up of the face—all from Cohen's memory as described to the artist.

Leterhaus was grateful. The fingerprints collected from the hotel room turned up as Cohen's and the dead chambermaid's, and the thorough German police tracked down the three previous guests who had used the room to match against other prints found there. They were left with one half-thumbprint with no matches in their computer records.

"You can help," the inspector general had told Cohen, "but you are not to step outside channels."

Cohen pressed on. He had carte blanche in the archives, as long as if and when he found something he reported it to CID, which would then pass it through proper Interpol channels to the Germans.

So he spent most of November in the back attic of the Russian Compound. He sat by a round window he pushed open at the very end of the long row of shelves stacked with boxes and cartons, going back to the days when the British packed up the building Allenby had captured from the Russians in 1917, the police station that in the days of the British was known as Bevingrad, and the Jews called the Russian Compound, when they turned it into *their* police headquarters in West Jerusalem.

Box after box, folder after folder, he searched for cases he remembered that involved relocation to what was then West Germany. He cross-referenced to the stories he told in his book about the years the Israelis dumped criminals who turned state evidence and needed relocation to a safer place than tiny Israel.

Sometimes he found himself daydreaming, remembering too well. Sometimes he studied the flimsy pages with amazement at how much he had forgotten. Most of it was detail, tiny, though telling; he had refrained from digging like this into his past while writing his book, not needing the paper to remember what he wanted to say. Now, he realized it was part of his hubris, for as he went through the folders that he gradually built into a pile for yet a second read in case he missed something the first time, he realized that no matter how proud of his memory, no matter how trusting of his intuition, even his version of the events was far from objective, no matter how hard he tried to stick to the truth as he could prove it.

So reading over the sad case of the green-eyed Bernstein brothers, for example, in which an identical twin murdered his brother in a jealous rage over their sharing of their little sister, he could see now that he should have spotted the insanity that lay behind the crime far sooner than he eventually did.

The sister was the key, of course. She became a state witness—while the district psychiatrist said she had suffered severe trauma, there was nothing to prevent her from testifying in the case. The Jerusalem branch of the family was ruined by the scandal, and Cohen, as happened so often— too often, he sometimes thought—took responsibility for the victim, making the arrangements for the girl to be sent, yes, to Cohen's hated Germany, to a maiden aunt on the girl's father's side, who promised to look after her. There, far from the scandal of tiny Jerusalem, she could get a fresh start. He put her on the plane promising her that things would work out for the best. He hoped he wasn't lying, but knew that for the pretty teenager with the cold green eyes, life had already chosen its tragic course.

He had doubts in many cases. There had been Abu-Hassan, an Old City dealer looking for a heroin route to Europe. Cohen should have never allowed the student from the Bezalel School of Fine Arts to carry that second shipment of the drug into the trap Cohen was laying for the dealer.

They were typical of the things he found in the search. There were dozens of cases, and each contained its small success and failures that added up to its closure. None seemed to logically lead to an assassination attempt twenty years after the informant or witness was relocated to Germany.

By the middle of December, he had almost finished a full second read of every file he found. Dozens of files were missing, of course. Some were lost, as sometimes happens to files. Some had become of interest to the Shabak. A few to the Mossad. And they could always step in to ask for what they wanted from the police.

He looked for anyone he ever sent to Germany. Informants and state witnesses, petty crooks and ranking underworld figures; during the seventies he sent many—on his first round through the files he found thirty-seven he remembered because he personally handed over the envelope of cash and the new passport.

And there was the rub. It was a secret operation: the German authorities knew nothing about it, and for it to work the secrecy had to extend all the way to the underworld itself. Sure, the informants and bosses both knew that state witnesses could get relocation, if the evidence was good enough against a good enough target. But only when the process was complete, when the target was behind bars—or otherwise incapacitated—and the witness ready to be moved, did they find out where they'd be going.

Leon Hadani testified, for example, about how Avi Hakatan used a razor blade hidden between his fingers as an ultimate weapon of fear to collect his weekly payments from the stall-owners of the *shuk*. It took Cohen a month to convince Hadani to talk. The promise of a new name and start in *hutz la'aretz*—"out of the country"—finally turned him over.

Shimmy Rozen's wife, Vered, turned her husband in for selling a crate of grenades to an Old City hood. She walked in off the street, and because of her information, the grenades were found in the basement of a Ramallah villa, where they were being fitted to timing devices. All Vered wanted in exchange for the information was a new name on a passport and a new life in *hu'l*—the slangy acronym for overseas. Israel was too small to hide someone, the Israelis didn't have a continent in which to hide anyone. But they also did not have the clout to guarantee a relocated witness a first job, nor the money for a well-padded landing. Germany was an easy country to pick for the purpose, and not only because of the past. Foreign guest workers were flooding the big cities of what was then West Germany. The working-class Israelis who needed the refuge could easily fit in.

It took two and a half years for the Israeli underworld to figure out what was happening, and another year before the Germans noticed shadows of a growing Israeli criminal community in their cities. In a four-eyed meeting with his German counterpart, the Israel interior minister rued that yes, "part of the normalcy of the Jewish state is that now we have criminals," but he denied any knowledge of a "systematic transfer" of Israeli criminals to Frankfurt and Hamburg. The minister wasn't lying.

There was nothing systematic about it, which is why it managed to be one of the better-kept secrets in a country full of secrets. But as such, it made Cohen's work that winter in the attic of the Russian Compound, looking at twenty-year-old pieces of flimsy, faded paper, much more difficult than simply collecting names from old folders and passing them on to Helmut Leterhaus.

Some had insisted on passports for their wife and children. He tried not to promise them more than he could guarantee, or knew they could achieve.

The names, the faces he had tried so hard to forget now came back to him. Vered Rozen's cheerless hope that things would be better for her in Frankfurt; Hadani's fear of what his life would become. The horror in the Bernstein girl's eyes.

If half the reason he had put their names and faces out of his mind at the time was to help preserve the very secrecy required for the success of their relocation, the other half was his feeling of doubt about exile as a solution.

Cohen carefully collected the names. The trouble was that as part of the secrecy of the operation, nothing existed in the records about the informant's new name. So his first round through the boxes and folders was to jog his memory and the second was to shake it hard, trying to remember the new names in the new passports.

It became a routine: Sunday through Thursday, every afternoon at five o'clock, Cohen walked the two kilometers to the Russian Compound, hoping that if there was indeed an assassin out there after him, the killer would try to make an Achilles' heel out of the habit. But nothing, absolutely nothing, jumped out at him in the dark on his way home at midnight. No shots were fired at his window, though TMC was doing its best to keep the story of the attack alive in America and Europe.

He turned down every publisher in Israel who wanted his book. There were no explanations offered for anyone who managed to get his new phone number, which he had given to barely ten people. By December he was already deliberating ordering yet another new phone number that only a handful would know.

"So write a new one, for us," said the Israeli publishers. But Cohen just said no.

A week after Frankfurt, he had finally tracked down Lassman in New York at Tina's office. They spent less than two minutes on the phone, with Cohen ordering Lassman not to discuss the case publicly. "No story, no interviews, nothing," Cohen instructed. "Not until I say so."

"You can't stop me from digging up what I can find," Lassman pointed out. "And I'm going after that crowd of Kaplan's. Those nuts paying for other nuts to make religious war."

"Dig wherever you want. Just make sure none of the dirt lands on my yard," Cohen warned.

"But—"

"No buts about it," Cohen interrupted. He spent five minutes on the phone with Tina, and made clear to her that the investigation into the assassination attempt was very delicate, and any public appearance by him was too dangerous to make. He wasn't giving interviews.

"You're a regular Salman Rushdie," Tina exclaimed. "How can you not let us make press about it?"

"Do what you want. Just don't give my number to anyone. And do not compare me to Salman Rushdie. No state, no religion, has declared war on me. Yes, someone might have tried to kill me. But nobody has taken credit for it. Not Jews. Not Moslems."

Occasionally he spoke with his former assistant, Nissim
Levy, sometimes calling with a question to clarify a point
raised by one of the documents he found in the archives,
sometimes because Nissim called to ask for Cohen's advice.
Now chief of Intelligence for the Southern District, Levy
had become a rising star in the police after a couple of
years of suffering in small-town exile in the Negev as a
result of his affiliation with Cohen's own unhappy departure from the force.

Nissim's skills as a cop—as one taught by Cohen—
shone in the dusty development town where he was sent so
ignominiously after being assistant to chief of CID in
Jerusalem. In three years—in no small part because of two
changes of police minister, as well as an investigation that
Cohen accidentally handled in a private capacity—Nissim's
reputation improved enough to take him to the Southern
District headquarters as deputy chief of Intelligence, and
when his boss died of a heart attack the previous year, Nissim had become acting intelligence officer for the district.

Even if Nissim now lived in the south, had a wife—and
soon a baby—and they only saw each other when Nissim
was in Jerusalem for a meeting because Cohen hated traveling, they were as close as father and son. Cohen was,
after all, almost old enough to be Levy's father. And Nissim was worried.

"Nazis?" he had asked Cohen the first time they discussed the events in Frankfurt, that first week Cohen was
back. Cohen had reassured him that the German police
were looking into that possibility. Cohen had no inten-
tions of digging in that direction.

And like Leterhaus—though with a far better understanding of the situation—Nissim asked about the radical
right in Israel.

"Since the Rabin assassination they've been lying low," Cohen said.

"Yes, but now they've got a government they like," Nissim said. "Friends in high places."

"All the more reason for them to lie low," Cohen said. "Besides, they know I'm out of things," he reminded his former assistant. "And with even the government they like meeting Arafat, they realize they're in the minority."

"All the more reason for them to act."

"I'm not in the force anymore," Cohen emphasized.

"No, but you helped out in that Temple Mount business."

"That was more than three years ago. Nobody's heard from me since."

"The inspector general says that . . ."

". . . I'm one of his 'closest friends,' " Cohen finished the sentence bitterly. "That's politics," Cohen reminded Levy. Cohen had established a scholarship fund for the children of police officers, but the fifth floor wanted a recreation center for policemen's families. "And don't you ever forget it," he reminded Levy. "Especially when he's putting his arm around you."

"He's always asking me about you," said Levy.

"You mean about me funding the recreation center?"

"Yes," Levy admitted. "He usually mentions it."

"You see," Cohen pointed out, "politics."

"So which way are you looking?" Nissim asked.

"Into the past," Cohen had said, almost dreamily. "But I'd rather hear about your present," he told Levy.

"I've got Shvilli mapping the Russians, and have begun working with the Palestinian Authority police on stolen car rings. The Jordanians are incredibly cooperative. If things keep up this way, we'll finally shut down the Bedouin smuggling routes across the Sinai and the Negev for good.

Eilat's booming. Gambling. Massage parlors. Tourism's down a bit, but they still outnumber residents. I asked for Shvilli. He's doing a good job."

"Why not?" Cohen had said.

"Well, you know. He's had his share of troubles."

"He's a good man. The best when Russians are involved."

"I know, I know, you don't have to convince me. It's Bendor who needs convincing." Ya'acov Bendor was Southern District commander, Nissim's boss.

"You've got the inspector general behind you." Cohen smiled. "You told me yourself."

"That was almost a year ago," Nissim pointed out. "You know how the flag flies on the fifth floor. The immigrant party's not happy about high-profile task forces against Russian Mafia. And Bendor's complaining about the budget."

Cohen had laughed at the time.

"What's so funny?" Levy had asked, almost offended.

"You sound just like me in the old days," Cohen had said.

So it continued through the weeks and months following Frankfurt. But by the end of the year, three months after the incident, Leterhaus was deep at work on a case involving a serial murderer working the brothels of his city, and the BKA and BND were busy with their own agenda. Leterhaus still had flags out for anything related to Cohen coming out of neo-Nazi circles but nothing came in. His interviews with the known Israeli criminals in town came to naught, not even a rumor that might have led further. The two who gave any reaction at all to Cohen's name when Leterhaus interviewed them, described an officer who had been fair and helpful, even if he wasn't friendly.

The Mossad and Shabak both were convinced, like

Cohen, that the violent right wing might be angry at him, but Cohen wasn't an important enough target. He began to believe it had all been a mistake, an accident. He even suggested that Leterhaus dig back into the hotel records for other guests who might have been targets. He didn't let down his alert completely, of course. His search in the archives was still not over. But gradually, Cohen cut back his visits to the Russian Compound attic to only three times a week, instead of four, and then only twice a week he spent sitting beside the round window, even if it was only cracked open to a winter rain, reading files, and breathing the dusty air of his past, sometimes even forgetting for a moment what exactly he was seeking.

· 11 ·

The storms attacked simultaneously from Africa and Asia, two low-pressure areas colliding over the intersection of three continents. It became a national emergency, taking precedence over everything, even the latest development in the peace process, and the brewing constitutional crisis over the Supreme Court's authority.

Falling snow began sticking to the ground that Friday afternoon in Jerusalem. By dusk, there was no way Ahuva would allow Cohen to drive down to Tel Aviv for the weekend. By eight o'clock, the snow in the street outside his house was ankle high, and if he intended to surprise her the weather prevented it. He had chains in the trunk of his car, but the radio reports were pleading with Jerusalemites to stay out of their cars unless it was an absolute emergency.

He spent much of the day on the Net wandering from Web sites about food to sites about history, following links as he followed clues, sipping cognac, and enjoying the sense of travel without having to leave home.

But just after ten o'clock, the electricity fell in the neighborhood. He went to bed and slept deeply. Saturday, he stayed home all day. A stiff chill clamped the city beneath heavy gray clouds that threatened more snow. The municipality was salting the icy roads, said his transistor radio. The army had sent plows to clear thoroughfares. But the ice was devilish, and the emergency regulations regarding driving remained in effect. "The worst snow storm in sixty years," said the Voice of Israel. Army Radio said it was the worst in forty years. The electricity flickered back on for a moment in the afternoon but then crashed again. The weather did improve: rain, not snow, fell, sweeping away the small banks of snow and turning the ice into slush. Only at dusk did the electricity return completely. He put Daniel Beernbaum's Beethoven piano concertos into the CD-ROM that evening while he surfed for pleasure, finally going to bed around midnight, planning on reopening the 1974 boxes in the attic archives of the Russian Compound the next day when he continued his search into his past.

Just before dawn that Sunday morning, as one of his several recurring nightmares reached the point of gunshot, alarms, and a sense of breathlessness from running as fast as he could away from the sound of ringing bells, he realized that it was the phone chasing him from beside his bed. Reaching for it in the dark, he knocked the receiver to the floor.

"Avram? Cohen? Boss?" High-pitched and urgent, it sounded vaguely familiar but he couldn't tell if the tinny sound was a calm woman or a nervous man. It came from the floor where he fumbled the phone into the darkness. His hand found the spiraled wire and he yanked the receiver to the bed, dropping it on the pillow beside his head. His eyes still closed, he mumbled a hello.

"Boss?" the voice asked again.

It had been a long time since anyone called him boss. "What time is it?" he demanded to know from whomever in his past suddenly intruded on his sleep. "How'd you get this number?"

"Yeah, that's you," the caller decided, and finally Cohen recognized the voice. "It's five forty-five, boss. In the morning," he added, just in case some of the rumors about

Cohen were true and he really was working at night and sleeping during the day.

"Shvilli," Cohen said, finally recognizing the voice.

It had been more than five years since Shvilli worked for Cohen. The last time Shvilli called his former boss was a year and a half earlier, to invite Cohen to a wedding. The Georgian-born, Soviet-trained polylinguist, whose favorite sport as a youth had been boxing, was giving away his first daughter, to a young lawyer she had been dating for less than a year. "I don't know whether to hug him or kill him," Shvilli had confessed to Cohen. "A lawyer," he complained. "With an earring."

Cohen laughed then. Now, he asked, "What's wrong?" Shvilli wasn't calling to invite him at dawn to invite him to a *brit*.

"I've got bad news."

"Obviously," said Cohen. "Just tell me, Misha," he ordered, using Shvilli's first name deliberately.

"Nissim is dead."

Pain propelled by memories shot through Cohen's mind like rain driven before the wind. He closed his eyes and for a moment thought he might be dreaming, that everything he expected in the nightmares he knew so well had suddenly given way to a new dream from which he'd yet awake sweaty, afraid.

Memories flooded him. Levy asking a question, Levy answering a question; from Levy's first days in Cohen's office, to the last—and beyond, when Levy's natural loyalties to Cohen made the junior officer suspect to the fifth floor of national headquarters. It would take nearly two years before Cohen could repair the damage his reputation did to Levy's career.

"Boss, you all right?" Shvilli finally asked.

Then, as suddenly as the phone call woke him, indeed as

the too-familiar gunshot in his nightmare always inevitably arrived, he was alert and focused like so many times in the past when survival required it.

"Hold on," Cohen said, seeking light, and a way to squelch the sour taste of alcohol-induced sleep that made his mouth feel glued shut. He pulled the little chain on the heavy brass night lamp on the table beside the bed. It illuminated a pale puddle at the bottom of the water glass he used for the cognac and water he drank before going to sleep. He downed those last few drops to get some moisture back into his dry mouth, smacking his lips with the sudden burn.

"How?" he asked.

"Looks like an accident," Shvilli said.

"Car?" Cohen guessed sadly.

"Yes," Shvilli admitted tersely.

"Where?"

"Down near Eilat."

"In this weather?" Cohen asked, with as much curiosity as anger.

Flooding wadis could sweep across a dip in the road and take a car dozens of kilometers away. What looked like a puddle as a car started into a dip on the road could suddenly be window high, smashing into the car, carrying it kilometers off the road. Buses, even loaded trucks, were known to be shoved aside by the rage of one of those flash rivers. Cars sometimes ended up in the deep ravines, dropping from the Negev plateau down to the Jordan Rift, the lowest place on earth. "He was out on the road in this weather?" Cohen repeated.

"Yes," said Shvilli.

Nissim took all the driving courses, coming out at the top of his group in every driving course offered by Israeli security. But he was always too quick on the gas pedal for no reason, to Cohen's mind, and used the siren a bit too much.

He wasn't reckless. But as always, self-confidence—and readiness to take risks that Cohen, older, and yes, wiser, knew were unnecessary—sometimes went a step too far. He wasn't fearless, but Cohen sometimes worried Nissim was too brave for his own good. So in that moment, Cohen realized that it wasn't inevitable that Nissim might die in a car accident. But it wasn't surprising.

"Was he alone?" Cohen asked. "What about Hagit?"

"The report says that as far as they can tell there was only one body."

"What was he working on?" Cohen asked.

"I don't know. He had a lot going."

"Maybe something you were working on with him?" Cohen wondered. Soon after his appointment as Intelligence branch commander for the Negev subdistrict of the Southern District, Levy brought Shvilli south from Jerusalem to map the Russian underworld operating in Beersheba and Eilat.

Shvilli paused before he spoke. "Could be. But he didn't tell me he was going down south this weekend. You taught him, after all."

Like Cohen, Nissim compartmentalized, keeping secrets from subordinates until they needed to know. Your methods, Shvilli was saying, without any mean intention, just pointing out the fact that explained Levy's behavior. It was a cop's approach and it was true and Cohen knew it, even if it only added to his pain the feeling that he was responsible for Levy's death. He went back to business, trying to keep focused, working at controlling his emotions.

Shvilli broke the silence. "He kept a lot going at once," Cohen's former undercover man repeated.

"Where are you?" Cohen asked.

"Beersheba station. Just dropped into the office. Saw

the bulletin on the desk. Called you first. Thought you'd want to know right away."

"What about Hagit?" Cohen snapped, almost bitterly, nearly angry that Shvilli thought of Cohen, not Hagit, first.

"SOP already kicked in. The social workers are probably already at work."

"So what do we know?" Cohen asked.

"Trucker caught the car in his headlights. Reported it to Eilat station. It came into District about ten minutes ago."

"Where they taking the body?" Cohen asked.

"You mean the pieces," Shvilli said bluntly. "It sounds like the body's a complete mess, smashed up as badly as the car."

"How'd they get an ID?" Cohen asked.

"From the plates, I guess."

"So we don't know for sure if it's Nissim's body?"

Shvilli paused for a minute. "We have to assume for now it's him."

"Maybe his assistant will know what he was working on," Cohen said. "What's her name? Jacki?"

"Yeah, I'll call her as soon as I get off with you," Shvilli promised.

"All right, I'll meet you at their house," Cohen decided, "if the weather doesn't hold me up. Meet me there." He started to hang up but paused, and deliberately using Shvilli's first name, he added, "Michael, thanks for letting me know."

He heaved himself off the bed and went to the thick curtain at his window, yanking it open angrily, starting grimly at the weather for what it did to Levy. The snow was mixed with a falling rain that had washed away the white of the night before. The storm had moved.

HIGHLAND PARK PUBLIC LIBRARY

Only the branches of the eucalyptus tree in his garden wore white sleeves of snow, making him sigh. He forced himself back to work building that wall in his mind, shoring up its foundations to make sure it stayed up, preserving Nissim's memory but allowing Cohen to continue with his work. He picked up the transistor radio on top of his wooden bureau, carrying it around the small apartment as he went through his little routine: he started with the kitchen, where he put on the kettle for hot water, and then to the bathroom where the radio played music while he showered. First he stood for a long while under hot water and then cold, until finally he was truly awake, just in time to shave while the six A.M. Army Radio news magazine on the first day of the workweek in Israel began to tell him the news.

They began with the weather, and its toll. An elderly woman had been found by her son, frozen to death in her unheated Jerusalem flat. A kerosene heater tipped over in an Arab villager's house, causing a fire that sent four people to the hospital, including a baby. In Tel Aviv, electricity remained out in most of the southern half of the city. In the north, snow kept falling throughout Galilee, with three fatalities. "And in the Negev," said the broadcaster, "flooding across the road north cut Eilat off from the rest of the country, and so far one fatality is reported." No names were yet attached to any of the victims of the three incidents. That meant next of kin were not yet told of the disasters that just struck them. Levy's parents were both dead. Hagit still didn't know.

By the time Cohen was dressed, standing in his living-room-turned-study, sipping his thick black mud drink made like instant with Turkish ground coffee, the broadcaster finished with the weather story and was talking about Israel's latest demands in the peace process. Cohen checked his watch and turned on the television to CNN.

The American weatherman spoke softly as he moved across the screen, blocking Spain and giving Cohen a view of the Eastern Mediterranean. Two low pressure areas had converged at the intersection of the three continents. From Africa, a band of clouds raced across the Sahara from southern Libya up into Egypt, thickening as it stabbed into the Mediterranean where it met the second swirl of clouds that bulged down from Greece and Turkey.

He glanced at his umbrella in the corner by the front door and again at the TV screen. The fast motion satellite picture's cloud cover flipped forward, showing the storm's breakup starting in the south. From Beersheba south, the sun would be shining in the Negev. He didn't need a raincoat, he decided, despite the rain pattering evenly on the glass canopy above the seventeen steps down to the back of the garden. He trotted past the deep green foliage of his garden, around to the front of the house, almost slipping when he jumped a puddle to avoid getting his sneakers wet.

Slowly but surely, he drove through the empty streets of the early morning city until down the mountain to the coastal plain, and heading south on the highway to the Negev, he was beyond the ice and able to speed.

· 12 ·

Sunk in his memories, he drove automatically. By the time he reached the bridge over the wadi north of Beersheba, Army Radio was carrying Nissim's name as part of their report on the road death toll. To Cohen's ire, they were specifically noting Levy was a senior police officer, so his death in a car accident made a natural peg for their daily traffic death report. "Even trained police officers," the broadcaster was saying, "have to be careful on the roads. This month's road accident death rate already set a new record."

Leaving the mumble of Beersheba behind, he felt his head clear as the speedometer rose and the clear air left behind by the departed storm rushed in from the open window, chilling his face even while the sun tried to warm it. Like the struggle of sensation on his face, his memories of the dead challenged him not to weep. He didn't, but his face was grim as two hours and seventeen minutes after leaving Jerusalem, he turned left onto an avenue wider than the two-lane road from Beersheba to Eilat and entered what had once been a gray little town but which was growing some color.

Nissim had helped in the town's self-improvement campaign, of that Cohen was sure. But what really made the difference was on his left: a low-slung high-tech park made of one- and two-story light blue buildings sat behind a row of newly planted palm trees that grew a little taller than the

dark blue Mercedes gliding out of the park under an elec-
tronically operated barrier, which was guarded by a security
guard in a simple uniform. Cohen drove another fifty
meters past another three palms in the median strip before
reaching a billboard promising a country club at *Neve
Darom,* the southern oasis.

He followed the arrow to the right, and headed toward
the new neighborhood of misproportioned two-story
apartment blocks with slanting red-tiled roofs where Nissim and Hagit had bought their first home. The houses
stood in awkward rows a couple of hundred yards into the
desert, on a still-new black asphalt road already scarred,
Cohen noticed, by tire rubber laid down by bad drivers or
teenage joy riders. The country club would have a swim-
ming pool and health spa, tennis courts, and an audito-
rium, said the signs hanging on a wire fence concealing the
hole in the ground where the foundations would go for the
complex. The last time he had been there, for the housewarming, there had only been a sign inviting people to the
model home at *Neve Darom.*

Just a month ago, Levy had been in Jerusalem for a
meeting and had dropped by to see Cohen's plans for the
house. Nissim had been proud that all the homes in the
neighborhood had been bought. "People are already coming around asking if we're selling," Nissim had announced,
pleased with his investment.

Cohen turned into the street where Nissim and Hagit had
planned to have their first baby. It was wide enough to park
at an angle in front of the houses. Their house was on the
corner, first on the left. About half the houses on the street
had a car parked in front. Outside Levy's house stood half
a dozen cars, including an empty blue-and-white, a van,
and an upper-range Peugeot, its three-digit license plate
identifying it to Cohen as a district commander's. Cohen

scowled, guessing the identity of the owner. A uniformed driver slouched in the front seat, reading the sports pages.

He walked on to the front gate, a low-slung iron arabesque set into a low stucco wall already traced by ivy. "I'm gardening," Nissim had told Cohen proudly. He paused for a second and looked up at the black bunting of the storm to the north. To the south, the blue was almost white in its clarity, without even a wisp of cloud in the sky. He knew that he might never know what really had happened when the flood took Levy to his death, because the storm would have washed away the evidence.

He looked around. The last time he had been there, half the homes had still stood empty. Now, parked cars, tricycles, and other children's toys, and a pair of spaniels and a poodle playing in the middle of the street gave life to the short, wide block. The sidewalks, however, were not completely paved. Three stacks of bricks, stacked on wooden palettes and still wrapped in their steel band, stood like sentries to the desert at the end of the street. Almost every front yard had at least one sapling and some shrubs. Levy had planted ficus on one side of the walk and a pair of palms on the other.

Finally, hesitantly, he looked at the house and found himself in the wide-eyed sights of a uniformed police woman with dyed yellow hair and a nose beaked into a sculpture on her flat face, heading down the walkway toward him, hand outstretched. "Yoheved Ginsburg," she said, sticking out her hand, "but everyone calls me Jacki."

"I know," he mumbled. Shvilli—unshaven, in sneakers, jeans, and a sweater under a blue police-issued bombardier's jacket—appeared in the doorway. His face confirmed what Cohen had hoped against hope he would not have to hear. It was indeed Levy who had died in the car.

"How's Hagit?" Cohen asked.

"Her mother wants the funeral in Jerusalem," said Jacki, "and wants Hagit back in Jerusalem for the shivah."

Cohen had met Hagit's parents twice—first at the wedding, then, two years later, at the housewarming when the young couple had bought the house in the desert town, and made public the announcement Cohen already knew, that Hagit was pregnant. At the wedding her parents had seemed proud of their daughter. At the housewarming, they kept to themselves, unable to hide their disappointment in their daughter's decision to make a home in the desert town so far from the family, unable to understand why Nissim had been sent so far south, unable to fight the transfer. They ran a small *makolet*, a mom-and-pop grocery store, on the border between Jerusalem's upper middle-class Rehavia and working-class Nahlaot. "With a university education, she decides to live in this place," the mother had complained to Cohen at the housewarming. He had used his empty glass as an excuse to get away from the embittered woman and her meek, silent husband.

"She'd rather stay down here," Shvilli pointed out. "They made a lot of friends here." Just then, as if to confirm his assessment, a blonde in her early thirties came out of the front door of the next house carrying a platter of food. Because of the waist-high wall separating the gardens, she had to walk down her walkway to the still-unpaved sidewalk, onto the asphalt street, around a ten-year-old gray Subaru sedan pulled up onto what would have been the sidewalk, past the parked police cars, and only then enter the path to the house. She sidled past Cohen, Shvilli, and Jacki, mumbling "pardon me" with a Russian accent before disappearing into the house.

"Do we know why Nissim was out on that road?" Cohen asked in a voice as low as the neighbor bringing food to the house of the mourners.

"It could be anything," said Jacki. Shvilli just shook his head sadly. Jacki's wide mouth squirmed downward into a frown, and she, too, shook her head no.

"And Hagit doesn't know, either," Cohen said in a tone that made the statement into a question to which he already knew the answer. Shvilli and Jacki exchanged glances but their expressions didn't need words to confirm Cohen's guess.

Cohen looked back at the district commander's car. "Does *he* know?" Cohen asked, indicating District Commander Ya'acov Bendor's car.

"He knows how to jump out of airplanes. He wouldn't know how to fill out an accident report, let alone read one," Jacki said.

Shvilli frowned at her, but, uninhibited by the responsibility of active service, Cohen could smile. Like her, he was not necessarily impressed with army officers' trading in their greens for blues. It took most of them too long to learn that the police might wear uniforms and have a chain of command, but that civilians were not the enemy. Ya'acov Bendor had come out of the paratroopers' brigade as a colonel who realized he'd never make general, and parachuted into the police where he was promised a promotion to commander—the equivalent of a general in the army.

A sudden sob from inside the house broke the quiet. "Who else is here?" Cohen asked Shvilli.

"The social worker, two neighbors, her school principal."

"What else do we know?"

"Hagit says he left on Saturday morning," Shvilli reported. " 'Work,' he told her."

"Early? Late? A sudden decision?" Cohen rattled off the questions. He didn't want to have to interrogate the widow. He knew he would nonetheless. A sudden gust of wind carried the sound of a motorcycle's sudden downshift on the highway a kilometer away. Shvilli's expression changed as he glanced off toward the distant bike, as if the sound were a scent he knew.

"Jacki?" Cohen called on her, like a teacher calling on a student. He feared the worst, needing preparation for what lay ahead, knowing Nissim learned much from him, but worried he might have learned too much. Secrets are the true trade of the investigator. Sometimes, Cohen taught Levy, to bring one secret into the open, another must be hidden in the dark.

But the throaty acceleration of the motorcycle and Shvilli's reaction to its arrival distracted her.

"Just what we needed," Shvilli muttered cynically as the all-black Intruder, its rider in black-and-blue plastic overalls and wearing a scuffed white helmet, rumbled down the wide street toward them.

"*Sha*," Jacki commanded, even though Shvilli was three grades above her in rank. "I heard he was down there. Maybe he knows something."

"He's a vulture and you know it," Shvilli shot back, "they all are."

"Press?" Cohen asked. Though he didn't completely agree with Shvilli, his distrust of journalists was legendary. He had used a few, but only when he had both the upper hand in the relationship—a shared secret that Cohen, not the reporter, controlled—and a need to move the investigation further.

Jacki nodded. "The Beast," she added. "That's what they call him. His name's Phillipe."

"French," muttered Shvilli.

The biker pulled up in the space between Cohen's car and the district commander's. He made a small ceremony of dismounting, starting with stopping the engine and kicking down the stand. Then he took off his black gloves, unstrapped the helmet, and finally swung his leg over to get off the motorcycle.

"Jacki?" Cohen called her aside as Shvilli headed down the walkway toward the biker, who went to the back of his bike where he unlocked a large box plastered with bumper stickers of every political stripe, thus mocking them all.

Levy's assistant tore her eyes away from the photographer and stepped closer to Cohen.

"Tell me," he said.

"Nissim went out some time after nine o'clock on Friday night. Hagit was tired and decided to go to sleep after the news. Nissim said he'd stay up. On Saturday morning, she found a note saying he had to go out, for work. Nothing out of the ordinary. Usually if he worked on Shabbat he'd be home by sunset. They made it a tradition, to try to have sunset together on Shabbat."

"But he wasn't back by sunset," Cohen pointed out.

"He called her."

"When?"

"Saturday afternoon. Said he'd been delayed. And would probably be back late."

"It was pouring. A flood. Didn't she say something? Tell him to wait until morning?"

When Jacki didn't answer, Cohen added another question. "Didn't you ask?"

"I didn't want to make her feel guilty."

He sighed but didn't criticize her. He would have criticized Levy if under different circumstances it had been Levy who had had a chance to ask a witness questions. He would ask Hagit the question. Jacki was looking down, trying to avoid his eyes.

"And she didn't ask where he was?" Cohen asked in a tone of voice that said he knew the answer.

"You know her. She didn't want to know anything about

his work." She paused, then lowered her voice. "If you ask me, she treated the job like *it* was the crime."

Cohen did not want to argue with the assistant. "Is Bendor asking questions?"

"He tried, but Hagit . . ." she paused, interrupted by a loud voice at the end of the walkway, making her eyes shift from Cohen's weary gaze to Shvilli with the biker, who without his helmet revealed a totally bald head over a thick neck.

"He was my friend, too," the newsman biker suddenly shouted from the sidewalk.

"But you're here to work, aren't you?" Shvilli answered back.

"Oh God," Jacki blurted, "I don't know why Nissim put up with him," she said to Cohen, apologizing for the Russian.

"Shvilli!" Cohen snapped, making Shvilli pause. The Beast looked toward Cohen, wonder on his face about the identity of the white-haired man in the windbreaker, gray twill trousers, and white scuffed sneakers who had the power to protect him from Shvilli. The Georgian stepped back, as if called by the bell to his corner, a sly smile on his face. The Beast nodded respectfully toward Cohen, grinned at Jacki, and then even more ceremoniously than before, turned his back on Shvilli and began unpacking his camera bags.

Cohen turned back to Jacki. She was smoothing back her hair with one hand, her eye on the photographer. "But Hagit what?" Cohen pressed, interrupting the unconscious preening for the camera.

"You know her, she's very, very . . ."

"What?" Cohen asked, knowing the answer.

"Emotional," Jacki decided, not wanting to ire the old detective. "She said she is waiting for you to show up so she can finally, finally . . ." Jacki wasn't able to find the words.

Cohen helped her out sorrowfully. "So she can finally lay the blame," he mumbled, to himself as much as to Jacki. She nodded ever so slightly.

He gave one final glance to the photographer, ignoring Shvilli's glare, and headed into the house to meet his accuser.

· 13 ·

During the years he had worked for Cohen, Levy had dated a lot of women, usually only one at a time, usually a beauty (with a preference for blondes), but always, only, someone with whom to share fun—when Cohen gave him time off— and never for a long-time commitment. So Nissim didn't prepare Cohen for an introduction to the woman he announced would be Mrs. Levy. One day he just showed up with Hagit and said she was the one. Cohen could only believe that Nissim, by virtue of the unprecedented announcement, was serious. Yet knowing Nissim's past, he wondered if the commitment would last. So for a while, whenever Cohen encountered Hagit—perhaps half a dozen times during the first year she was with Levy—he watched her with a natural curiosity that she clearly interpreted to mean suspicion. There was also no doubt in his mind that she was also suspicious of him. Levy looked up to Cohen, all the worse, as far as Hagit was concerned, because Nissim loved Cohen and Cohen loved the police, so Nissim loved the police. Hagit did not.

She made no secret of her distaste for the job—the way it kept Nissim away from home, indeed, put him in danger. But she also loved his self-sacrificing readiness for public service.

Complicating matters, Nissim lapsed into adultery a year after the wedding, confessing the indiscretion to Cohen, whose response was simple. It was not an order or a suggestion, merely a statement of fact, the logical conclusion deduced by the evidence.

"If you want to save the marriage, you will confess," Cohen had said simply. Nissim did.

A year later, Hagit was pregnant and they bought a house with a government-subsidized mortgage, a loan against Nissim's pension plan, and the dowry that Hagit brought to the marriage. As usual, Nissim turned down the money Cohen had offered to help.

Now, less than a month before the due date, Nissim was gone and Cohen had to face Hagit alone. He shuffled into the house, past the narrow staircase that led to the second floor, left to the living room. It turned into a semiopen kitchen at the rear, beyond which lay a green lawn of tightly mown buffalo grass bright under the desert's yellows and the white sun rising into the pale blue of an almost cloudless sky.

The furniture was simple, a living room set with a matching three-person sofa, a two-person couch, and a single armchair. Beyond it was a small oval table covered with platters of food, paper cups, open bottles, and a tall electric kettle boiling away, all for the coming week's visitors.

Two women were in the kitchen area. The blonde neighbor who arrived just after Cohen was washing dishes. A tiny elderly woman with dark leathery skin that brightened the fading colors of her flower print dress fussed with a dish towel, wiping down the counter, keeping beady eyes on the living room and entrance.

District Commander Ya'acov Bendor, his uniform tailored to fit his huge girth, occupied the three-person sofa, alone. His entire posture indicated that he was a man without any regrets. Opposite Bendor was a slender woman in her mid-thirties, wearing a business suit and with a stack of papers on the slope of a lap made by her crossed legs.

As Cohen entered, Bendor was listening intently to the

woman. She was leaning forward over the stack of papers, speaking in a low voice to the district commander. Her black hair was streaked by white shocks at the temples. Too well-dressed for the Beersheba station's social worker, Cohen thought. The principal, he decided. Hagit's boss. Bendor's gaze floated back and forth between the principal's eyes and her long legs. Neither noticed Cohen at the door.

Hagit was nowhere to be seen. Cohen walked through the living room without pausing, silencing the principal and startling the senior officer on the sofa by ignoring him. Spotting an open jar of instant coffee, Cohen scowled, but he picked up a spoon from the counter and looked for a spare coffee cup. The blonde neighbor turned to him with one in her hand.

"Where's Hagit?" he asked her. Bendor eyed him with curiosity for a second longer, then returned his gaze to the principal, who resumed speaking in a low voice.

"Upstairs," the neighbor whispered. "With the social worker." Just then, Bendor heaved himself upward from the sofa with a grunt. Cohen took the cup from the blonde woman and asked if there was any mud coffee—finely ground Turkish coffee that must gradually settle at the bottom of the cup before it can be drunk. "I'm sure Nissim must have kept some," Cohen said softly. The blonde neighbor started looking in the cupboards. Bendor cleared his throat.

"Perhaps someone could tell Hagit that I had to go," said the former paratrooper, heaving himself to his feet with a grunt and the order. It was not a bellow but an announcement, loud enough for everyone in the house to hear, whether on the first floor or the second. But while he spoke to the room, his eyes were on Cohen. They had never met, but Cohen was sure that Bendor recognized him.

Cohen's eyes shifted to the district commander's ranks on the epaulett, and ever so slightly nodded respectfully to the olive branches and the star. He would have traded all his money in exchange for the authority—and responsibility—the grades gave their owner. But instead of looking back at Bendor's eyes, Cohen noticed movement on the stairs to his left, over Bendor's shoulder. Hagit was coming down the stairs. It was difficult to tell if she was walking slowly because of her mourning or because of the weight of her pregnancy, but she took each step carefully, almost regally. She wore a housecoat that made a flowing tent hanging from the circumference of her stomach. Her dark brown hair, thick and curly, had fallen from its braid, and framed her tanned face with a tangle that almost hid her eyes from everyone until she reached the district commander, held out her hand, and softly said, "Thank you for coming."

Ben-Ya'acov took her hand but her reflexes were quick as she stepped backward just a moment before he began leaning forward to offer her a fatherly embrace.

"It will be very hard to replace him for all of us," he said. "For you, and for us, too, he was family."

Hagit nodded, and then, noticing Cohen behind the overweight district commander, froze and shifted her stare to Cohen's tired face, suddenly ignoring the senior officer.

Cohen put down the coffee cup and turned his palms to Hagit, as if to show he hid nothing and that he had nothing to offer that could comfort her except his embrace. It was an instinctive reaction, but she made him wait, and in her eyes he could see her trying to make up her mind whether to accept his silent condolence.

"Shalom, Avram," she finally said, walking toward him, reaching into his hug. "You loved him so much," she whispered into his ear as they leaned toward each other, Cohen careful not to bump her belly, so ripe and ready for birth it made him wonder if the baby would wait for its due date during the trauma of the coming days.

Hagit pulled a thick curl of hair away from her face. Her light green eyes—usually bright, now deadened—looked directly into Cohen's own sorrow-struck face. Her eyes gave away her mother's European roots, but her father was a North African, and he gave her light coffee skin and deep brown, curly hair.

In the sandy town she hated so much at first, she had found a place to be herself. Trained to be a high school teacher, when Nissim was thrown by the job into the desert town right after Cohen's fall, Hagit found herself in front of a classroom full of elementary school kids. By the time Cohen could face facts and realize he wasn't going to get back his active duty badge, Hagit was in love with the town and Nissim was moving up the hierarchy fast with a promotion to Beersheba.

"I can get there in twenty minutes with the siren," Nissim had bragged, finding his own rationale for looking ahead rather than behind. "And I can lift a chopper if I have to get somewhere fast. But the drives in the district are beautiful—and the roads are getting better all the time. The road from Mitzpe to Eilat—it's a lot more beautiful than the Arava ruler. And the peace, Avram, the peace . . ."

Already, Levy twice met with his counterpart from Jordan, to begin a practice of coordination along the border. Tourism across the Jordan Rift Valley was already changing the landscape. With two border crossings to Jordan, and one at Taba to Egypt under Levy's purview as chief of Intelligence for the Negev, he saw a great future for the region—and a lot of work for him as a cop. "I'll bet that a Southern District commander gets to be inspector general by the end of the century," he had vowed to Cohen, as if promising to carry Cohen's flag on all the way to the inspector general's job. Nissim was always ambitious.

It all went through Cohen's mind as he looked at the

young woman in front of him, ten years younger than her husband, now dead before he reached forty.

Cohen knew her future was not destroyed. In her eyes he looked hopefully for her understanding of that truth about the loneliness that still lay ahead, that her sorrow would pass to become an ache and then turn into a strange whisper late at night that came back not to haunt but to remind one of love. Instead, all he could say was, "I'm sorry," so softly that only Hagit could actually hear him.

Bendor hitched his trousers. Behind him, Jacki and Shvilli came in, followed by "The Beast," carrying two cameras and a large bag over a safari vest that went over the overalls, which were unzipped in the front far enough to reveal a thermal undershirt. Between the photographer's oversize appearance, the district commander's own huge girth, and the social worker coming down the stairs the room was becoming crowded.

"Come outside with me," Cohen ordered Hagit, holding her left hand and leading her through the kitchen. He slid open the glass doors to the garden at the rear of the house, and she followed him out into the crisp air warming fast under the rising sun.

Flower beds of geranium and petunia, watered with drip irrigation from black tubing, bordered the lawn. He marched to the end of the garden, to the wall where the desert began abruptly on its other side. Except for a short rise of the highway over a last lip of hill to the far right, no sign of civilization marred the view beyond the backyard lawn Levy had planted.

They stood side by side staring out at the wild land just past the neighborhood's edge. The sun was above the house, and in the precision of the clear air, their shadows lay long ahead of them on the rough texture of the ground. A large boulder within his shadow's grasp made Cohen play with the illusion and grab for the rock like a giant. Then a distant truck on the road south shifted gears, its sound caught on a breeze driving across the surface of the desert. Cohen's shadow let go of the rock as the highway sound dissolved into chimes hanging somewhere down the row of gardens. Then there was nothing except the wind.

"This won't last forever," he finally said, waving his hand at the view. Two nearby mounds partially framed a far-distant horizon marked by stubby plateaus, like a row of gapped teeth. But he was referring to her sorrow, not to the pristine view.

"I know," she said. There was another pause. "I don't blame you."

"Don't blame him, either."

"I blame myself," she admitted. "If I had let him tell me about his work . . . but I said no." She spoke with deadly bitterness. "I wanted to believe in the good of people," she said softly. "He worked with the evil." There was a pause. Cohen waited. "I closed my eyes, and now," she said, her voice trembling, "Nissim's are closed. Forever." She heaved a deep sigh. But she did not let the tears flow or the anguish buckle her knees.

Cohen put his arm around her. "He was lucky to have you. Good for him. He was happy."

"Because of this," she said, patting her stomach.

"And a good reason, too."

"He used to love *me,*" she wept quietly.

"He did."

"Not as much as I loved him," she said. "That's why I didn't want him to talk with me about his work. To free him to be himself, to be free to be with me. I wanted him to relax, to—"

"You see," he interrupted. "We both tried to teach him something," he said, trying to soothe his own conscience.

115

"But he didn't learn, did he?" she sobbed again, as if reading his thoughts.

"Nobody's perfect," he said, and realized that an unintended grin crept across his face, for he saw it mirrored in her own. Her smile in response came hesitantly at first and then turned wry, indeed resolved. For the first time since they met, he felt they had shared their love for Nissim, gone but not forgotten.

· 14 ·

Dealing with sorrow is as difficult the thousandth time as the first, but practice makes perfect, so that it became easier over the years for Cohen to seal his sorrows away in secret vaults that only he could open. The signs pointing to those moments of mourning could be seen on his face. The lines carved around his eyes and mouth, parallel and askew, creating junctures of expression that signified yet another riddle solved—or left behind as an eternal mystery—could be specific or so vague that sometimes even he, glancing in the mirror, wasn't sure if he recognized the emotion that had caused his face to thus fall into place. He liked to think of himself as simple, though the world saw him as complicated, and over that bridge he walked all his waking hours. Now, wanting to console her, all he could think of were the facts he knew and didn't know and how they fit together to explain what had happened. Cohen was sometimes ready to take enormous risks, but with simple things he preferred to be cautious. Like driving when time was not a factor. He realized he was hoping to learn that Nissim's death wasn't an accident, because if it was, it would have been Cohen's greatest failure that Levy had died senselessly. He needed information.

"We need to know how he died," he tried.

"An accident," she snapped at him, then regretting the bitterness, apologized. "It was bound to happen, wasn't it?

I knew it would happen. It's why I never wanted to know. If I knew, I would think about it. I'd imagine him in those places, dangerous places, horrible places."

"We need to know what happened," he said again softly. "As close to the truth as we can. What exactly killed him."

"I already called the hospital. I told them they can use whatever they want from his body. For transplants. There should have been a card in his wallet, but they told me he was in the water, the mud, . . . oh God," she bawled, and Cohen grabbed her to give her support. But she didn't want his support nor need it, wresting her body away, surprising him with an agility disguised by the majestic bearing of her pregnancy. She pulled a handkerchief from a pocket and blew her nose. Then she sighed heavily, and nodded. "I'm okay. I will not break down."

"You will eventually," he told her simply.

"Not in front of all these people," she said.

"You might," he pointed out. "I'm worried for the child."

"I'll be okay. He'll be okay."

"I'll provide for the child, whatever is necessary," Cohen said.

"I know," she admitted. She had never fully fathomed Nissim's refusal to take financial help from Cohen.

"Good," he agreed.

They stood together quietly for a long moment of silence, each with their own thoughts. Cohen finally broke it. "He called you to say he'd be late. When?"

"Shabbat afternoon."

"I thought you made a tradition of the sunset."

"When he was home," she said angrily.

"Did he say when he'd be back?"

"He said it would be late, after I went to sleep. It's happened before. You taught him, after all. The job's the life," she said, trying not to be bitter.

"And he didn't say where he called from? Eilat? Mitzpe? Beersheba? Did he name any place at all?"

Hagit began to shake her head, but stopped, suddenly remembering something much more important. "They told me a wadi. Not where," she said. She laughed slightly to herself. "You know, for the first time I want to know. Where, when, how, all of it. Every detail."

"We need the autopsy, the traffic report, and most of all, some intelligence from the field."

"What do you mean, 'intelligence from the field'?" But before she could wait for an answer, understanding crossed her face. "You mean they don't know where he was?" she asked him. "They don't know what he was doing there?"

Cohen didn't know whether to shake or nod. He just looked at her.

She almost laughed, realizing something. "It was bound to happen," she said. "He deserved it, the bastard," she added, "taking all those chances. It's why I didn't want to know."

"But now you want to know," he pointed out. He was about to ask her for a full recounting of her phone call from Nissim when they were interrupted by a voice calling out Hagit's name. Cohen turned a moment after Hagit.

The sun that created such perfect shadows was suddenly in his eyes. He reached into his windbreaker pocket for a pair of black sunglasses. By the time he had them on, a squat bald man in a light blue shirt over a round belly and a bright-colored tie hanging below a reddish neck tight in the collar was reaching out to Hagit from two footsteps away. "Our mayor," Hagit muttered under her breath to Cohen. And then she was letting the politician wrap his arms halfway around her. Despite lowering his voice, the politician's condolence—"It's a loss to the entire town"—sounded like an announcement. When he added, "and to me personally, of course," it sounded like a question.

The frown in the lines of his face gave him the proper mourner's expression, but his eyes gleamed with expectation, waiting for Hagit's thanks. It was a symptom of an addiction Cohen knew all too well, the politician's need to be acknowledged as helpful. Nissim had enjoyed that narcotic as well, Cohen had to admit.

Hagit was right, he thought. This was wrong. They should all leave her alone until the shivah began.

"Hagit?" he tried, "perhaps . . ." But she interrupted him, perhaps misunderstanding his tone of voice.

"Rafi," she said to the mayor, "this is Avram Cohen. He used to be Nissim's commander."

The politician nodded at him. "Nissim pointed you out to me at the housewarming. But unfortunately we didn't get to speak then. Now, to all our distress, we meet under very different circumstances."

Cohen racked his brain trying to remember the politician's last name and political party. A clansman, Cohen remembered about the politician, able to call on a whole wing of a tribe for his campaign activists, distantly related through marriage to at least two members of the Knesset. The newspapers predicted a bright future for him when he was elected as a young Turk with big plans for the sleepy town. So far, Cohen had understood from Nissim, the politician had delivered on at least some of his promises.

In the quiet of the lawn under the bright morning sun, for a second Cohen thought he could almost hear Nissim's voice that afternoon six months earlier at the housewarming. "If Rafi decides to head for the Knesset, Hagit thinks I could get elected mayor." Nissim said it with irony, indeed with just enough curiosity about Cohen's reaction to make the old detective realize that Levy had not ruled it out of hand. "Do you think you could get elected?" Cohen had asked then. Nissim was proud. "I did a year on foot in uniform inside this town. I know everyone and they all know me. They look up to me. They listen to me. Maybe she's right." Levy had ended the conversation with a wave to a neighbor coming into the garden, and a quick grin at Cohen before heading back to the barbecue grill. That was six months ago, the last time Cohen had seen Levy, when Hagit was barely three months pregnant.

"Uzan," Cohen finally said, remembering the politician's last name. It made the mayor's greedy smile spread even wider. Cohen was still not used to the looks of expectation on the faces of people who know he was suddenly rich, and hoped for a handout.

"A tragedy. A tragedy. Poor Nissim," Uzan said, the smile on his face at odds with both the words and their tone. "He did such good work here. A role model to the young people." He lowered his voice. "And I understand you were like a father to him."

"He was an orphan," Cohen stated bluntly, for the record. "But father or not, I think there's too much going on here right now for her." He squeezed Hagit's shoulder slightly, "Hagit?" he asked her, his eyes on the mayor, determined to send them all home.

But when he felt her body tense under his hand, he looked at Hagit and saw the glare of anger drying her eyes. The Beast, followed by Shvilli, Jacki, and the principal, came out into the garden.

Hagit licked her lips, readying herself to speak. She opened her mouth, but there was only silence. Jacki stepped forward. But then Hagit found her voice.

"No." She made the single word an announcement strong enough to make everyone pause. "No!" she repeated even more emphatically, her eyes darting from face to face. "I will not have people telling me what I am feeling, or what I have to do, or what I want."

She turned on the mayor. "I know, Rafi," she said, trying to keep exasperation out of her voice, "you want him buried here. My parents want me in Jerusalem. The DC," she added, emphasizing the two syllables in a slightly louder voice, in case he was still inside the house, "wants him in the policeman's plot in Beersheba."

And then she looked back at Cohen. "It's crazy, isn't it? Completely crazy. You know," she said, looking at him. "None of them even care what Nissim wanted. Tell them," she demanded.

Cohen's eyes turned to the people gathered on the lawn, each standing separately at a respectful distance from one another as if posed in tableaux and away from Cohen and the rotund mayor. "Nissim wrote a will."

"And?" blurted the mayor.

"For one thing, he didn't want a religious funeral, no *Hevre Kadisha*," Cohen said.

"Bravo," said The Beast, just loud enough for all to hear.

"Not even the police rabbi," Cohen added to the district commander, who just then came out into the garden. "A memorial service—if Hagit wants. If the hospital—or the medical school—can use parts of his body, it is theirs."

"Fantastic," the photographer repeated. He began to lift a camera, but Cohen glared at him and The Beast relented.

"Please, everyone, come back later," Hagit said softly. "Tomorrow. The day after. Nissim's gone, that's true. But I will still be here tomorrow. And don't worry, Shula," she said, suddenly raising her voice to address the school principal, whose face was pinched into a worried frown. "I'll be all right."

Finally, Hagit turned to Cohen. "I think I will lie down now," she said, "I'm very tired." She said it with deliberate quiet, touching his hand, then leaning forward to kiss him on the cheek before walking through the still garden, as if none of them were there to watch her. The DC stepped aside. Hagit paused at the social worker, whispering something that made the woman frown and say something quietly to Bendor.

Cohen watched as Hagit passed Jacki. The police woman raised an arm to put around Hagit's shoulder, but the widow raised her hand and seemed to pat the air, repelling Jacki's offer. The policewoman looked at Cohen. He nodded to her, so Jacki followed the pregnant woman into the house, while Cohen and the DC met in the middle of the lawn.

"Do you know what Nissim was doing this weekend?" Cohen asked.

The DC frowned and shook his head no. "But I'm sure we can find out."

"Bezek should check his home phone for Friday and Saturday," Cohen said automatically.

"We know what to do," the DC cracked back.

Cohen stared at the oversize man. "I want to know exactly what happened," he said slowly, the words sawing the air.

"We all do," said Bendor. "But from what I hear, it looks like an accident."

It was a standoff, broken by The Beast's beeper going off, a second before Bendor's cellular phone, strapped in a holster on his waistband like a second pistol, rang. The photographer drew his communication device first. The DC reached for his little phone like a gunslinger.

The district commander said "yes . . ." paused to listen, and then, glancing at Cohen for a second before moving away, said "yes" again. Cellular phone to his ear, Bendor scowled and walked to a corner of the garden, to keep secret any more specific dialogue with his caller. The mayor and principal huddled momentarily, and then left via the backyard's wrought iron gate to a pavement stretching the length of the row of houses facing the empty desert. The pedestrian path took them around the house.

"You," Cohen called to the photographer. "Phillipe," he added, making The Beast's naturally mean expression suddenly soften into a smile. "Come here." The photographer approached. "I heard you were at the scene," Cohen said.

"That's right," said the photographer, his brown eyes narrowing into two thin openings in a sun- and wind-burned face that itself was buried beneath a black beard just on the edge of being either brand new or fully grown. "Some good snaps."

"Good," Cohen said.

"I don't sell pictures to the cops. Except wedding pictures. I'll do them if I need the bread. What are you, Internal Investigations? National HQ?"

"My name's Cohen," said Avram. "Avram Cohen."

"Ah," Bensione responded. "Are you the one with the book? The bomb? In Germany?"

"I used to be Nissim's commander," Cohen answered. "In Jerusalem. You have a card?" he asked.

The photographer just stared at him resentfully. From his windbreaker pocket Cohen pulled out a plastic pen and a palm-size pad of thin paper with a yellow cover made of thin cardboard. "Your number?" he asked.

"Why?" Bensione demanded.

"In case I need to see your pictures. I'll pay double what any newspaper pays for your pictures."

Cohen could see greed in the photographer's eyes, but suspicion, as well.

"You sure you're not going to give 'em to the cops?"

Just then Bendor approached, holstering his cellular phone. "Cohen? A word." The district commander officiously repeated the name when Cohen ignored him. Bendor grabbed Cohen's biceps to get his attention. "In private."

"You see?" said Cohen, his eyes still locked with the photographer's. "I am not from the police," he managed to get in before Bendor led him away from the photographer. The DC dropped his grip after a long stride that nearly made Cohen stumble.

"That was the inspector general," Bendor said, again using force—this time the position of the highest-ranking police officer in the country—to hold Cohen's attention. "He sends condolences," said Bendor, "but he asks that you—"

"Leave this to the system to take care of," said Cohen. From the corner of his eye he noticed the photographer watching carefully from the distance.

" 'Despite the personal nature of his relationship to the deceased' were his exact words."

"I'm sure," said Cohen.

"Please, Mr. Cohen," said the former paratrooper, emphasizing the mister, "don't make this harder for us."

"Never crossed my mind," Cohen answered. Even he wasn't sure if he meant it. Just then, he was aware of The Beast holding a camera up to take their picture. Cohen turned instinctively away from the camera while Bendor turned just as spontaneously toward the lens.

"About the memorial ceremony," said the senior officer, "he'll get a salute, of course. Fulfilling his duty, and so forth."

"Of course."

"My office can make the arrangements."

"It can wait," Cohen ordered. "Let Hagit decide. There's time."

"Good," said the former paratrooper, suddenly patting Cohen's arm.

"We're coordinated." The Beast approached the two men, and Bendor's tone changed and he checked his watch.

"I'm due at the border to meet my Jordanian counterpart. His first visit. I'm putting out a red carpet for him."

"Shit," said The Beast, who now arrived beside them, smacking his palm against his forehead as if to punish his brain. "I completely forgot. I'm supposed to cover that."

"I'd better not see you on your bike trying to pass me, trying to get there first," the big man laughed as he left The Beast with Cohen.

"Here's my card," the photographer said, stuffing it into Cohen's hand. "Call me around five. I'll have pictures for you." He then trotted out of the garden on the heels of the district commander, leaving Cohen in the garden, alone with his memories of Nissim Levy.

His first two years as chief of investigations, Cohen worked without a full-time assistant. But Jerusalem had grown overnight after the Six Day War, and then steadily with both the country's highest birthrate—and the pilgrims. The more difficult life had become, the more people had wanted God to give them answers, and anyone moving to Jerusalem knows God's supposed to be just around the corner.

He had gone through half a dozen aides, assistants, and helpers until Levy had asked for the job. Cohen had known little about Levy when the dark-haired junior officer in uniform had approached him that day in the hall. Levy's name had already been mentioned at a staff session by Schwartz, the patrol chief, who had complimented Levy for spotting drug traffic at a newspaper kiosk in Kiryat Yovel. Schwartz had called Levy "a good cop," a few weeks before Cohen had fired Gershon Yalowitz with a bellow heard all the way to the holding cells.

"If you have the brains to match your courage," Cohen had said to Levy that day in the hall, "you can try it." For the first few years, Cohen would tell Levy that it was his handwriting that had saved him his job. He had joined Cohen's office in the years before computers. Even typewriters were rare in the system. Everything had been done by hand, from taking down witness and suspect statements to court transcripts—often in the hand of the judge.

In addition to his street smarts, Levy had handled paper better than anyone in the system Cohen had seen. Cohen had hated handling administration as much as he had loved reading the case files. They were a perfect match—even if Levy's ambitions sometimes had outrun his abilities.

As Levy had learned, and as Cohen had kept raising the standards, something more than the loyalty of a trusted assistant had taken over their relationship. Cohen's only child had died unborn with its mother less than a year after Cohen's marriage, right after the Six Day War in one of the PLO bombings in the city. It had never been said directly between them, but for Cohen, Nissim had been the closest he had ever had to a son. Nissim's own loyalty meant that when Cohen had fallen out of favor, so had Nissim. And when Cohen's star had risen again—even if he was no longer on the force—so had Nissim's.

So more than anything else, Nissim's suffering for Cohen's failures or successes was the reason for the sadness the old man felt that morning alone in the bright green garden at the edge of the desert. He lay down on the grass and listened to the sound of his heart beating and the wind, closing his eyes against the warming sun, thinking about Nissim.

· 15 ·

"Boss?"

Daydreaming, dozing, or sound asleep, Cohen had been thinking back to his last investigation for the police, when Nissim had taken a knife in the shoulder blade from a suspect trying to get away. In his hospital bed, Nissim had opened his eyes and smiled at Cohen, saying, "Boss?" But this voice was different. "Boss, you okay?" it asked.

Cohen pulled his hand away from his brow, where it had been shading his eyes. Shvilli was looking down at him. From the grim expression, Cohen had the feeling it was more bad news. He looked at his watch. He had slept nearly two hours.

"What happened?" he asked.

"They got the body out of the car."

"And?" Cohen demanded.

"It wasn't an accident. Nine-millimeter slugs. At least one in the head."

Cohen sat up straight, gasping for air, coughing until he could say, "Who could have done it, Misha?"

"I'm going down to Eilat to find out. I thought you might want to come."

Cohen rubbed at his forehead. "Do we know for sure that he was in Eilat?" he asked. He crossed his legs, sitting like a Buddha, while Shvilli dropped a knee to the ground before him.

"I've been over the map a dozen times," Shvilli said. "The nearest settlement is Kibbutz Haran. The only thing going on there for us was a pair of Australian volunteers caught growing some grass last summer. Nothing else. My bet? He was either ambushed at the corner where he went off the road, or dumped there. But he came out of Eilat."

The assassination of a policeman was extremely rare in Israel. Years could go by without an attempt, and suddenly there would be a flurry of armed attacks. Twice while in office, Cohen had been targeted by his own targets. Once it was shots fired at him near his home. The other time, he luckily decided that day to bring his car in for a lube job, and the mechanic found the tampered rear-wheel brakes.

Usually, underworld assassins used car bombs, as well as drive-by shootings and ambushes. And, like police everywhere, the security establishment took such attacks personally. In those two cases where Cohen was targeted the investigation went quickly, with the entire security network of the country thrown into the case. The same thing would happen now. The Shabak would attach an officer to the special investigating team, to be appointed by Bendor, and vetted by the inspector general.

Cohen wanted to be involved. And he knew it was impossible. Yes, there might be some on the fifth floor ready to vote for him, but he knew none would dare nominate him. Should he call the inspector general and volunteer? He knew the answer. "No," the IG would say, and for good reason that could be summed up in one word: Policy. So how long, Cohen wondered, could he investigate on his own without the police finding out? A few days perhaps. A week. He could trust Shvilli and had no choice but to trust Jacki.

"Who would put out a hit on Nissim?"

"If you ask me, it was one of my Russians. There's big

Russian action down there. Run by a pig named Yuhewitz. We know he's got three whorehouses and at least two floating casinos. When he's in town, he stays on his glamor ship at the marina."

"But was he down there this weekend?"

"I've been putting out some calls."

"Would Yuhewitz order a hit on Nissim?"

Shvilli's face turned grim. "He knows Nissim had an eye on him. He has a lot to protect. Maybe Nissim was down there spying and got caught. Cowboying it."

Was that like Nissim? Cohen wondered. Yes, by learning from Cohen, Nissim had learned to act on his own when necessary. No, because unlike Cohen, Nissim's loyalties were to his career as a professional within the system, and not to the truth for its own sake.

So he asked Shvilli, why would Nissim be down there, on his own, in danger, alone? If he was going down for a confrontation, why alone? And if it was a long-standing contract, why did the killer wait until a wintry night on a weekend? Shvilli had no answers.

"Help me up," Cohen said, holding out a hand to his former junior officer. He had sent Shvilli into dangerous places alone in the past. He had done the same to Nissim. He had gone alone into dangerous places more times than he cared to remember. But in the months since Frankfurt, he had often brooded over why he had run. Had he been afraid that night? No, he had decided. Not of bombs. But of the exposure. He had resolved not to get involved in the investigation of that strange incident in Frankfurt because, he said, he was done with investigating, done with that life. He lied. To himself, mostly, as usually happens with liars. Ahuva had shown him that. But it took Shvilli telling him that Nissim was murdered to finally make him see through the lie. For a few moments, just before dozing off in the cool fresh air at midday in the desert winter, he had indeed considered letting the system handle it all.

The traffic forensics and the autopsy, the clarification of what Nissim was doing south that wintry night; his thoughts raced, coming back to the realization that the inspector general would be correct. He had no right to get involved. He had reason perhaps, but he didn't have the privilege and the authority—and responsibility—that comes with it.

"What's going on?" Jacki asked, coming into the garden.

Cohen looked at Shvilli. The Georgian-born boxer with a talent for languages and disguise had an expectant look on his face, as if much more had been said between them than actually was turned into words.

Jacki was impatient. *"Nu!"* she demanded. "Tell me."

"On the other hand," Shvilli said, grinning a pair of gold teeth at Cohen, "you could give me a job."

"Michael!" Jacki hissed, shocked. "You are so rude."

"C'mon, sir," Shvilli said. "It could be great. Privatization? No? Isn't that the key word nowadays? What do you say?"

"Michael Shvilli, have you gone out of your mind?" Jacki cried out.

"Shh," Cohen ruled. "Is Hagit sleeping?" he asked. Jacki nodded. The master bedroom window, he remembered, overlooked the garden.

"Does she know about the shooting?" he asked, looking up to the second floor. A pale blue curtain billowed slightly in the soft breeze.

Jacki shook her head.

"So what do you say, boss? We have a deal?" Shvilli wanted to know.

Cohen shook his head sadly. "Not like this, Misha. Not in a storm."

"You left in a storm," Shvilli protested.

"They pushed him out," Jacki reminded Shvilli.

"He was there," Cohen reprimanded her with a reminder that she only heard the story from Nissim.

He looked into their eyes, and then into his own soul. "No," he decided. "I am not going to take responsibility for you two making rash decisions. I am not making any rash decisions. You asked me if I want to go with you. I do, but—" The phone ringing inside made him stop. "Jacki?" He asked her to answer it, but before she could respond, after two brief rings it stopped.

"Hagit must have answered," Shvilli realized first. Cohen looked at Jacki. And from the upstairs window above their head Cohen heard a scream. Jacki was the fastest of the three back into the house and up the stairs. Shvilli came in second. By the time Cohen reached the second-story landing, Jacki was shouting "her water broke, her water broke!" and Shvilli was at the phone, calling an ambulance, while Hagit lay on the floor where Jacki found her, a lopsided puddle growing on the carpet beneath her, sobbing, "he was murdered, he was murdered. They told me it was an accident, but he was murdered."

And for the first time since Shvilli called him that morning, Cohen felt his own tears creeping into his eyes.

· 16 ·

Only when the baby boy was wrapped in swaddling and the mother was sleeping soundly did Cohen feel free to act. He called the inspector general from the pay phone in the maternity ward at Beersheba's Soroka Hospital.

"You know I can't allow that," the inspector general said.

"Yes," said Cohen softly.

"You aren't going to run off investigating on your own, are you?" the inspector general warned.

"I'll do what I can to help," Cohen promised.

"To help. Not interfere," the country's top cop ordered.

"Who got the *tza'ham?*" Cohen asked, using the bureaucratic acronym for the special investigating team that would be formed.

"Shuki Caspi."

"Who?"

"Caspi. A good boy. Born in Beersheba. Knows the territory. Bendor brought him in from the paratroopers, and he learned fast."

"I heard that Russians, in Eilat . . ."

"See, that's just what I mean," the inspector general complained. "You think we don't know that? Avram, the force didn't stop working just because you're retired."

The inspector general's secretary came onto the line, reporting that the prime minister's office was asking for him.

"I've got to go, Avram. I'm sorry about Nissim. We all

are. That's why I promise we'll do our best to find his killer. I promise. If Caspi needs you, he'll call. And when we have something, I promise personally to call you and let you know."

Cohen hung up. A red-eyed woman was staring at him, waiting for the phone. He stepped away and considered his course of action.

Down the hall, Jacki was still at Hagit's side, joined by Hagit's parents. Shvilli was back at police headquarters, trying to get onto the *tza'ham*. "If you're going to work for me," Cohen had said, "my first order is get onto that *tza-'ham*." Shvilli took the command at face value, trusting Cohen.

"Too much perhaps," Cohen muttered to himself now, considering his options. A sign in the little lobby where the elevators opened to the maternity ward told him that pathology was in the basement. The elevator stopped at each floor, going all the way down. He stood in the corner and watched as gurneys rolled on and off, visitors searched for departments, and doctors and nurses cursed the elevator's slow pace. In the basement, he followed the signs through a maze of windowless tunnels that finally came to an end in front of wide-swinging doors. An empty gurney was parked outside the doors. He looked through the little glass window in the left door.

It was dark. He pushed open the door and pulled out his cigarette lighter for some light, then added a cigarette to his palm, lighting it to kill the smell of chemicals that the air-conditioning couldn't hide. The six slabs were all clean stainless steel with basins built into the surfaces. No bodies were in sight. He moved slowly through the large room, heading toward a row of filing cabinets against a distant wall. Beyond the cabinets was a door wide enough to allow two gurneys to pass.

The first was locked. They were all locked. But on the desk was a computer monitor glowing with the blue and yellow of a program's menu. The screen's light illuminated a stack of files on the desk. The third folder was Nissim's. A registration page reported the arrival of the body at 03:13 that afternoon. That was more than five hours ago, Cohen thought angrily. The pathology should have been done as soon as the body arrived, even if it meant the pathologists had to work around the clock.

He scanned the form listing the various tests that the pathologists would seek. Another document in the file was the donor's card found in Nissim's wallet, saying the body's parts could be used. The fourth was a piece of hospital stationery. A doctor's scrawl that Cohen held close to the computer screen light to read reported that a preliminary examination found an entrance and exit for what appeared to be a bullet. "A general workup for suspected murder" was to be performed the next day, the doctor ordered. Cohen slapped the folder closed and left the lab, losing his way twice in the maze of underground tunnels before finding a set of stairs that took him to the first-floor lobby of the hospital and then the elevators back to the maternity ward.

It was close to nine, and the last of the relatives and friends of the new babies born or about to be born that day were on their way out. Hagit was in the last room on the right of a long corridor with four wards of four and six beds on each side. Her bed was beside the window. Her parents sat with their backs to the view of the dusty city. Jacki stood behind them. Hagit had woken, cried, and taken gratefully the sleeping pills provided by the head nurse on the floor, said Jacki. "She's coming home with us, as soon as the doctors let her go," Hagit's mother whispered angrily at him. Her husband kept his eyes on the sleeping woman. Cohen remained silent. "Look at her, does she look like she's in any condition to take care of herself right now, let alone a baby?" the mother demanded.

"First let's hear from the doctors that she's all right," Cohen finally said. "Jacki?" he asked the policewoman to join him in the corridor.

"This is all your fault, you know," Hagit's mother hissed at Cohen's back as he left the room. Hagit's father looked up at him, and even from across the room, Cohen could see the old man had been crying.

Jacki and Cohen waited in the hall while a family including three children, two new grandparents, and a pair of great grandparents—each held by the arm of one of their children—walked slowly by, stage whispering about the latest new member of the family.

"More problems," Jacki told Cohen after the family was gone. "Misha called. He says the investigation's totally locked on Kobi Alper—and they won't let Misha into the team."

Cohen sighed. Alper was Nissim's first big case when he went from Yeroham Station to Southern District headquarters as deputy chief of Intelligence.

Nahum Nahmani and Buki Abutbul, brothers from two different fathers, had disappeared. They had run the meat processing plant their mother inherited from a third paramour. One night, they just never came home from work.

Levy had made forensics return three times to the plant. He had worked informants on the street and case files from the past. Kobi had had to discipline the two younger competitors. If they had only tried to steal the brother's territory, it would have been a dangerous situation. But they stole Kobi's own drug supply, to capitalize the move against him. It took Nissim three months, but he managed to bring Kobi to court. The judges sent Kobi to Ramle for two life sentences. It would be at least twenty years before Kobi had any chance of getting out. Kobi had made it clear—first in interrogation, and then in court—that he would get Nissim. "You tilted the balance, you maniac," he had shouted at Levy when the sentence was handed down. "You'll pay for it."

That had been more than a year ago. Cohen had followed the case in the papers. Nissim had called the night Kobi went down. "What do you think he meant when he said I tilted the balance?" Nissim had asked.

"You were a new force in town. Maybe there were arrangements you disrupted," Cohen suggested. "Just keep your eyes open. And watch your back."

"I'm worried about Hagit," Nissim had said.

"Can Kobi run a contract from Ramle?" Cohen asked.

"I doubt it. He was all force himself. He had to pay his followers. And he's running out of money. I hear he needs a new lawyer for his appeal."

It took Levy a month to make absolutely sure that Kobi had no more friends on the street and another month to convince his wife that behind bars Kobi was no danger to either of them.

"Was Kobi making a comeback?" Cohen asked Jacki. "Making new friends?"

"Enemies, more like it," Jacki said.

"What else did Shvilli say?"

"They told him he could do what he wanted with the Russians, but as far as they were concerned, Kobi ordered it."

Cohen shook his head. "Where is he now?"

"Ramle, of course."

"No—Shvilli."

"Making phone calls, he said."

"He said he wanted to go to Eilat. Someone named Yuhewitz?"

"Boris," said Jacki.

"Shh!!" a nurse hissed at them, striding up the corridor from the nurses' station. "Visiting hours are over. You aren't supposed to be here," she ordered, then walked past two steps to look into the ward where Hagit's parents were still at their daughter's bedside. "You'll have to go, too."

While Hagit's parents gathered up their belongings, Cohen asked Jacki where he could find Shvilli. "The Rendezvous club," she told him. "It's Shvilli's main hangout. You can't miss it, on the lefthand side, leaving town south into the Negev."

Cohen nodded and headed for the elevators behind the nurses' stand. "Just remember that I'm in," Jacki said loudly to his back, making the nurse shush her. Cohen waved a hand to show he'd heard. He didn't stop at the elevator, taking the stairs two at a time down the four flights to the ground floor and then out to the parking lot to his car.

· 17 ·

Was he conducting his own investigation? Was he ignoring the inspector general's strict orders not to get involved? He couldn't say right then. But he did know that he was doing the only thing he could do and not feel dead. It took him less than fifteen minutes to reach the other side of the desert town, which except for the mall—OPEN UNTIL MID-NIGHT shouted the banner hanging outside, trying to drum up business—seemed to have gone as deeply to sleep as the new mothers back at the hospital.

But at the Rendezvous nobody was sleeping. A Sunday night is ordinarily quiet even in Tel Aviv's hottest enter-tainment spots, let alone sleepy Beersheba. But the Ren-dezvous was full. Mercedes and Hondas, BMWs and two Rovers—all cars costing more than twice what an average Israeli family needed for two years—were lined up in the dusty lot outside the low-slung building at the edge of an industrial park still more under construction than built.

A bored blonde in a low-cut leotard greeted him at the door. The sound was deafening to his ears. A man with shiny black hair, wearing a blowsy red satin shirt and tight black pants, was singing in Russian, accompanying himself with an electronic keyboard sitting on a stand beneath his fingers.

More than two-thirds of the tables—and there must have been at least fifty—were taken. Some of the tables were lined up in long rows, filled by groups of families or friends. At other tables, couples dined alone. Many were singing along with the entertainer.

"You want to sit down?" the hostess asked him in Hebrew heavily accented by Russian.

He ignored her, scanning the smoky crowd for Shvilli. Finally he spotted him, at one of the long tables in the center of the room, sitting on a chair pulled up to the head of the table but slightly away from it, beside a squat, neckless man who was concentrating on pouring a shot of vodka into a short glass. Shvilli was leaning forward, whispering something into the fat man's ear. The man finished pouring, put down the bottle, and then, still listening to Shvilli, picked up the glass. Shvilli suddenly sat back, keeping his eyes on the man, who held up the glass, and appeared to shout something in Russian. Cohen wouldn't have been able to understand it, but he also couldn't hear it because of the crowd's enthusiasm for the song. But he saw the lively party sitting around the length of the long table in front of the fat man gradually turn to him. So did the people at two other tables nearby. The man was making a toast. Many at his table picked up their glasses. From almost twenty meters away, Cohen could see that nobody cheered as the fat man downed his glass in one shot, followed by everyone else at the table—including Shvilli.

"You Russian?" the hostess now asked Cohen, in Russian. But he was concentrating on his former undercover man. As Shvilli lowered the glass he had been holding, he noticed Cohen waiting at the entrance to the restaurant.

Shvilli said something to the fat man, then stood up, patted him on the back, and wound through the crowd, clapping over his head with the crowd, encouraging the singer.

The hostess must have noticed Cohen's reaction, for suddenly she was much more interested in him. "You know him?" she asked in Russian. At least that's what he assumed she asked from the tone of her voice.

But he didn't answer, watching Shvilli's face for a clue of whether to greet him or ignore him. The truth was that Cohen did not know the details of Shvilli's cover. So he shrugged, with honest ignorance and feigned apathy.

Shvilli waltzed past like a slightly drunk celebrant regretfully on his way out to his car to go home, grabbing Cohen at the neck like a dancer in time to the tune, and turning the older man, who nearly stumbled.

But as they made the turn, Shvilli said in a low voice, "make sure nobody's watching and follow me out as soon as I'm gone," and then he was, indeed, gone, out the front door.

Cohen stayed at the doorway for another ten seconds and then handed the menu back to the waitress and said, in English she barely understood, that he was a tourist and was looking for a "quiet cup of coffee before the drive to Eilat" before he slipped out the door after Shvilli.

Grateful for the night air and the drop in decibel level— the music could still be heard out in the parking lot off the road to Mitzpe—he found Shvilli in the shadow of a lonely palm tree a few strides away from Cohen's car.

"Who was that?" he asked Shvilli about the bald fat man.

"Yvgeny Yudelstein. An arbitrator. Solves problems between gangs."

"Does he know anything?"

"He knew a little. Not much. Now he'll find out more."

"Why?"

"You see him give that toast?"

Cohen nodded.

Shvilli said something in Russian, mimicking a hoarse, high-pitched voice.

"I'm sure it's a precise replica of the original," Cohen said. "But what does it mean?"

" 'To the State of Israel, where there is rule of law,' " Shvilli translated, adding, " 'and people know that there are limits.' " He translated for Cohen.

"A real patriot," Cohen said.

"He thinks if it's a Russian, it'll give the community a bad name."

"Does he know you're police?"

"I trust him," said Shvilli.

"Don't be foolish, Misha."

"It's not that he knows. For sure, I mean. He suspects maybe. He likes to joke, that's all. And only when it's just the two of us. Never in public. And he's the only one who's ever even hinted about it. Like I said, privately, between us."

"And what does he say privately to others, about you?"

"Well, that's it. He'll never say a word to any of them. Not directly. And never anything bad. Not in public."

"See?" Cohen pressed, worried for Shvilli.

"Look, if they can trust him, I can trust him."

Cohen pulled out his flask. All day he had been careful not to take it out. But now, the cold desert at night made his shiver of fear for Shvilli turn into a physical shudder. "Want some?" he offered his former junior officer.

"Cognac?"

Cohen nodded.

Shvilli scowled. "I've been drinking vodka. I don't mix grape and grain."

Cohen smirked. "What about this Yuhewitz?" he asked.

"We were closing in on him. He's a regular slave owner. Promises girls work as models in Israel, lends them the money for their tickets, gets them ID—even immigration grants—but when they arrive, he puts them to work on their back. They have to pay for their tickets if they want to get their passports, and their passports are usually forged. It's a vicious circle."

"Why haven't you busted him?"

"We're working on it," Shvilli said angrily. "What do you think we've been doing? We've closed down his houses three times in the last two months. The girls are thrown out of the country. His lawyers keep getting him out. The last time Yuhewitz got out, Nissim took it personally . . ." Shvilli paused, waiting for Cohen to fill in the blank. Worried, Cohen didn't.

"He made a scene. At the yacht. In front of a lot of people. I know. I was there."

"What did he do?" asked Cohen.

"It was a party. Six weeks ago. Nissim would never get away with that kind of behavior in Moscow. At least not in public."

"What happened?"

"It's one of Yuhewitz's parties. Maybe a hundred guests. Russians, mostly, from around the country. Some with wives, some with their girls. There's a casino onboard and enough girls to keep the juices flowing. Just before they raise the steps for the sunset cruise, Nissim shows up. Stands on the dock shouting, not letting the sailors loose the ropes, shouting for Boris to get out on deck."

"Does he come out?"

"Yes."

"People are watching?"

"Yes."

"What does Nissim say?"

"That it was 'the last time.' "

"The what?"

"That it was the last time Nissim would let him get away with it."

"Why? What happened the last time?"

"A house gets busted. Three girls get arrested. Boris isn't touched, of course. The girls are deported. A few days

go by. One night, the border patrol comes in with one of
the girls. Dehydrated, almost dead. She went to Cairo, flew
back to Sharm el Sheikh, took a bus up to Taba, and then
walked north, looking for a place to cross the border. She
had to go far past Eilat. Turns out she had a niece, a child,
who depended on her. Yuhewitz's lawyers could have
helped her, at least. Nobody told the judge . . ."

"Why didn't Nissim know?"

"We found out too late."

Cohen sighed. "So he feels guilty and makes a bigger
mistake as a result."

It was Shvilli's turn to sigh. "Yes. He let all his anger
show. I was downstairs, already in the casino. I heard the
shouting. Everyone heard it."

"More about who was at the party?"

"Friends, hangers-on."

"How did Yuhewitz respond?"

"Nissim was shouting in Hebrew. Called Boris a murderer. I thought the guns would come out. But instead,
Boris just smiled and said his Hebrew was not good
enough to understand everything Nissim was saying. People laughed. 'Come on board,' Yuhewitz invited him."

"And?"

"Nissim suddenly caught hold of himself. He just
turned around and walked away."

"Did Nissim write a report? Tell Bendor?"

"I don't know."

"Did you?"

"I reported only to Nissim."

"Afterward, when Nissim left . . . did people talk about
it? What did Yuhewitz say?"

"Some of the wives were a little shocked at first. But his
people kept things smooth for the rest of the ride and the

weather was great—clear, cool skies. Nobody got seasick. But I know Yuhewitz was mad."

"How do you know?"

"There was someone important there. Alex Witkoff. It's said he owns three banks in Moscow. Made aliyah a few years ago. Brought a lot of money. A very lot. And it bought him some very high windows. He shows up with the main players we've spotted. But it's hands off when it comes to Witkoff. He's a real success story, no? By the time we spotted him with Yuhewitz, he was already getting press as an example of a successful immigrant making use of his connections back there and here to make business. Big business. And he's got at least three ministers on his side. Hands off. He's in and out of the country at least three times a month."

"What else?"

"At first, I thought he was just another newly rich Russian enjoying his money. He played the tables and used the girls—the best, of course. He lives in Tel Aviv, so we don't see him often. But he's been showing up more often, and not for gambling. He and Yuhewitz spent a long time talking privately that night."

"Would he want Nissim dead? You say he's a banker."

"I'm not saying he did. Want Nissim dead. But he's big. Very big. You want to know about the Russian Mafia? I'll tell you. It's all about banking. Money laundering. You know how much money was stolen in Russia since the wall came down?"

"No."

"Some say it was a hundred billion dollars. Some say a trillion. Finance scams. All sorts of scams. Forge some fake payment documents for money due. Get credit from a bank for those documents. Send the money overseas into bogus companies that send the money on into a third layer of foreign accounts. Disappear. It's as simple as that. Or get a letter of guarantee from another bank and use it to open an account. How much do you think you have to bribe a bank manager somewhere, working for a couple of hundred dollars a month, to sign a letter of credit? Or pay someone to forge such a letter?"

"What about verification systems?" Cohen asked.

"They're starting from scratch. Things are improving. But it's taking time. Meanwhile, we know how Yuhewitz makes his money. But we don't really know where Witkoff's came from."

"Does he know he's a target of investigation?"

"I don't know," Shvilli admitted. "I've never been able to get very close to him."

"What's your cover?" Cohen asked.

"All they know is that I'm here since the seventies. Came right before the Yom Kippur War. Made money in real estate up north and am enjoying a very early retirement. I'm around because I like the action. Girls, gambling."

"Do you?"

"What?"

"Like the action?" Cohen asked.

"Dont't worry, I know which side I'm on. And I know my limits."

"What about drugs?"

"I'm neither a seller nor buyer, don't like junkies, and at parties I pass the joints politely. It's worked for almost a year."

"That's a long time, Misha. A year."

"It got me close."

"But being at the house today probably won't help keep it safe."

"What was I going to do? Pretend nothing happened?

We were as close as this," Shvilli said, rubbing his two fore-fingers together.

"What about your family?" he asked.

"I see them."

"How often?"

"Once, twice a week. You know what it's like . . ."

"When this is over, you're done with the assignment."

"So we're going into business?"

"I'm not becoming a private investigator."

"You do it anyway," Shvilli pointed out.

"Why didn't you tell me this before?" Cohen demanded.

Shvilli remained silent, obviously embarrassed. Cohen didn't press any further. Now at least he knew. But he disappointed Shvilli with his next question. "What about Kobi Alper? Maybe he really did manage the hit?"

Shvilli glared at the cigarette burnt to a stub between his fingers. "Look, maybe they're right and I'm wrong," he said, shrugging. "I don't know. I do know one thing. These boys play in a different league than Kobi. Much bigger. Maybe Caspi's right. Maybe Kobi arranged it. But I'm betting it was one of mine."

· 18 ·

Cohen reached Ahuva's just after midnight. She was sitting on the four-seat sofa opposite the television, which was playing CNN special coverage of a massacre in Africa while she read a thick typed manuscript of an opinion in draft form, marking it with a red pen for retyping.

"I heard about Nissim," she said.

"Thank you for not asking why I didn't call," he said, not taking off his windbreaker and going directly to the liquor cabinet beside the television to take a tall water glass that he filled halfway with cognac. He raised it to his lips, watching a distant star in the night sky over the sea become a plane coming into Israel from Europe. The plane was still at least a minute away from the coastline. He drank only half the glass then looked at her, blinked, and sat down in the matching chair beside the sofa, facing the horizon out the window. "The radio still says it was an accident," Cohen said.

"It wasn't?"

He shook his head. "At first it looked like an accident. But he was shot." He took another sip from the cognac and put the glass on the glass coffee table in front of the sofa.

"I can read your face, Avram Cohen. There's something else, isn't there?" she asked.

He nodded. "Hagit had a baby. Three weeks premature. A boy."

148

"As a result of the death?"

He nodded. "Four hours of labor. Baby's fine. They're at Soroka maternity. Hagit's mother hates me. When she wakes up, Hagit will probably hate me, too."

Ahuva remained silent, waiting for the rest of his testimony.

"She was fragile at first. When we thought it was an accident. But when she heard it was a shooting, the water broke."

"Better that than her mind," Ahuva said.

He shook his head sadly. "She answered the call from some young chief superintendent. He told her on the phone. An idiot."

Ahuva pursed her lips then plucked at her earlobe. "You were once a young chief superintendent."

"Who at least had the brains to know how to break news like that to someone," he said angrily. "We were all there. People who knew Nissim, who know Hagit. Especially Jacki and Shvilli. Either one of them could have told her so much easier. We thought we would when she woke up. Instead, she answered the phone."

"It's not your fault."

"The worst of it is that this Shuki Caspi is locked on a theory, which will make them blind to what's in front of them. It makes me very unsure that they're going to find Nissim's killer. At least not quickly."

"You think it might be someone else?"

"I don't know. I do know that you don't decide who did it before you look at the evidence. We still don't know where Nissim was when he was killed. We know there was shooting, but did it cause the crash? Was he trying to avoid it or was he surprised? It's all in forensics. And I don't have access. But meanwhile, I have a trustworthy source who has listed a lot of good reasons why it might be Russians.

149

He's going down to Eilat looking for one. I'm supposed to find another one up here."

"And then what?"

"Find out if they did it."

"Just like that?"

He nodded.

"Maybe you're locked onto a theory, too?" she asked quietly.

"Don't think I'm not aware of that," he said, a slight moan in his voice.

"Are you sure you should be doing this?" she asked. "On your own? If this man is so ready to kill a police officer..."

"He didn't. But he might have arranged for it to happen. Paid someone to do it. He was one of Nissim's targets, and my source says he probably knew it. But if they chose assassination as a method, it meant Nissim was getting too close to something. But I don't know what—even if—he knew what it was. And I can't trust a blind system to find out for me."

She set aside the paper on her lap and stood up. She was wearing a satin three-button nightgown that Cohen loved to open, each undone button revealing a stretch of lush warm skin. She came around the coffee table and kneeled beside him, picking up his cognac glass and taking a sip, then passing it to him. He finished it and put it back on the table.

They sat that way in silence for a while, her arm on his thigh, her hand on his stomach, his hand over her shoulder, resting lightly on her breast.

"Avram," she asked softly. "First that bomb in Frankfurt, now this? Should I be worried that they are connected?"

"I don't see how," he said truthfully. He grinned at her, then leaned forward to kiss her.

"Just be careful," she said, just before their lips touched.

"I promise," he said, while his hand reached for the nightgown's top mother of pearl button and then reached into the warmth of her body as their lips met in a deep kiss.

After Ahuva was asleep he got out of bed. He pulled on his trousers and bare-chested and barefoot went down the stairs to the first floor of the apartment. He took a cigarette from the packet in his jacket pocket and went to the broad picture window, slid open the glass, and stood in the cold night air watching the traffic six stories down on the north-south boulevard. Nobody was out on the beachside boardwalk. The storm that had raged over the eastern end of the Mediterranean had created a new measure of relativity regarding how cold that winter could become. The air was almost still, cleansed on Friday by rain, dried on Saturday by the bright sun. Tomorrow it would be warm again, almost fifteen degrees centigrade in Tel Aviv, the weatherman on the radio had promised.

A siren turned into a patrol car racing south toward Jaffa.

He finished the cigarette, stubbed it out on the railing, and crossed the living room to the kitchen, where he dumped the butt in the trash bucket beneath the sink. Then he went to the phone beside the sofa. It rang twice after he punched in the number.

"Kochinski," mumbled a man's voice.

"Raoul, it's Avram Cohen."

There was a brief pause. "The deputy commander?"

"Yes."

"You're not police anymore."

"I need a favor."

"I've heard that before," Raoul said. "It usually meant being on my feet for twelve more hours."

"You heard about Nissim?"

"The accident. You always said he drove too fast."

"It wasn't an accident."

"So they'll send him to me."

"No, the body's with the medical school."

"David Rath is a good pathologist. He turns out good doctors—"

"Please, Raoul," Cohen interrupted. "I just want to be sure they cover everything. I want—"

"Every detail," Raoul interrupted, knowing exactly what Cohen would say. "Yes, yes. I'll call down in the morning."

"And I'll get back to you around noon."

"I'm sure," said the pathologist.

"And Raoul," Cohen added, "this is between you and me. Nobody needs to know we spoke. For your sake, as well as mine."

Raoul sighed. "Under the circumstances, I didn't expect anything different."

Cohen laughed and hung up, then went back to the bedroom, finally feeling sleep coming on. He lay down on the bed beside Ahuva's still body, resting his hand on her thigh as he closed his eyes and welcomed the darkness.

· 19 ·

"Remember," she wrote at the end of the short note he found on the breakfast table that Monday morning, "you're not alone—and it's not all dependent on you."

Yes, he knew in his belly that she was right. But in his head he had doubts that had nothing to do with distrust of her love, or Shvilli's loyalty, or Jacki's eagerness, which was so much like Nissim's own enthusiasm for the job. The doubts were about himself. Ahuva's innocent question about a connection between Nissim's death and Frankfurt sparked a tiny corner of tinder in his mind. There was neither fire nor smoke, not yet, but he could feel the molecules moving. If not for Nissim's death, he had figured on another two weeks to finish going through the files in the dusty attic of the Russian Compound. Now, he wondered if he would have to go back again to the beginning, once he reached the end.

The water for his coffee boiled. He dumped a tablespoon of Turkish ground coffee into the bottom of a glass, added a half a teaspoon of instant coffee, a tablespoon of sugar, and poured the boiling water onto the mixture slowly, into two stages, stirring the first time when the glass was barley a third full. Before the swirling stopped, he filled the rest of the glass and set it aside beside the morning's *Ha'aretz* newspaper.

The court order was working. Nissim's death was a

storm-related accident, not a murder. But his reputation won him a brief obituary that mentioned in three paragraphs Levy's background as Cohen's assistant, the Kobi Alper case, and Levy's sometimes controversial lobbying for a full-fledged special task force on the Russian underworld.

The coffee powder had settled at the bottom of the glass. He took a first sip to test the black drink, then two more deeper drains on the glass before leaving the apartment.

Downstairs, he cut through the glass lobby that over-looked the beach to one side and Hayarkon Street to the other. Ahuva's building had seventeen stories. The first floor was commercial—a couple of boutiques, a small jew-elry store, a little shop selling books, magazines and news-papers, tobacco, perfumes, and film.

A cafe occupied the corner nearest the outdoor patio entrance to the building. Sunlight splashed across the patio from the sun rising in the east and a waitress was unfolding chairs beside half a dozen tables outside. He ordered an espresso from the barman and with the platter and coffee in one hand and the two tabloids he bought at the kiosk in the other, he went out to the patio.

Like *Ha'aretz*, the two tabloids also carried the story on the pages with their coverage of the weekend storm and its effects. But the court order couldn't prevent *Ma'ariv* and *Yedioth* from calling Nissim's accident "mysterious." Noth-ing was said about bullets, but the reporters did report that a special investigating team had been established under Caspi's management.

Ma'ariv carried everything *Ha'aretz* reported, but also ran a rare photo of Nissim in uniform, with District Com-mander Bendor at his side, on the steps of the Beersheba District Court the day Nissim testified against Alper. No mention was made of Big Kobi Alper's threats, although his arrest and conviction was included in the list of Levy's accomplishments in the last year and a half. "Now it can be revealed," wrote the reporter looking for an angle, "Chief Superintendent Levy was a key lobbyist for the police to establish a special task force to coordinate the investigations into Russian-led organized crime in the country."

As he read, he began rubbing at his forearm. The eczema was trying to come out on his arm above the six-digit tattooed number on the vein side of his forearm.

The last time it itched in that part of his body was in Frankfurt, but as the days and weeks passed, the rash shrank back until it was only a tiny red spot in the little web of flesh between his forefinger and middle finger on his left hand and then finally it was gone. Now it was returning, but only when he finished reading the obituary, which included a mention of Levy's eight years under Cohen in Jerusalem did the detective notice his hand rubbing at the faded navy blue of the jacket sleeve.

He stopped, trying to still the voice telling him to roll back the sleeves of the windbreaker and his shirt and attack the itching, concentrating on telling it to go away. That didn't work either. His cortisone cream was at home in Jerusalem.

He looked up to take his mind off the itching. A bleached blonde in a two-piece outfit that revealed age as well as skin had become the second customer of the hour for the cafe, taking the seat at the end of the row from Cohen to his far left. Like him, she was enjoying the warmth of a bright sun after the days of cold and rain. When she smiled at him he looked at the little notebook he bought at the kiosk where he got the papers and began making a list. It was only three lines long to start. He didn't think about how long it would grow.

His first errand was to a shop at the northern end of Dizengoff Street where cellular phones were sold on the spot with already active telephone lines. It took an hour, including the half hour wait for the phone line to be turned on. Once he understood all the functions of the phone, he paid with a credit card and crossed the street to a half-empty cafe. An enthusiastic young waitress promised everything was made by hand. He ordered a croissant with an apricot filling, and when she was gone he began working the phone.

He started with Laskoff's office, asking Rose for the earliest appointment possible.

"It's good you called," she told him. "Mr. Laskoff asked for you."

"What about?" Cohen asked.

"He didn't say."

"Is he in now?"

"Unfortunately not."

"Here's my number," Cohen offered.

"Mr. Cohen!" she exclaimed. "You, with a cellular phone?"

"Yes, Rose. Even me," he admitted. But it was the only way he could manage what he had to do.

His next call was to Jacki. He dialed the direct line to Nissim's office.

"Head of *tza'ham*," a nasal man's voice said at the end of the line, surprising Cohen.

Cohen asked for Jacki, using the acronym for her title as assistant to chief of Intelligence.

"It's for you," he heard Shuki Caspi say. "Tell whoever it is to call back later."

"Hello?" Jacki asked

"It's me, Avram Cohen," he said, "but don't let him know. Just take down this number, and call me back as soon as you're alone."

"No problem," the woman said.

Cohen gave her the number and she hung up with an

officious "thank you." He wondered what Caspi was telling her—or asking—and cursed the fact that it was the young officer searching Nissim's desk, and not Cohen himself.

At Abu Kabir forensic labs, they told him Raoul had gone down to Beersheba for a consultation at Soroka. That made him smile. But when he tried Shvilli's cellular phone number, he was dismayed when a female voice recording told him the subscriber was off-line at that time.

He then spent a few minutes with Tel Aviv information getting in quick order the phone number of Witkoff Chemicals and Trade, where a man with no Russian in his accent said that Witkoff was not expected that day, "but if you leave a message, I'm sure—"

Cohen closed the connection.

Almost immediately, his new cellular phone rang for the first time, surprising him. Expecting Jacki, he heard Laskoff's voice.

"So, my friend. Even you succumbed."

"To what?"

"The miracle of the mobile phone," said Laskoff.

"Just don't be giving out my number," Cohen growled. "Listen, I need some information."

"Obviously," Laskoff said.

"Does the name Alexander Witkoff mean anything to you? A Russian."

"Russian?" the Hungarian-born banker asked warily.

"Yes. I've heard he might be part of one of the consortia bidding for the banks."

"I can make some calls, see what I can find out."

"Good, please. And whatever you can learn, please let me know."

"You don't have to tell me that," Laskoff said. "But for once, perhaps you could tell me why you need to know. Or is this one of those affairs where it's best I don't know?"

"Just be discreet," Cohen warned.

"I'll get onto it this week," Laskoff said.

"Today," Cohen pleaded.

"Av-ram . . ."

"Please, Ephraim. It's important."

"What about your house?" the banker asked. "I thought *that* was important. We're down to the last two signatures. They're pressing for another twenty thousand dollars each."

"I'm having second thoughts," Cohen said, shocking Laskoff.

"What are you talking about?"

"I'm getting tired of the greed. Not just their greed. All the greed."

"Look Avram, we've been over this—"

"I don't want to discuss this right now," he interrupted. "Tell them I'm thinking about their offer. But first find out what you can about Witkoff."

He slapped the mouthpiece closed, hanging up the phone, and turned his attention to the croissant. Just as he was about to take a bite into the roll, which he had carefully spread with an apricot jam, the phone rang.

It took him until the end of the second ring to set the croissant down. He licked his finger where some jam slid off the knife before he finally answered the phone.

"I can't believe that idiot," Jacki moaned over the phone.

"Who?

"Shuki Caspi."

"What happened?"

"Yes. Misha called in from Eilat. He said that he found a watchman at the marina who remembers Nissim on Friday night."

"Yuhewitz has a boat at the marina," Cohen said.

"Right. So I tell Caspi that. What does he say?"

"What?" Cohen asked.

"That the Alper brothers kept a boat down there for years."

"Where's Shvilli now?"

"Eilat."

"When you reach him, you hear from him, give him my cell phone number. Meanwhile, I need everything you can find in Nissim's files."

"Caspi's in a meeting with Bendor. But he'll be back soon."

"Start with the Alex Witkoff file. Shvilli told me he lives in Ramat Aviv Gimel. I need whatever Nissim had. I'll wait."

It took only two minutes for her to return to the phone, asking what he needed from the file.

"How much is there?"

"Let's see. Not much. Some correspondence with Moscow, Interpol. Witkoff's wanted for questioning in Russia and France."

"The Germans?" Cohen asked, instinctively.

"No."

That disappointed Cohen.

Then she laughed, surprising him. "His driving record. He likes fast cars. Five tickets in the last two months."

"He should have had his license bounced," Cohen muttered. "Any of those tickets in the south?"

"Three."

"When?"

She gave him the dates—all were within the last six months.

"Anything else?" he asked.

"Let's see. What's this?" she asked herself. "Hold on. There's a little notebook in here. It looks like a log. Dates. Names . . ."

"A log of what?" he asked impatiently.

"Just a second," she answered, almost as impatiently.

159

"Eilat. Hotels, mostly. A few addresses. The marina. Wait a second. Damn. I can hear Caspi outside, talking with someone. I'd better close . . ."

"Wait. I want Witkoff's address. And photocopy the entire file and fax it to me."

She dictated the numbers and street name, added a "no problem about the photocopying," and hung up just as Caspi must have entered the room, for Cohen could hear a man's voice asking "who's that?" Cohen could only assume Jacki would have an answer.

More calls needed to be made. He dug out Phillipe Bensione's card. The photographer's cellular number was busy.

Cohen took a bite of croissant, surprised at how good it was, and used the redial button twice, trying to get through to the photographer to no avail.

He had hopes for better photos of the scene than the one that *Yedioth* splattered on page one. The photographer had crouched between the sun rising over the Arava, and the car had settled into about thirty centimeters of almost yellow mud on the highway beneath the Negev's eastern cliffs. The wide angle showed all the way from the white-on-red license plate that identified it as a staff car for the police to the tip of a winch crane mounted on the back of a tow truck. There it was, the head slumped against the steering wheel, the black-and-white mop of curly hair muddied by the yellow of the wet desert and the newspaper's tabloid ink. The only red in the picture belonged to the license plate. But there was no doubt the man in the picture was dead.

· 20 ·

He stopped at a bank and wrote a check for cash for fifty-thousand shekel. The teller looked at him disbelievingly, but her expression changed after she called his bank branch in Jerusalem. "In two-hundred shekel notes please," he said. Sometimes, he knew, cash could be much more effective than a weapon.

The teller, in her early twenties, probably just out of the army, said she needed the manager.

"No problem," said Cohen, waiting another twenty minutes before finally pocketing the cash into five bulky envelopes of ten thousand each, which he stashed in the inside pockets he had sewn into his windbreaker.

Half an hour later he was turning off the Haifa Road into the north Tel Aviv neighborhood of Ramat Aviv Gimel. They had begun building the neighborhood just north of the university in the seventies, but in the mid-eighties, with the opening of the commercial center and the completion of its country club, Ramat Aviv Gimel had flourished so that eventually it had become the setting—and name—of a television soap opera about a family ruling a fashion empire from the flashy address.

Cohen found the building at the most northwest corner of the neighborhood. He drove slowly through a parking lot. It was half full. Jeeps, family sedans, passenger vans, and at least three sports cars. Jacki had said Witkoff liked

161

fast cars, Cohen remembered. He paused, foot on the brake, in the middle of the lot, thinking, looking. Three cars, lined up beside one another, caught his eye. A BMW sports car, a Mercedes two-seater, and a Land Rover. Their license numbers were consecutive, registered at the same time. All were models that could not be bought directly off a showroom floor, brought into the country as private imports. When Jacki called back to ask what to do with the photocopies, he'd ask for Witkoff's registration numbers. They should be on the driving record.

Then he pulled out of the lot to park across the street on the north side of the building. Beyond, there was only the green and yellow wild mustard scrub that covered the sand dunes stretching all the way to Herziliya. To his right below the rise on which the entire apartment block sat was the Haifa Road carrying cars and trucks north. Beyond the road were more sand dunes, but Cohen imagined that from above the penthouse one would have a view of the landing strip at little Sde Dov Airport. And beyond that was the sea.

He got out of the car and lit a cigarette, smoking as he leaned against his car looking at the twenty-story-high building. All he could see of the penthouse was that Witkoff had turned the open space on the roof into a garden.

A mother and a teenager who was wearing a leg cast and was on crutches came out of the building's lobby and down to the sidewalk where the mother unlocked a gray sedan too old to belong to the building. "You heard what the doctor said," he heard the woman say to the boy. "You were very lucky. Lucky, you hear me? So I don't want to hear any more about motorcycles from you." She didn't even glance at Cohen after she made the U-turn and drove away.

He flicked away his cigarette and crossed the street to the building's main entrance, facing north toward the southern sand dunes of Herziliya. No security guard that he could see was watching from inside the glass lobby, but nonetheless a video camera was pointed at him from under the ceiling of the exterior lobby where he checked the mailboxes, looking for Witkoff's name. Yes, he had the right building. The penthouse was apartment number thirty-nine.

He went to the panel of intercom buttons, standing so the camera would only get a shot of his back, and pressed Witkoff's once, a full beat long. Nothing happened. He tried again, shorter. Still nothing. A third tap at the button.

"*Da, da,*" a female voice answered, then asked in a tone that Cohen understood, even if he didn't know Russian, "Who is it?"

"From the electric company," Cohen said in Hebrew.

"I no know electricity," the woman stammered in pidgin Hebrew. "Video, video," she instructed.

"Electricity," Cohen said. "I'm not the cable man. Electricity."

"*Televizia.* Look *televizia,*" the woman's voice said.

He turned to face the camera, smiled at her, and then pulled out his wallet and showed her a business card. It was the photographer's. But he doubted she could make out the writing, let alone read the Hebrew. "Electric company," he tried again, giving a quick grin to the camera then turning to face the door.

The buzzer went off. Cohen pushed through the glass door into the lobby. Enough sun had poured into it to make the central heating redundant. He wiped slight beads of sweat that gathered on his forehead.

When the elevator opened he found himself in a small corridor with only one door. A young platinum blonde woman in jeans and a blue shirt tied into a halter was peering through the crack in the open apartment door as he came out of the elevator.

"We had a report about a problem here," he said, opening the fuse box cabinet set into the wall opposite the elevator doors.

"No. No problem here," the woman said in Hebrew with a whiny Russian accent. But she opened the door a little more.

He wiped sweat from his forehead. "Hot." He smiled at her. "Water?" he asked, with an exaggerated pantomime of a man drinking, smiling at her with all the charm he could muster.

She smiled, and leaving the door open, left the entrance and disappeared into the apartment. He followed the clicking of her heels on the marble floor.

Through a short lobby, he came into a broad expanse of living room with a sixteen-person dining table and two distinct sitting areas, including one for a wide-screen television screen and a baby grand piano. A broad wooden desk stood in the near corner, holding an elegant pen set and a switchblade for a letter opener. No papers or ashtrays, no coffee cups or opened books littered its surface.

Cohen was looking for anything that would give him a sense of Witkoff the person. So far, all he had was a neatness that was almost unnatural. There were photographs, all including a man with short cropped gray hair. He assumed that was Witkoff.

In the kitchen, immediately to his right, he heard a cupboard close, then the clink of a glass on a counter.

Just then, his eyes fell on the last thing he expected to see: on a side table next to a rocking chair, he saw something that truly shocked him: a copy of the German edition of his book.

In the kitchen, water was running in the sink. He strode across the room, his sneakers silent on the stone floor.

The clicking of her heels on the stone floor suddenly

resumed. He put down the book, but remained standing in the middle of the room.

"Hey!" she cried.

He flung up his hands, showing he had not touched anything, surrendering to her. It made her pause and look at him thoughtfully for a second, and then she found the word. "Out, out. Now." She said it like she was shooing a stray animal.

He smiled again and took a step forward, telling her in Hebrew and gesturing that he was sorry, but asking to use the bathroom, as well.

Again that made her pause, considering her alternatives. Sweat beaded on his forehead. She nodded.

"Thanks," Cohen said. "Which way?" he signed, pointing at two doors and a corridor entrance that exited from the main room, itself easily bigger than his entire apartment at home in Jerusalem.

She sighed and pointed at a door to his right. He patted his belly softly, as if to say it was very weak, and closed the door behind him. His stomach was fine. He dropped the toilet seat so she could hear, if she was waiting beyond the door. Then he waited. Thirty seconds went by. He grunted slightly, then sighed, wanting to make her think he'd be a while.

Sure enough, after another few seconds, he heard her mutter something to herself, and then her footsteps tapped their rhythm away from the door. He waited another few seconds, then opened the door a crack. It gave him a view of most of the big room. He peeked around the corner. She wasn't in the room.

He strode to the book, picked it up, and thumbed through it quickly. It had been read. Maybe twice, or more. A coffee stain marred one page, another was dog-eared. It was the chapter that explained the witness relocation program to Germany.

A phone rang through the apartment. He froze for an instant, and then the ringing stopped. He heard her voice, speaking in Russian. It gave him more time. He thumbed through the pages again, looking for notes, anything to indicate why Witkoff would have the book. This time he found something that he missed the first time. It made his hand shake slightly.

The book was inscribed "With gratitude." No date was added to Benny Lassman's autograph. Nor did the handwriting say to whom the gratitude was addressed.

The clicking of the woman's heels on the stone floor suddenly began approaching from somewhere behind him in the depth of the apartment's other rooms.

For a second he was tempted to take the book. But its absence would draw attention to his presence. He didn't think the woman was reading the book, but he had the feeling that as long as he left it in its place she wouldn't make the connection between the grim face on the cover and the electrician with the smiling pantomime of drinking water.

So he put down the book exactly where it had been and went back to the bathroom, closing the door behind him.

"Finish?" she asked through the door.

He flushed the toilet, running water in the sink for a second before he opened the door, drying his hands on a small guest towel. "Thank you," he told her, relief on his face, walking past her with a smile that turned grim as soon as she closed the door behind him.

· 21 ·

"No interviews about me," Cohen had said that night in Frankfurt, when, on Cohen's heels right up to the boarding gate for the flight to Rome, Benny had kept insisting that they had another best-seller to write. "No," said Cohen. He didn't want to deny Lassman the chance to make a living. He just didn't want to draw any more attention to himself. "There's nothing I can do to stop you. But I don't have to cooperate," he had explained to the writer.

"I've got a good relationship with Leterhaus," Lassman had said, referring to the German cop running the case. "I can do it from his point of view. Hell, I can do it from my point of view."

"In fiction," Cohen warned.

"I can't let this get by me, Avram," Lassman had tried, appealing to Cohen's loyalty. "You've got to understand that. You can afford to let the moment pass. I can't."

That was when they were still in Frankfurt. Cohen sighed then, as he did now, speeding on the highway to Jerusalem, using one hand on the wheel, the other on the cellular phone, trying to get through to the reporter. The number had been busy since he left Tel Aviv. It was still busy as Cohen crawled through the constantly clogged entrance to town, past the foreign ministry and through the Valley of the Cross until he was at the Gaza Road. There he took a left, and three streets into Rehavia, he took a right, then another, finding a parking spot half up a sidewalk at the end of the cul-de-sac.

Lassman lived on the ground floor in the back of a six-flat apartment building in the neighborhood. The weight of the wet snow from the storm had broken tree branches that Cohen had to skirt as he strode down the slate path around the building into the back garden. The sun had been almost warm in Tel Aviv. In Jerusalem, the mountain altitude cut the heat, and even in the ostensible shelter of the buildings around him there was a strong breeze. In the shade of the old Rehavia trees that enveloped Lassman's unkempt garden and patio, very little sunlight gleamed through the leaves. It was cold.

"Benny?" Cohen shouted, banging on the peeling white door.

"Who is it?" Benny called out from inside.

"Cohen."

"Avram?"

"Open up, it's cold out here."

Instinctively, by habit, Cohen slipped a foot into the door as Benny, unshaven and red-eyed, wearing a bathrobe over a T-shirt, trousers, and two pairs of thick mismatched army socks, opened a crack to the cold.

"What the hell is your connection to Alex Witkoff?" Cohen demanded, pushing past Benny into an overheated low-ceiling living room and study.

Lassman's computer screen glowed in the semidarkness of the room, along with a table lamp on the desk and another bulb burning over a small kitchenette.

"Who?"

"Witkoff, Witkoff," Cohen said impatiently, unzipping his jacket. "Owns a chemicals and trading company. Lives in Tel Aviv. Russian millionaire, possibly dirty. Probably," he added.

"Believe me, Avram, I don't know who you're talking about."

"You autographed the book for him. 'Thanks for all your help,' you wrote. 'with gratitude,' " he added, quoting directly.

They were eye to eye. Cohen could smell Lassman's breath and sweat and realized the writer was sick with the flu. "That's what you signed in his copy of the book."

"I signed a lot of those books," Benny protested, then coughed so badly he bent over, grasping his lungs, grimacing in pain.

"You wrote 'With gratitude,' " Cohen pointed out again. "For what?"

"I don't know what you're talking about," Lassman said anxiously, then broke into a cough.

Cohen took a deep breath, trying to regain control.

"I was just about to make a cup of tea and cognac. I've got this flu," said Benny. "You have no idea how sick I am."

There was a dry and claustrophobic smell in the room, which was overfurnished with Lassman's landlady's old heavy upholstered furniture.

"Alexander Witkoff," Cohen repeated.

"Why don't you sit down," Lassman offered. "Calm down, tell me what this is about. I was about to make some tea." He didn't wait for Cohen to sit down, and instead shuffled toward the little kitchenette attached to the main room that Lassman had turned into an office.

Cohen's glance naturally went to the desk. Lassman was untidy, not sloppy. No overflowing ashtrays or unwashed cups and glasses were to be seen. But on the floor around the desk and on level surfaces in the room, stacks and piles of papers, magazines, and books were probably organized in a way that only Lassman could understand.

"I heard about Nissim," Benny said, his back to Cohen,

who was glancing over the papers on the desk. "I said to myself," Lassman continued, "it was bound to happen. That guy took chances. Big chances."

"He was murdered," Cohen said bluntly.

Lassman turned, the bottle of cognac in his hand. "What are you talking about? The radio said an accident."

Cohen shook his head. "There was a shooting."

"Who did it?"

"The system says it was Kobi Alper. But I'm looking at Russians. And one of my Russians had the book. Alexander Witkoff." He repeated the name. "You signed his book."

"Could be, I don't know. I'll have to check the notes."

"Now."

"Why don't you sit down?" he asked Cohen, pointing at a stack of papers on the seat of an armchair. "Just drop the pile on the floor." Lassman turned back to the kitchen counter to prime the two cups of tea with shots of Extra-Fine, a cheap brown brandy sold only in Jerusalem.

Cohen reached for the pile of magazines and photocopies sitting on the chair. The top document was a photocopy of a three-inch clipping from a Texas newspaper. Headlined "Book Fair Bomb," it was a wire service version of what happened in Frankfurt.

Underneath that little clip was a glossy American magazine that compared the Cohen case to the Rushdie case. The next was an article that analyzed Cohen's book and reached the conclusion that the mystery bomber was ideologically motivated by Nazism. Still standing, Cohen leafed through the thick pile. There were photocopies of book reviews and letters to the editor, there were original magazines and ragged tear sheets from newspapers. In one way or another it was about him, his book, and the bomb—and why Nazis did it.

"What is all this?" he asked, "all these articles?"

Lassman turned around with the two cups of tea. He passed one to Cohen with a long reach, then put his own cup down on this desk and picking up a blanket crumpled on the floor beside his chair, wrapped himself like a mummy, and sat down at the desk. One hand held the blanket closed, while the other he used for his tea. He smiled at Cohen. "Clips, research. Notes. Books. What it looks like."

Cohen knew very well why he didn't want to give interviews, why he didn't want to cooperate with the journalists. What he didn't know, until then, was just how much attention his case had received. He had stopped asking Carey to send him reviews even before the Frankfurt Book Fair. Leterhaus only sent news when there was some, which had become less and less frequent.

Tina, too, had a life that would have to go on after Cohen. He only asked that she keep the media away from him. He let her sell translation rights, but nothing else. And yes, he'd let the book be sold to Hollywood, on condition they "don't use the title, don't name the character Cohen, and don't ask for interviews," and then, just to make sure she understood, he added, "and I don't have to go there." He eventually compromised. They could use Benny's title. But he knew his conditions precluded any sale.

At first, Tina called almost once a day, each time asking with a nervous giggle, "So when do you think the coast will be clear?" He'd say only when the murderer was caught. Gradually, the calls dropped off to once a week and then every other week, until finally, she stopped calling entirely. Her office staff was efficient, of course. As the checks came in, she wired the money—less her commission—to the proper accounts. But Laskoff handled that side of the matter for Cohen.

He was looking around the room at the piles, astonished by the amount of material. "It's not all about you, of course," Lassman said. "The Nazi stuff is on the couch. Messianicists over there," he added, pointing to the left of the desk, "and Israeli criminals in Frankfurt over here."

"What's this?" Cohen asked, pointing to the pile he put down on the floor.

"Stuff that still needs to be filed."

"And where's Alexander Witkoff in all of this?"

"How should I know?" asked Lassman. "I'm not looking at Russians. At least none have turned up in my investigation . . ."

"I am not interested in your investigation," said Cohen angrily. He pushed himself to his feet from the armchair. Lassman looked surprised, and was even more surprised when Cohen stepped over a pile of files toward the desk. Cohen knew that despite all the semichaos of the room's surroundings, Lassman was meticulous about saving information in his computer.

"I'm telling you, Avram," Lassman said, standing up and away from the chair in front of the computer. "I haven't come across any Russians on this story."

Cohen sat down in front of the computer. He gave the mouse a little shake to clear the screen saver of bouncing quadrangles. An array of icons was laid out on the screen. "Top righthand corner," Lassman said, sighing.

Cohen clicked on the icon of a telephone named "contacts." A spreadsheet listing names and telephone numbers in columns opened up. He clicked for the find menu and typed Witkoff's name into the window. "Not found." said the box that appeared on the screen after a few seconds.

"See," Benny said, watching from over Cohen's shoulder.

Cohen typed "Alex" into the box.

Lassman laughed. "It's going to find hundreds of names. At least two dozen from Alexandria."

"Egypt?" Cohen asked.

"No, Virginia. You wouldn't know about it. Did a great cocktail party there. Collected a lot of business cards. And do me a favor, when it gets to Alexandra, remind me of her last name. She picked me up in Chicago. Amazing woman."

"Shut up, Benny," Cohen muttered, slapping the return button with a growing anger as one by one the machine found every instance of "Alex" in the spreadsheet. Lassman did collect a lot of business cards with Alexandria, Virginia, addresses. And Alexandra's last name was Swartz. But no Alexander Witkoff showed up in Lassman's computerized phone book.

"Maybe if you gave me a description," Lassman suggested.

"I only saw his picture."

"And?"

Cohen thought about the pictures he had seen at Witkoff's penthouse. Could he even be sure the man he had seen in the photos was indeed Witkoff? Most of the pictures had shown the man with famous people—a minister, a singer, a television talk show host. One photo had stood out, because in it the man had been alone, at the *kotel.* He hadn't been praying, but rather posing with the big stones against his back. It had been afternoon, Cohen could tell from the picture, both from the squint in the man's eyes and a hint of shadow on the wall behind the man. He had been wearing a *kippa* perched with unfamiliarity on his head; a new tallith, edged with gold embroidery, had glistened white in the bright sun. The man had not really been smiling, but there had been an almost smug self-satisfaction in his expression.

"Short hair. Cropped close. Very short hair. Fifties. Maybe forties. Thin eyebrows. Thin lips." Cohen thought a second longer. The photo had been full-frame, but had cut the man's legs just below the knees. However, the tallith, conservative-style and embroidered with gold at the neck, had reached only to Witkoff's waist. "Tall," Cohen concluded.

Lassman shook his head. "You have to understand. I spent a month on the road in the States touring for that book. I signed hundreds of those. Mostly to strangers. Like Alexandra." Lassman went to the kitchen counter to add a shot of brandy to his tea. He offered the bottle to Cohen, who shook his head no.

"It was the German edition," Cohen suddenly realized. "The German edition. But you signed in Hebrew. You signed it for an Israeli. Not a foreigner."

That's when Lassman remembered. He didn't say so, not yet. But Cohen could see in the split second that Lassman's hand paused on the cork cap of the liquor bottle that the reporter remembered. "Tell me," said the old detective.

Lassman added another shot of cognac to his glass tea cup, then shuddered as the alcohol steamed into his system. Finally, he sheepishly turned to face Cohen. "I can't be sure it's him. I never did get to meet him. But maybe. Maybe."

"What?" Cohen asked.

"I told you I was planning to do a story on the slave trade. After Frankfurt. I even started researching. But then there was the bomb."

"How did he get the book?" Cohen asked, spacing the words with an exaggerated patience that indicated he was losing his.

"I wanted to meet someone—anyone—from high up in the organization. A boss of bosses. I asked Nissim for help. But he brushed me off. 'Premature,' he had said. And the girls weren't much help. Half of them didn't even realize that he existed. And those who did had no idea of his name. I went to house after house, trying to get lucky. And

I did, I thought. An owner—a woman, and that's rare in that business—offered to help. She wouldn't give me a name. It was too dangerous, she said. But she told me that if I gave her a copy of one of my books, and a letter, she could make sure it got to the right person."

"Why?"

"Why what?"

"Did she want to help?"

"I paid her," Lassman admitted.

"So you sent *my* book."

"The author's copies had arrived the day before," Lassman admitted sheepishly.

"How do you know he could read German?"

"I didn't. But I was down to my last copy of the American edition. I had asked Carey for more. But they only came the next week."

"Why not send one of your own books?"

Lassman shrugged, embarrassed. "I'm down to my last copies and they're both out of print."

Cohen refocused on his purpose. "Who's the woman? The madame?"

"Her name's Sonia. At the Exotica. It's in Tel Aviv. I even have the card here somewhere." While Lassman looked for the card, he kept explaining what he did. "I brought a book and attached a letter with the questions I wanted to ask."

"Which were?"

"How the business works. How they get the girls. Who they bribe."

Cohen couldn't help but laugh. "Why did you think he'd give you any answers?"

Lassman paused from where he had hunched over the desk drawer, rummaging for the business card. "The letter said I wanted to write a book about how his business is a

175

business like any other business. I complimented him on
his organization, flattered him. I promised that if he didn't
want to be quoted by name, I had no problem with that.
All I wanted was to understand how the system worked. I
appealed to his ego."

"And you thought that would get through to him?"

"It's worked in the past. I appealed to his obvious love
of capitalism."

"You didn't even know his name."

"If he's really the man for all those houses, then he's
brilliant. I estimated that he's making at least a million a
week. To build a business like that in less than five years,
it's impressive. I said so in the letter."

"Did it work?"

"I never heard from him again."

"You didn't try?"

"I called Sonia a couple of times over the next two
weeks, but she said she hadn't heard anything from him.
And then there was Frankfurt. And the bomb."

"And the chambermaid," Cohen reminded him.

"Yes, and afterward . . . wait, here's the card." He presented the little business card embossed with a florid script
reading EXOTICA, held up by a pair of line-drawn nude
girls. Beneath was an address and phone number in Tel
Aviv.

"What?" Cohen asked. "What happened afterward?"

"I became obsessed," Lassman said simply. He waved at
the piles of folders all around them. "This, it took precedence over everything."

"You never heard from him again?" Cohen asked.

"Never," Lassman said sadly.

"I'm sorry," Cohen said. He meant it.

· 22 ·

He had a claustrophobic headache from the overheated flat and a gnawing guilt over the writer's obsession with the Frankfurt bombing. Worse, though he still had nothing more substantial than Witkoff's reading of his book, it created a connection, tenuous, unclear, ambiguous but nonetheless a connection between the Frankfurt bombing attempt and Nissim's murder. And if they were connected, then Hagit was right. Cohen was to blame for Nissim's death.

So perhaps more than anything, right then, Cohen feared the pain that would rock him if indeed he was to learn that the shaky link was in fact a strong rope between the two affairs. Death. More than ever, he was determined to find Nissim's killer.

It was barely a kilometer from Lassman's garden flat to Cohen's place in the German Colony. But two blocks from home, traffic onto Emek Refaim was stopped by a pair of patrol cars.

He waited ten minutes until the sirens announced the prime minister's passage. Until the assassination, such a progression had meant two silver-gray cars. Now, the convoy included at least two motorcycles, three jeeps, and an American-made, four-wheel-drive van, as well as two bulletproof sedans, one for decoy and the other carrying the premier.

Cohen never liked sirens. Levy loved them. Cohen scowled at the politician's party as it whooped past, and then the two young policemen who stopped him at the corner let him pull into Emek Refaim Street. Two turns later, his car was in the little tin garage and he was on his way up the stairs to his apartment on the second floor.

Suspect, the old tomcat that lived off and on at Cohen's apartment, was asleep on the middle of his bed, a privilege the cat was allowed to enjoy only when Cohen was away from the apartment. The cat opened one eye, looked at him briefly, then closed it indifferently for a second before rising. It stretched from paw to paw for another long second before it walked to the edge of the bed and jumped down, disappearing past the door into the little hallway between the living room study and the kitchen.

He showered and changed into a clean white shirt and gray twill trousers. He made a cup of black mud coffee and tried calling Shvilli again. It worried him that there was no answer so he tried Jacki again at her office, asking her why Shvilli's phone wasn't on. She blamed batteries and holes in the cellular net down south.

"As soon as you hear from him, tell him to call," he said.

"I made those photocopies," she added.

"Fax them to me," he ordered, giving her the number. "How's Hagit?"

"Last I spoke with her," Jacki said, "she was demanding that they let her and the child go home already."

"What do the doctors say?"

"They want her in a couple of more days. For observation."

"Send me the fax," he ordered, and hung up.

A few minutes later, he heard the computer answer the phone, open the fax reception program, and command the printer to make hard copies.

Comparing the license registration numbers on the speeding tickets to the notes he had made when he went to

Witkoff's place in Ramat Aviv Gimel, he identified the red BMW 328 convertible parked beside the Mercedes and the Land Rover.

Nissim's logs named Yuhewitz and Witkoff, among several other names that Shvilli had mentioned. The dates were as recent as the three days before the murder.

He called Abu Kabir to ask for Raoul. But the forensics expert wasn't going to be back in his office that day, said the secretary. Cohen left his cellular phone number in case the pathologist called and then tried Bensione again. But the photographer, too, was unavailable. Frustrated, he reached for the phone on his desk a third time.

But his cellular phone rang.

"Yes?" he answered.

"Boss, it's me," Shvilli said.

"Where are you?"

"Eilat."

"And?"

"Nissim was here."

"Yes, Jacki told me. The watchman saw him at the marina."

"Yes, but there's more. I know for sure he was at The Crown on Saturday night." It was one of the resort town's luxury hotels.

"He stayed overnight?" Cohen asked, surprised. Nissim would have called Hagit if he had been going to stay overnight at the hotel. Of that, Cohen was certain. There was crackling on the line, and then a shallow silence, and then Shvilli's voice.

"It's my fault," the undercover cop was saying, "it's my fault . . ." Then the connection fell into silence again.

"Hello? Hello? Shvilli?" Cohen tried. "I can't hear you."

". . . I didn't. And I don't know how he found out, but . . ." Again the line dropped.

"Shvilli!" Cohen yelled. "The line's breaking up. Call

me on a regular phone. Take my number. Can you hear me?"
He dictated his Jerusalem number into the phone, not at all
certain that Shvilli could hear, and closed the cellular phone,
waiting for the phone to ring. When it didn't after ten minutes, he used the asterisk code on his phone to redial the last
number that had called him. It was busy. He tried again.

"Shvilli? Can you hear me?" he tried when the ringing
stopped.

"Yes."

"All right. Maybe the line's okay now," Cohen hoped
aloud. "You said something was your fault. What was your
fault?"

"There was a meeting. All the bosses. From all over the
country. I should have known about it. I didn't. But Nissim obviously did."

"Russian bosses?"

"Yes."

"And?"

"Maybe they spotted him. I don't know. But I do know
that he was here. Remember Pinny Shimoni from
mounted patrol? He left the force a couple of years ago
and moved down here. Got a job in security for the hotel."

"He saw Nissim?"

"On Saturday night. Definitely on Saturday night."

"About what?"

"He was with a woman," said Shvilli. "That's what Pinny
told me. In the lobby."

Cohen said nothing, thinking. He wasn't surprised by
the report. Disappointed, yes. And more. Confused.

"Pinny knows her?"

"He wished."

"Description?"

"Young, short black hair. Long legs. 'Serious pussy'
Pinny told me."

"So was he down there for the woman or the bosses?" Cohen asked Shvilli. At first he thought Shvilli's silence was a sign of deliberation, but it went on too long. "Shvilli?" he tried. "Was Witkoff there?" But the cellular phone connection had fallen again.

Cohen sighed and hung up, then used his regular telephone. Opening the very first of the little yellow notebooks he had been filling since the morning he began the search through his memory in the attic of the Russian Compound, looking for the Frankfurt bomber among the informants he had sent to Germany, he went over his notes.

The forensics from the Frankfurt hotel had yielded very little. There had been the bomb, of course, but nothing in its design and construction had contained a tell-tale signature in any of the counterterror or police archives in either Germany or Israel.

Cohen's fingerprints, and the dead chambermaid's, had been all over the room. Cohen had no memory of gloves on the hands of the chambermaid he had nearly stumbled over in the corridor on his way to his room that night in Frankfurt. And the artist's sketch he had had drawn up and sent to Germany had proved useless.

As long as the Germans believed the case of the murdered chambermaid and the bomb might have roots in some form of Nazism—whether the old-fashioned kind or one of the neo versions, punk or not—they felt driven to solve the case.

In his book, Cohen had admitted to killing "more than fifty" Nazis in more than a year of vengeance after liberation. But he had detailed only two specific executions—his first (and the satisfaction it gave him) and the last (and the self-disgust he felt).

The rest, he said, didn't matter, though he had catalogued the many ways he, as one of the *nokmim*—the avengers—operated: "We hanged and shot and strangled. Knives, clubs, whatever was appropriate for the execution's circumstances. Sometimes we hunted, sometimes by accident we came across a target. One simply died of a heart attack as soon as he realized what the three strangers on his doorstep wanted," he had written.

So in Germany, archives had been opened, historians questioned, old newspapers scanned. There had been hundreds of such murders in the wilderness of Europe's collapse and into the beginning of its reconstruction. Nobody suggested prosecuting Cohen. But the German enthusiasm for focusing on the bombing and murder had declined as the days went by and the press had caught another story and the experts had said it could take years to track down the children and grandchildren of Nazis killed by avengers after the war. Nonetheless, a few were found in those first few days after Frankfurt. One had actually heard of Cohen and his book. After the news story about the bomb at the book fair, she had bought the book. She loved it, she said. Her father had been a colonel in the SS. She had no memory of him. Much younger neo-Nazis, punk or not, were also questioned. They laughed about the bomb and the dead chambermaid. But none of the known activists could be placed anywhere near the hotel in Frankfurt, and none knew any woman—or transsexual—with a mole on her jawline. Even the relatively educated leadership knew only what they had read in the newspapers and seen on television. Nobody among them, of course, felt bad either for Cohen or the dead chambermaid. She was, after all, a foreigner. They all recommended the German authorities ask the Jew if he planted the bomb.

Cohen's apparent conviction that his potential assassin might have come from inside the Israeli criminal community in Germany had also been a distraction to the Germans.

His contact for all his efforts was Helmut Leterhaus, the German officer whom he had met that night at the hotel. Cohen had sent him faxes with vaguely remembered new names given to the informants relocated to Germany. Indeed, the apparent ambiguity of Cohen's memory made it even more difficult for the German officer to take his suggestions to seek out criminals from the past.

By Christmas, the Germans were rapidly losing interest in the case. In mid-January, the pretty high school daughter of a prominent banker was kidnapped. At first it looked like a clumsy terrorist group, then a purely criminal gang, but by the end of the month the police were guessing that it was psychosexual. Cohen even caught a glimpse of Leterhaus standing in the second row of officers at a Frankfurt press conference about the case, picked up by CNN.

Leterhaus didn't need to spell it out for Cohen. The official policy was becoming that the Israeli author's case was just that, an Israeli case, and if someone had tried to kill him, the Israelis should figure it out. There was a conspiracy-minded reporter from a small left-wing paper who wondered occasionally in print why Cohen had been allowed out of the country that night. He should have been the suspect.

The reporter's stories asked why nobody that first night thought to wonder if Cohen planted the bomb as a publicity ploy for his book. Indeed, the question had arisen that night, but had been quickly knocked down by all the witnesses to Cohen's clear dislike for publicity of any sort. Leterhaus had said not to worry about it. The newspaper's anti-Zionism made it anti-Semitic. That didn't convince Cohen, who sympathized with the reporter's real complaint—that the police seemed more interested in the bomb than in the murder of the chambermaid, the native-born German child of an immigrant family imported to the country.

That was something that Cohen had noticed right from

the start with the policeman. The bomb was much more interesting than the murder. "Yes, yes," Cohen would try to explain to the Frankfurt cop, "the bomber is the killer, but the murder is the more serious crime committed. Remember, the bomb didn't go off."

But just as the Israeli cops investigating Nissim's murder were focused on Big Kobi Alper—or for that matter, Cohen was focused on Witkoff—the Germans were more interested in the bomb. And after months of *gornisht*, nothing, even Leterhaus didn't seem to care much more. Yet when Leterhaus had called to say he was ordered to suspend his activity on the case in favor of the missing teenager, he had reassured Cohen that if the Jerusalemite came up with any leads, "I will do my best." Now a stranger answered the phone at Leterhaus's direct line. Cohen asked for his contact man.

"He is gone," said the officer at the other end of the line. He spoke German.

"Gone?" Cohen answered in English. Before he could ask where Leterhaus went, the officer asked who was calling.

"Cohen. Avram Cohen," he answered obediently.

There was a pause, but not long enough for Cohen to add anything.

"The book fair bomb?" asked the German officer.

"Yes."

"You're the policeman. The one who wrote the book."

"Yes," Cohen admitted.

"Didn't like it," said the man, adding, "hold on. Transferring."

The book critic in the policeman made Cohen smile, but the long wait for the call's transfer made him uneasy. He held the phone between a cocked shoulder and his ear, leafing through his notes, looking for Leterhaus's home number.

"Oberpolizeirag Maerker," a woman identified herself.

"My name is Avram Cohen," he began in English, "I am trying to reach Polizeirag Helmut Leterhaus. I have some new information—"

"You haven't heard?"

"What?"

"Leterhaus is dead."

His heart missed a beat, a bead of sweat grew in his palm clenching the phone. Suspect the cat, sitting at the half-open windowsill, deliberating whether to go out or remain sitting in the warm sun, must have sensed the sudden tension. As if escaping, the cat suddenly leapt out the window. It was as short a jump from Cohen's bed to the floor as it was from the window to the roof of the wooden-and-glass pergola over the outdoor stairway from the garden to Cohen's second-floor flat.

"Hel-lo?" the woman modulated the syllables into two tones, to catch his attention.

"How?"

"An automobile accident."

"A car accident?" Cohen asked.

"Yes. Two weeks ago. A drunk."

There was something in her curt tone that for a second made him think that she meant Helmut was at fault. For all his flaws, as far as Cohen could tell, Leterhaus was not a drinker. Cohen was the one with the reputation as an alcoholic, but at least had the sense to use a driver when he did drink, even if the driver couldn't tell from anything except Cohen's breath that his boss had been drinking. Leterhaus, on the other hand, looked like he never drank.

Cohen hesitated, but then asked the obvious question.

"No," she replied. "The other driver was drunk. Ran a red light. Both were killed."

"Oh" said Cohen, relieved. "I'm sorry to hear about it."

"Yes, a tragedy," said the woman, almost bitterly, as if Leterhaus nonetheless was at least partly to blame. "How can I help you?"

"You have an open murder case. The chambermaid. Marina Berendisi."

"And the bomb under your bed," she added.

"Yes, of course."

"We continue to investigate, of course," the woman said.

"Of course," he said, disbelieving. "I have a name for you to check."

"Excuse me?"

"I gave Helmut names. Leads."

"Yes, but they were not as helpful as you seemed to believe," she said.

He bit his jaw, clamping down anger, trying to ignore the tone in her voice.

"I have another one. Helmut ran the other names through the databases."

"And spent many days and weeks searching for these people and interviewing them."

"Yes," Cohen admitted. He had to be careful. The call was made on a far-fetched hunch. He had no way of knowing for certain that it was Witkoff to whom Lassman had sent the book. And he certainly had no other reason than the fact he found the book in Witkoff's penthouse to see a connection between the Russian Mafioso and the incident in Frankfurt. He could not tell her the reasons for his request, lest she dismiss it as either a simple waste of time, or worse, meddling. He did not want to beg. "All I ask is you run it through your database. On the basis of what turns up you can decide whether to investigate further."

It was her turn to fall silent a moment. "What is the name?" she finally asked.

"Witkoff. Alexander Witkoff." He spelled it for her.

"He is one of your relocated informants?" she asked, with a natural disdain for another policeman's snitches and obvious disapproval of the Israeli police's former practice of using Germany as a dumping ground for criminals.

He thought for a second, still feeling the paranoiac jolt he experienced when she had told him Leterhaus had died in an accident. He had his phones checked regularly. Too many private investigators were on trial for wiretapping; and while the bureaucracy was still knee deep in old paper, the intelligence services had long pioneered eavesdropping through the phones. In any case, Cohen was tired of phones and Udi Hason had never found anything both times in two years that Cohen had called, suspicious there were bugs on his phones.

"He originates from Russia," he finally decided to tell her.

"Oh," she said. "Do you know what city, please?"

"Moscow, I believe."

"And he is an informant?" she asked again.

"No," he admitted. "But please, just check the name in your database. Please." He was begging. Hating himself for it, he added, "a few seconds of computing time. Helmut was able to check the computers at the BKA and BND."

"I see," she said, making him think she didn't. "Is that all?" she added.

"It is rather urgent."

"Excuse me?" she asked, offended by the idea that he could impose his schedule upon her.

"Helmut often looked up names while I waited . . ."

"Mr. Cohen," she said, "I assure you this will be handled with all due speed."

"Please, take my phone number. Call me any time of the day or night . . ."

But instead of making the promise, she said, "Of course,

if we need you further we will be in touch. Thank you for calling, good day."

"No, if anything turns up, you let me know," he shouted down the line at her. But by the time he added, "that was my deal with Leterhaus," the line had fallen dead.

· 23 ·

He could understand the German police. Many times he had wondered how he would have treated such a crime if it had occurred on his patch. Understaffed, pressed by the daily crunch of events, the attempted bombing of a famous tourist visiting the city would get a lot of attention at first, but with the author gone—and the innocent bystander only one of the city's thousands of hotel workers—how much time would any top floor of any police department allow a full press on the case? If within the first seventy-two hours they didn't make an arrest, the likelihood of one dropped daily, as would the effort, until the investigation became a routine hour—a week, a month, a year—of noting that nothing new had turned up.

He couldn't blame them. It was a peculiar case, so with each passing day and week that the Israelis turned up nothing on the radical Jewish right, the Germans found no leads among the Jew-haters, and Cohen himself had failed to provide Leterhaus with a useful name from the past, Cohen's case had become his alone.

His own impassioned plea for the peace process in the epilogue of his book had made all the experts rule out an organized Arab gang picking him as a target. His position as chief of CID in Jerusalem had indeed made him part of the war effort, but never, in all the years that he had run CID, which had arrested thousands of Arabs in the city for

189

both all the mundane and extraordinary reasons that the police had made arrests in Jerusalem, had any Palestinian group ever targeted him—or indeed any other police commander—for vengeance. Several radical right-wing Jewish groups had, however, named him as a traitor.

He found Leterhaus's home phone number on his yellow pad. Beneath the phone number was Leterhaus's home address, which the German police officer had given Cohen in the hopes that one day the Israeli might come back "under different circumstances" and they could visit as friends.

At the time, Cohen had doubted he would ever do that. Now, he wondered if he should write a condolence note to the dead officer's wife. But before he could decide, the cellular phone rang.

"Boss, it's me. I'm back in the office." It was Shvilli.

"Can you talk?"

"They picked up Kobi Alper's little brother Itzik this morning—at the airport. They're convinced he was trying to get out of the country because of the hit."

"Nearly three days later—ridiculous," Cohen pointed out.

"Don't be so sure. They started looking for him on Sunday morning and only found him today. The last time he was definitely seen was sunset Friday at his mother's. The Alpers never miss their Friday evening dinner with their mother—unless they're in jail."

"You were telling me about Nissim meeting a woman in the lobby of the hotel," Cohen reminded the detective.

"Yes. 'Young,' Pinny said. 'Flashy.' "

"A working girl?"

"From Pinny's description, maybe. But from a very high-quality house. Yuhewitz owns a house like that."

"Was she registered in the hotel? Did Pinny find out?"

"He only saw them for a minute. They were leaving together."

"And Pinny hasn't seen her since?"

"I don't know."

"Ask him. Find her. And another thing. Nissim's phone records."

"I know, I know," Shvilli protested. "Jacki says she's trying to get them. But Caspi's cheap, real cheap. He's a shit. He's trying to prove he can fill Nissim's shoes. Carry all the weight himself. Someone ought to tell him that police work is teamwork. And Bendor loves his ass because Caspi came from the paratroopers. Besides, Caspi never liked Nissim. And he knows I was close to Nissim. Believe me, boss, I'm not getting much cooperation from him."

Cohen let Shvilli get the resentment off his chest. "Michael," he finally said softly. "Forget Caspi. Tell me about the Russians. That meeting? What were they discussing?"

"I'm working on it, believe me. I've got a source who was inside. But it's like he's disappeared. 'You just missed him,' 'he was just here'—everywhere I look for him, he's gone or hasn't been around."

"Witkoff? Could he have been doing business in Germany? In Frankfurt?"

There was a long silence. For a second, Cohen wondered if again the phone line was to blame.

"You mean if he had something to do with what happened to you there?" Shvilli asked back, disappointment in his tone, as if he had just discovered something he wasn't sure he wanted to know about Cohen. Now it was Cohen's turn to think hard before answering. He did not want to sound paranoid, even though, if asked, ever since he had heard Nissim was dead he had simply followed intuitions dictated by emotions. But before he spoke,

Shvilli added a request to his question. "I have to ask you something, boss. About that business."

"Frankfurt?"

"Yes."

"Go ahead."

"Is it true you didn't want to help?"

"Actually, I've been digging in the archives," said Cohen. "An old case, perhaps . . ."

"But that night, you left, you could have stayed. It's like you . . ." Shvilli was asking if he had been afraid.

"Ran?" Cohen filled in the blank.

"Yes."

"I was leaving anyway," Cohen said, not wanting to explain, not needing to explain, suddenly certain of his intuition, if not the evidence. "Find out, Michael. From Yuhewitz, from Yudelstein, whoever you can ask. Does Witkoff have business in Frankfurt?" It was his last question before hanging up.

He checked his watch. He wanted to make sure of something Lassman couldn't tell him. Did Sonia actually pass the book onto Witkoff or did the Russian get it from someone else? He was pondering these questions, knowing that he needed more than a hunch, when the phone on his desk rang again.

"Raoul?" he answered hopefully.

"Hello, Avram," came the reply. Recognizing the voice, Cohen clenched the receiver tightly, knowing that he had failed to keep his efforts a secret. A call from Meshulam Yaffe meant only one thing: politics. The ultimate survivor in the police bureaucracy, Yaffe was now a special assistant to the minister of police. He had survived three ministers in three years, specializing in keeping the hem sewn between the professional needs of the police force with the political needs of his political masters. Just as he had a tailor keep his uniform well cut, he followed the fashions, tailoring his position according to the power balance between the fifth floor of police headquarters and the police ministry on the sixth floor of the government office complex across the valley in Sheikh Jarrah.

"What do you want, Meshulam?" Cohen asked brusquely.

"How are you?"

"Get to the point," Cohen ordered.

"My condolences. On Nissim Levy. I know how you two were close."

"Get to the point."

"Avram, please. Can't you for once be gracious!" Yaffe was an emotional man.

"I know you too well, Meshulam. There's something you want."

"Please, Avram, I'm serious. The minister sends condolences. Everyone here does, in fact."

"Thank you."

"See, that didn't hurt, did it?"

"What do they want?" Cohen asked a third time.

"It's what you want, Avram," Yaffe said, pointing out the obvious.

"Stop waltzing, Meshulam," Cohen demanded. "What are you calling about? I accepted your condolences. What else do you want? And please don't tell me about the academy needing new sports equipment for the gym."

"It's not about the equipment," Yaffe said.

"Then what?"

"I know that you spoke with the inspector general. And that he asked you not to interfere."

"With what?"

"Av-ram! Please."

They were in a battle of wits that they had played for years, going back to when Yaffe was the police liaison for all the foreign officials in Jerusalem. From diplomats to clergymen, if they got into trouble with the police, Yaffe was their official address at the police, while Cohen's department—often in coordination with the Shabak counterintelligence agency—ran the investigation. Yaffe's job was to prevent scandals. Cohen's job was to get to the truth.

While still on the force, Cohen had usually gained the upper hand. But it all was a matter of information. And right now, Yaffe definitely knew more than Cohen. At the very least, Yaffe knew how he learned about Cohen's inquiries. Had Witkoff already realized Cohen was asking questions? Did Shvilli let it slip that his information about Nissim in Eilat went first to Cohen? And where was Jacki—running back and forth between Hagit and Levy's old office now, according to Shvilli, already occupied by Shuki Caspi. He couldn't rule out a call from Frankfurt to Bonn to Jerusalem. And he wondered if there was something Yaffe learned at Ramle—where Kobi Alper was incarcerated—that made the politician's politician call him. In short, there was only one way to go—surprise Yaffe. He did so by suggesting they meet, to talk. That night.

Meanwhile, Cohen decided to get some sleep. He needed it for the night ahead.

· 24 ·

It was Yaffe's idea to meet at Balkan, in Tel Aviv. It had simple, obvious fare: grilled and baked meats, soups, and salads, but nobody ate there for the fare. It was the restaurant of choice for the power elite. Ministers and generals, industrialists and publishers—they all ate there.

For its first two generations, the restaurant was across the street from the wholesale fruit and vegetable market behind the defense ministry. The third generation closed the twelve-tables-and-a-bar place and joined the gentrification of the old port of Tel Aviv at the very northern end of the seaside boardwalk. The old storefront place could barely handle fifty people at a time. The converted warehouse next to the skin-diving club on one side and overlooking the Mediterranean on the other had tables and chairs to seat two hundred.

From a glum brown-and-green decor, the restaurant changed into a place brightly lit by the open sky of the western horizon. The menu also changed, now emphasizing seafood and pasta, much more fashionable than the Balkan-Jewish food the grandparents had cooked.

To reach the entrance to the restaurant, Cohen had to walk to the end of the parking lot, past the broad plateglass windows. Yaffe was looking out for him, and waved for Cohen to join him at the table of six. But Cohen shook his head and pointed at the entrance, for Yaffe to join him there.

"I thought you'd join us for dinner," said Yaffe. "Shaul Machnes is coming. He said he would like to meet you."

"The MK*?" asked Cohen.

"Yes."

Cohen shook his head. "I'm not here to socialize," he said, "especially not with an MK. Follow me."

Yaffe tried to protest with a "but," but Cohen walked into the darkness of the port's most western edge, beside the retaining wall that prevented the Mediterranean sea from rising onto the asphalt surface of the old port and washing the nightclubs and restaurants away. So Yaffe apologized to the waiter, whom he had told to bring a chair and add a setting for Cohen at the table for seven, and scurried to catch up with Cohen.

They walked beside the retaining wall until Cohen stopped, distant from all the parked cars, in a darkness Cohen estimated was impenetrable to anyone sitting inside the restaurant and at a place that gave him a view of all the cars entering the port. On the way down to Tel Aviv, Cohen had done the calculations in his head, reaching the obvious conclusion: If Yaffe knew that Cohen was investigating Witkoff, Cohen assumed that Witkoff himself also must know. He couldn't be sure, of course. That's why he was meeting Yaffe. To find out just how much Yaffe knew.

"Why all the paranoia?" Meshulam asked.

"You tell me," said Cohen. "You're the one who called, worried I would vandalize something."

"That's precisely the point. You are mistaken."

"About what?"

Yaffe sighed. "We understand that you take Nissim Levy's murder very hard," he began. "And obviously, if you

*MK: Member of Kuesset, the 120-seat Israeli Parliament.

have any relevant information, we'll be happy to take it, follow it up. But . . ."

"But what?"

"Do I have to spell it out for you?"

"That you can't do anything about the Russians?"

"No, that *you* can't do anything about it. Leave it to us."

"Meanwhile, I understand the investigation's focusing on the Alper brothers."

"Yes, that's true. We're holding one of the brothers . . ."

"Did you know that Nissim personally threatened Boris Yuhewitz?"

"Who?"

"See, that's what I mean. You don't even know what it's about."

"I know that you're asking about Alexander Witkoff," said Yaffe, losing his temper.

Just then a car pulled into the parking lot, sped up for about fifty meters, and then slowed down, turning to drive past them slowly. Before the headlights could blind Cohen, he turned away to look out to sea, smiling at the way, after all, Yaffe had been the first to name Witkoff.

And Yaffe went on, without prodding. "Yes, there are rich Russians. Very rich. Richer than anything you can imagine. Where everyone else saw chaos, they saw an opportunity. They took it. Yes, some of them made their money from the black market. And some even came here. Jews. And maybe even some who aren't Jews. But not all of them are Mafia. Not all of them are criminals. Did it ever occur to you that some of those businessmen are just that, businessmen? Legitimate businessmen. Avram, Avram, please, don't be naive," Yaffe complained. "The Russians changed the country and the country changed the Russians. But just because there are Russian whores doesn't make every rich Russian a pimp. And just because a person arrives from Russia with a lot of money, doesn't mean they are the Godfather."

"Money doesn't have a smell, you mean," said Cohen.

"You know what I mean," Yaffe shot back.

Cohen sighed. Though the storm was over, the winter sea was not calm. A wave crashed against the retaining wall and some spray drizzled down on them. He pulled out a cigarette and discovered that he was over his self-imposed limit. It made him scowl, but he lit the cigarette anyway.

Maybe Yaffe and his minister truly believed that Witkoff was clean. Maybe Shvilli was wrong. But still, he had found his book in Witkoff's house, and if indeed the book had reached Witkoff through Sonia, it meant that the Russian banker knew of the relationship between Cohen and Levy.

After all, for more than half the years Cohen headed CID Levy had been his chief aide. He was mentioned on many of the pages of the book's chapters about Jerusalem. So why, Cohen wondered, remembering that long moment when he had held his book trembling in the penthouse living room, why had the chapter about the witness relocation scheme been the most dog-eared part of the book he had found? The connection was tenuous, too tenuous. Indeed, the most tangible proof that he had about Witkoff's possible involvement in the case was that when he pulled at the thread by asking about Witkoff he found himself dealing with Meshulam Yaffe.

"How did you find out?" he asked.

"It's a very small world nowadays," said Yaffe.

"The Germans," Cohen guessed. "They called you when I offered them his name."

"It doesn't matter how I know," said Yaffe. "What matters is that you understand that you are on the wrong track. You want Nissim's killer found? Let Shuki Caspi, and all the good people on his team, do their job."

"I'm not interfering with them. But if they aren't going to investigate a possible lead, someone has to do it."

"And why should it be you?"

"Because Nissim was like a son to me," Cohen said bluntly. "And he was blamed for the sins of his fathers once before. I want to make sure that it won't happen a second time."

"What are you talking about?"

"You said you don't know who Boris Yuhewitz is. Let me tell you. He seems to be running the Russian scene down in Eilat. And a few weeks ago, Nissim Levy publicly threatened him in front of a lot of people."

"I'll look into it. Maybe you're right about this Yuhewitz," Yaffe conceded. "But that doesn't mean that Witkoff—"

"He was there."

"How do you know?" Yaffe asked, disbelieving.

"It's a small world," Cohen said, throwing the phrase back into Yaffe's face. Then he pulled another deep drag off his cigarette and told Yaffe the truth: "I don't know why. I don't know how, but I think that Witkoff might have had something to do with what happened to me in Frankfurt."

"That bombing?"

"A girl was killed. And someone tried to kill me. Yes. And from the way you're reacting, there's more to it than his being a banker."

"You're crazy," Yaffe protested, starting to walk away. "He's a banker, not a killer. And you, I'm afraid, have become completely paranoid. What is it the kids say nowadays? Get a life, Avram." Yaffe reached into his inside jacket pocket, for a second making Cohen even more paranoid. But instead of a weapon it was a comb that he pulled out, running it through his already neat white hair, patting it all into place. Then with a shake of his head at Cohen, Yaffe headed back to the restaurant.

Maybe he was paranoid, he thought. Maybe he had built a fantasy. There was only one way to find out. He took a last puff on his cigarette, flicked the butt over the retaining wall into the cold sea, and walked back to his car.

· 25 ·

The Exotica Club was southeast across town, in a neighborhood that by day was devoted to the car business and by night was a poor cousin to the gentrifying old port.

From new car showrooms to one-man tool-and-die shops, from used engine parts to motor scooter repairmen, the neighborhood was known for its traffic jams reported by national radio stations. At the critical junction of two main arteries crossing the city north to south and east to west, it overlooked the Ayalon Highway, the tiny country's central road ventricle.

At night the streets of the neighborhood were mostly deserted, except for clusters of cars parked outside cheap wedding halls and experimental discotheques.

That night, only one hall was hosting a wedding. Cohen drove past just as the bride climbed out of a balloon-festooned car. She gathered the long hem of the dress to avoid the grease of the sidewalk, then ran through the deepening night cold to her fluttering family at the fluorescent entrance to an office building with a street-floor display of Japanese cars.

Cohen drove on deeper into the neighborhood, past shuttered garages and cheap restaurants that served daytime garage hands, reaching a narrow street lined by three- and four-story buildings built in the sixties.

Scattered lights showed a few offices still occupied with

workers, impoverished start-ups that in their own way were gentrifying the neighborhood just as the restaurants at the old port had pushed out the ceramics traders who had used the old docks as warehouses.

He stopped at a four-way intersection where one road was named for a kibbutz and the other for a rabbi, before glancing one last time at the page of the road atlas on the passenger seat.

In front of him, the rabbi became a dead end. He pulled through the intersection slowly. A couple of blocks to his right, he could see the bright lights of the main thoroughfare.

To his right, the iron gates of a body repair shop were still scarred by old election posters showing only the hairline, forehead, eyes, and nose of a past candidate. The rest of the face was torn away. Past the garage, graffiti on the wall advertised a nightclub, and then the peeling plaster wall of the repair shop's offices were taken up by a gold-on-black poster advertising cheap flights to Turkey, competing with a larger black-on-white announcement for "returning to the answer." Three wise men from the Council of Torah Sages would teach lessons and raise a "great shout for redemption."

To his left, two different buildings were joined into a four-story office building. The street floor included a shuttered sandwich shop and a small printing plant. The second floor had lots of little businesses, judging from the jumble of signs in the windows. The third floor was shrouded in the dark of night, and only one dim light came from the fourth, incomplete floor of unglazed windows and cement block walls. None of the signs on the windows, nor at the three separate entrances to the building pointed to the Exotica Club. He pulled out the card Lassman had given him. Number 5. He rolled down the window to check. It was the place.

He made a U-turn, but instead of driving out he backed into a place between a Dumpster and the gutted remains of a car left out of the garage for the night. The rear of his car was up against a low retaining wall. The roar of a truck passing on the Ayalon Highway below made the cold night air suddenly seem even colder. He turned off his car lights.

Just then, a stairwell light from number 5 flashed on, splashing new shadows into the small street. Two young men came running out of the building, scrambled up the street, and tore around the first corner to the right. Then a burly man in tight jeans, shiny shoes, and a black leather jacket ran out of the building. He pulled a blackjack out of his pocket as he raced up to the intersection after the boys. He looked left, then right, raised a fist and shouted something in Russian, but he didn't run after the young men. He rolled his shoulders like a boxer and replaced the blackjack in his pocket with a packet of cigarettes, lighting one and rolling his shoulders again before checking his watch. The gold caught a sliver of light from the sole street light on the street.

Cohen slouched at dashboard level, watching from behind the wheel as the bouncer blew another thick cloud of smoke and hot breath into the chilly night air. He was obviously waiting for someone. Cohen waited, too.

There was a rumble of an old taxi coming into the neighborhood. Two men in business suits got out of an old Peugeot station wagon. One paid the driver through the window. The other, with a thin mustache and a white scarf, limped forward a few steps.

"Is Juliet here tonight?" the man with the mustache asked hopefully in Hebrew. He neither raised his voice nor whispered, but in the quiet of the little street at night his words carried on the cold air through the open window of Cohen's cold car.

The bouncer nodded. The taxi engine roared for a moment and then the car drove away.

"Yossi?" asked the other newcomer, putting away his wallet into an inside jacket pocket as he joined his friend and the bouncer. "You sure this is the place?" He spoke American English.

"Don't you worry, Harry," said the limping man. He spoke heavily accented English. "You'll see." Then he added in Hebrew to the bouncer, "is Sonia here?" Again the bouncer only nodded.

"So we go have some fun, yes, Harry?" Yossi said, putting a hand on the American's shoulder. As they followed the security man into the hallway, where the stairwell lights had timed out, Cohen heard the limping man say in Hebrew to the bouncer, "Sonia's going to love this one. A real gentleman."

With that, they disappeared up the stairs. A minute later, the hallway light went out and only the lampposts illuminated the street. Cohen opened his glove compartment and pulled out his flask of cognac. He sucked at the leather-wrapped silver bottle once, lit a cigarette, and took another sip. Only when he had replaced the flask in the glove compartment and finished his smoke did he roll up the window of his car and get out into the darkness.

· 26 ·

On the first floor, signs pointed to an orthopedic shoe manufacturer and a laptop wholesaler and several companies claiming to be limited, whether in universal, worldwide, or simply global trade. Nothing pointed to the Exotica Club on the second floor. But on the third-floor wall, instead of tacked-up plastic plaques announcing fledgling or veteran businesses with arrows pointing either right or left down the corridors, two doors greeted him.

Exotica Productions was written in an italic script across the reflecting glass door to his left. An arrow was drawn onto the wall with a red Magic Marker pointing at a button for a buzzer.

It took about ten seconds for the door to open with a click. He pushed through and found himself in a corridor draped by red velvet curtains. He pretended to be drunk, and keeled slightly to his left and then right, testing for the distance to a more solid wall or door, wondering if there were openings in the curtains. At the end of the corridor, which was lit only by a bath of low-watt little lightbulbs in the ceiling, he found himself facing another door.

He pushed through into a large lounge that included two sofas, half a dozen armchairs, a small but well-stocked bar where the bouncer was making himself an espresso, and, in one corner, a large office desk carrying a computer monitor. The lighting in the room was as dim as in the velvet corridor except at the desk, where a halogen lamp cast a spotlight on the clear surface. At the little bar, the bouncer put down a white porcelain espresso cup and turned on his seat to face Cohen. From behind the tall back of an armchair facing a large TV screen playing a video of two naked women frolicking in a field appeared the face of the mustached man from downstairs.

"Yes, this is the place," Cohen muttered, grinning at them all as if he were on stage and they the audience, and then asked much louder, "Is the highly recommended Madame Sonia here?"

Acting, he was removed from himself, able to take in details. There were seven women; four blondes, two brunettes, and a tall slender black girl with gravity-defying breasts barely camouflaged by a transparent black robe that fell open and closed, revealing long limbs as she danced quietly by herself to a softly weeping electric guitar playing blues from speakers hidden somewhere in the room.

"She'll be right out," the mustached man in the armchair promised, "but I was here first."

Cohen slightly raised two hands in mock surrender, "No problem, no problem. Are you the bartender?" he added, heading toward the bouncer at the bar. "A cognac, please."

The bouncer sighed and went behind the bar, taking down a bottle. Cohen took the second bar stool and leaned on the counter, looking at the women, smiling. The black girl danced slowly past him, her long arm stretching a long finger that gently touched his cheek until a fingernail, for a moment, scratched his two-day-old beard. He sat still. She floated away, hands on her buttocks swaying suddenly twice as fast as the music, keeping her eyes on him. Cohen smiled at her, then took a sip of the cognac the bouncer presented him.

One of the blondes said something in Russian, and two others laughed. A fourth rose from where she had been curled up like a cat in an armchair and went to the bar, joining the bouncer/bartender behind the counter, taking a glass and pouring some soda water, then holding it beside Cohen's glass so the bouncer, after filling Cohen's drink, could add a splash to the soda.

She was about to say something, except suddenly there was a flurry at one of the curtains and a laugh, and Sonia—for who else could it be?—appeared suddenly in the room with an elderly man before her, laughing cheerfully but at the same time giving instructions in Russian to the bouncer, telling Mustache in Hebrew that the American seemed very happy with Juliet, and asking the girls something in Russian, indicating Cohen with a long fingernail. From the tone of her voice, he decided, she was asking why one of them had not already captured his attention.

She was short, but full-figured, her breasts holding up a strapless dress. In the dim light, she might have been a beyond-her-years teenager or in her late thirties, or even early forties. She smiled at Cohen a second time, and asked him to join her at her desk. The bouncer, meanwhile, held open the door for the elderly man who was bidding farewell to each of the girls with a little bow and peck of their outstretched hands. One of the blondes on the sofa said something in Russian, pointing at the mustached man in the armchair. Sonia waved her off and beckoned her new customer, the barrel-chested, white-haired man in the gray twill trousers, sneakers, white shirt, and a gray windbreaker jacket. Cohen took his glass to the desk and sat down in the steel and leather chair.

"Can you tell me how you came to find our little place?" Sonia asked Cohen. There was no suspicion in the question. It was more like a customer survey.

"A friend," said Cohen. "You are Sonia? He especially noted your charms."

She smiled again. But now there was something in her eyes that showed more curiosity, as if there was something else she was supposed to know. "Your friend's name?" she asked.

He smiled at her. "Benny."

"Which Benny?"

"From Jerusalem."

"The writer?"

He nodded.

"A good boy. So did he tell you the rules?"

Cohen shook his head.

"You pay in advance."

He nodded, reaching for one of the packets in his inside jacket.

"We take credit cards and—"

"I'll pay cash. For *your* time."

"Barbara seems interested in you," the madam said, looking over Cohen's shoulder. Cohen turned to find himself facing the undulating hips of the black woman.

"She is very appealing," Cohen admitted, but he leaned forward and tried to smile with as much charm as he could muster. "Perhaps later, but for now, I think I prefer you."

"Later?" she asked, skeptical.

"Another time perhaps," he promised. "But you are the best here. Benny said so. And we both know that he is an accurate reporter."

She laughed. "A good boy," she repeated.

"He tries," said Cohen.

"Too much, sometimes," she said, suddenly a little scornful.

"So how much?" Cohen asked.

"For Barbara? Six hundred shekel. For me? A thousand. Unless . . ."

"What?"

"You have special needs."

He pulled ten two-hundred shekel notes from the envelope he opened inside his jacket and spread the red bills on the gleaming surface of her desk.

He lowered his voice. "I have special needs," he said.

She raised an eyebrow, suspicious, tempted, curious.

"Talk," he said.

He thought he saw a flutter of suspicion in her eyes, but then she smiled and slid the money into the drawer, waving a hand at Barbara, sending her away.

There was a little round of laughter from the Russian girls on the sofas behind him. "Yossi," she suddenly said to the mustached man with the limp. "I know you've done a good job this week. Bringing the American tonight was very good. But I'm afraid, darling, that you'll have to wait a little while. Unless of course you'd like . . ." she waved a hand at the girls, none of whom seemed particularly enthusiastic about Yossi.

The buzzer rang and she tapped the desk, making the computer mouse move and the monitor come to life. From where Cohen was sitting he could only guess there was a video card that enabled her to view on the monitor screen the person who had asked for entry to her kingdom. She sighed and pressed a button beneath the desk surface.

"Karin," she called out to a blonde in a red bikini, pushing herself away from the desk and rising, "you're in charge. I'm taking . . . you didn't tell me what to call you," she said to Cohen.

"Avram," he said.

"Avi," she changed it. He winced. She didn't notice, but spoke over his shoulder. "I'm taking Avi to my room for a while," she announced to Karin.

"What about me?" whined Yossi.

"You can have Juliet when your American finishes," Sonia offered, "or maybe you'd like Barbara." The dancing girl heard her name, grimaced, but then moved her dance toward the mustached man in the armchair, slowly descending in front of him as Cohen followed Sonia.

They went through a slit she knew in the curtain, leading to another draped and dimly lit corridor, long and narrow, lined by six doors on each side. Over two of the doors, a little light flashed, indicating the room was occupied. Vaguely through the first door they passed, Cohen could hear the rolling English of an American trying to speak French. Probably with Juliet, Cohen decided. Sonia led him to the last door on the right, opening it to a room about the size of his little living room study at home.

Instead of windows, there were mirrors on three of the four pasteboard walls that were covered with a wallpaper of swirling red, purple, and black paisley. Light came from low-watt bulbs, illuminating details like the fur-covered handcuffs on the night table beside the huge bed, which was covered in black sheets. He crossed the room to a brighter light coming through the beaded curtain. It led to a shower stall, bidet, and toilet, as well as sink and counter and the bright lights of a makeup studio mirror.

He doubted the room was microphone or camera free, but he was past the point of caring. She made it clear she was a professional at work. She knew the risks. So far, all she knew was that Cohen wanted to talk.

"I like talk," she said as she came into the room. "But it is not so easy for me. In Hebrew. In Russian I am much better. But I'm learning. Maybe you can teach me something new. A veteran Israeli like you . . ."

He took her hand in his and put an arm around her waist and said, "I'm hear for talk, not sex," in a very low voice.

"Information. Benny gave you a package to deliver. A book. A letter."

She went to the boudoir table, looked in the mirror, then plucked a tissue from a box on the cosmetic table. She dabbed at the corner of her lips, then slid open a drawer and pulled out a red lipstick that she applied carefully, leaning forward toward the mirror. Only when she was satisfied with her appearance did her eyes go to his, reflected in the mirror.

"Such a smart boy, and so foolish," she finally said. "Is there a problem? Is Benny in trouble?" she asked.

"Should he be?"

"I have not seen him for a long time."

"He's been busy," Cohen said. "Did you deliver the book?"

"Yes," she admitted.

"To?"

"Benny knows."

"No, he doesn't."

"Yes, he does."

"All Benny knows is that you said you would give it to a boss."

"I did."

"Who?"

"Why?"

"It was my book."

"Benny says it was his."

"Benny helped. It is my story."

She looked him up and down. "Police, yes? Remembrances? Yes?"

He nodded.

"I didn't read it," she reiterated, trying to make him believe her. "Just passed it on."

"To Witkoff," he said. "Alexander Witkoff." He stated it as a fact, and was surprised by her reaction.

"Who?" she asked, asking so bluntly, so simply, so honestly, that his instincts told him to trust her precisely because specifically, in that instance, an honest ignorance of Witkoff's name cost her nothing. He sat down, stunned by the surprise.

Misunderstanding his slump to the edge of the bed, she got up from the cosmetic table and crawled onto the bed until she reached his shoulders and tried to ease the tense muscle bunched at the base of his neck and across his shoulders.

"There, isn't that nice?" she asked. "Why don't we take a nice hot shower together. Why worry about Benny? So smart, so foolish. But you are different . . ."

He stood up, not so much angry as impatient, tired, and hungry. He wanted to move on, but he had to try again, just to be sure. "Alexander Witkoff?"

She pouted innocence. "Avi, Avi," she offered, reaching for his hand. "Yes, I know an Alexander. Several. Even Witkoffsky, a teacher when I was in polytechnic in Leningrad. But no, his name was Fyodr. Not Alexander. What do I care about a Witkoffsky?"

"Two people are dead because you gave that book to someone," he said.

"I'm impressed. So I must be careful what I say," she snapped, but it was boredom, not fear, that made her suddenly mean. "So, who is this Witkoff?"

"I thought he was a boss. Your boss. I needed to be sure, before I could . . ."

"I told you. I have no owner. Benny wanted to meet someone very high, very high. I know this man. He is very high."

"But he is not your owner?"

"I have no owner," she protested again. "I am a businesswoman. Partners, yes, I have partners. Not owners.

And the man is not a partner. He does not need places like this anymore. He comes to see me. For personal attention. Older men have special needs." She smiled at him. "If you let me, I will show you how well I know—"

"How much did Benny pay you?" he interrupted.

She scowled. "I know what Benny wanted. To meet . . . " she paused, not saying the name itself. "To meet this man. I know this man. Benny is a good boy. He tries too hard, but he is a good boy. He wanted some help. And what was the help? Deliver a book, a letter. What harm can that be?"

He decided that she was confident from the start. Confidence was her natural immunity. She was a professional, he decided.

"Here's ten thousand shekels," he said suddenly, surprising her, pulling out one of the envelopes and spreading the pale red cash on the black sheets. "I want the man's name."

She picked up one bill, holding it to the dim light, checking that the crisp new bill wasn't counterfeit. On one side, the country's second president, a poet and Zionist ideologue, looked out mournfully. On the other, a little girl with a pencil and eraser worked in a notebook, while in the background of the bill Hebrew letters floated in the red sky. 200 NEW SHEQALIM it said in English and Arabic beneath the girl.

She started to gather all the money. He grabbed her wrist much faster than she could have expected. She did not resist.

He looked for needle tracks. He found an old white-line scar of a suicide attempt perpendicular to the veins on her wrist. She smiled at him and said, "You underestimate me."

"I'm sorry," he said bluntly. "The money is yours," he added, still restraining her attempt to take the cash. "For the information."

She considered his hand on her wrist, the money on the bed, and then his face, looking into his eyes, shaking her head. "It's not enough."

"Benny didn't pay you this much."

"I didn't tell him a name." She considered the sum. "If I do this, if I tell you, if he finds out I told you . . ."

"I won't tell him." It was not the first time Cohen promised confidentiality to an informant.

"You know," she said, studying his eyes, "I believe you." But then she smirked, almost laughing at his innocence. "But he can find out."

"If he is as rich, as important as you say, why should such an important man trust a woman like you. Working in a place like this?"

Again she smirked at him and he became aware of her hand in his lap. "I am special, perhaps," she offered. "Especially with older men," she added.

"He's my age?" Cohen asked.

She patted at his shoulders, to test his fitness perhaps. "You, I think, have a better body." She looked back at his face and gently brushed back some of Cohen's white hair. "But your face is older. Maybe five, maybe ten years." She raised an eyebrow, and added, "maybe twenty. I'm impressed."

"So you are a toy for him," he asked.

She grinned at him. "A favorite toy."

"Why?" he asked. "Why?" he repeated, changing his tone to offer negotiation.

She looked at the money on the bed again and shook her head. "It's not enough."

"He is rich. If he likes you so much, why doesn't he take you out of here?"

"You are rich," she tried. "Why don't you?"

"How much?" he asked.

214

"To buy out my business? Let me retire the way I want? More than you have."

"He won't know you told me."

"Can you guarantee that? Can you be sure that if I tell you, if I help you, my life will not be in danger?"

"Your life is in danger here."

"You may have a strong body, but if you are threatening me, Andrei is a boxer."

Cohen pulled a second packet of cash from his jacket pocket. "Your friend won't know," he said, keeping his eyes on hers. The second ten thousand made her eyes flicker.

He could see her thinking, her eyes searching his to find out how much further she could stretch the negotiations. She was right. There was a risk, even if Cohen did his best to avoid divulging his source. But he was right, he saw her thinking, life is a risk. And to earn twenty thousand shekels in fifteen minutes for nothing more than a name was not an easy proposition to turn down.

She swallowed, said, "Zagorsky, Vlad Zagorsky," then reached greedily for the money.

"You are sure?" he ordered.

"Zagorsky, yes, that's who you want."

"Describe him."

She smiled, and he realized that she could do better than that.

"Pictures," he said.

She bit her lower lip.

"Don't lie to me, please," he asked, and maybe it was the age in his voice, the weariness or the pain, or simply her own fatigue, but after she thought a long time, looking at him and perhaps into her own soul, she nodded, and got up from the bed, making sure to take the cash with her.

A few minutes later, he was watching the television set in the corner of the room. It began with a black-and-white shot of the very room in which Cohen was now sitting on the edge of the bed. First Sonia entered, then a man.

Upon Cohen's chest a heavy weight suddenly fell and pressed. He lost his breath momentarily, gasping enough to make the madame worry a customer was about to drop dead in her place, but he waved away her sudden maternal instincts as she tried patting him on the back, as if he was choking on a piece of food. He took a deep breath, then exhaled in a shallow, painful sigh.

"You know him?" Sonia asked. "You know Zagorksy?" she asked again.

But what could Cohen say then, what could he tell her—or himself—that the man whose scarred face was turning from grimace into the repose of climax could not be a Russian Mafia boss of bosses, that it was improbable, impossible, inconceivable. For one thing, Cohen thought, the man on the television screen so enthusiastically enjoying Sonia's skills was not named Zagorksy.

· 27 ·

In the Russian Compound attic, among files that looked faint in daylight but clear under a little halogen light that he brought when he worked at night, Cohen had found a case file that at the time, while searching for his relocated witnesses, he had barely glanced at with interest. He remembered the case well. It was in the seventies, when for a few brief years, in exchange for wheat from America, the Kremlin had allowed a few thousand Jews a month out of the Soviet Union. And it was the first time that as head of CID in Jerusalem he had directly felt the heavy foot of interference from one of the big brothers—Shabak, Aman, or Mossad—suddenly trodding on his own as he tried to solve a murder.

The murdered woman had been a cardiologist in the Soviet space program who had become slightly famous in her struggle to win permission from the Soviet authorities to leave Leningrad for Israel. Her name was Masha Karlinsky, and she had been found, her throat sliced from ear to ear, on the sitting room floor of the two-room flat she and her husband had been assigned in what was considered the best new immigrants' hostel in Jerusalem.

Masha Karlinksy, the Russian-Jewish scientist who bravely, famously, survived the gauntlet of Soviet repression of her ambition to move to Israel was also, well, somewhat promiscuous.

There weren't many secrets in the hostel, with six stories of one- and two-room flats suitable for single people and small families, built on stilts on the steep slope looking west to the Valley of the Cross. "Passionate," said her supporters. "Greedy," said her detractors. The husband, Yevet, had put up with it stoically in Leningrad, said the gossips, because her position as cardiologist to the cosmonauts—and his, as a gynecologist who treated some of Leningrad's most powerful women—had provided them with privileges unavailable to more ordinary citizens of the Communist state. All those privileges were lost, of course, once they begun their campaign for emigrant visas, but they were lucky, nonetheless.

Both were handsome people who spoke English. Whether it was their striking good looks combined with obvious professional capabilities, or simply good luck, their cause quickly became internationally known, their faces appearing on posters at demonstrations from Jerusalem to Paris to London and Washington. In short, they managed to get out, landing in the Jerusalem hostel for new immigrants, and already before they learned Hebrew they were both granted jobs at Hadassah Hospital.

Their first year in Israel, they had managed at least to maintain the facade. But he was no research scientist—he needed patients, and he hadn't moved to the West to work shifts in a hospital. He wanted a private clinic of his own and hated Jerusalem's cloistered feel, traveling by bus to other towns in the country, looking for an opportunity to restart his career. She, on the other hand, was a researcher who had worked in a rarefied atmosphere and while she was having a harder time with Hebrew than he, her real problem was that while Hadassah had a good R&D budget, the nearly three years she had lost in her profession while campaigning for their freedom had had their effect.

No longer a star in her profession, she had become bitter, unable to appreciate Yevet's own efforts to find them an apartment they could afford outside of Jerusalem. In Leningrad, at least, her job had granted her a status that gave them a large apartment by Soviet standards of the time—four rooms for the childless couple—so each could have an office at home, as well as at their respective laboratories.

In the hostel, they had barely thirty square meters. Shouting had often been heard from behind their door. On at least one occasion, she had stormed out of the hostel late one night. He had chased her down the hall shouting "Whore!" all the way to the lobby. Only there had he realized he was only wearing his underwear. He'd returned to his room, glaring at anyone who dared catch his eye. She had been back in the hostel two days later, apologetic and demure, but the quarreling had resumed after a week. The murder had taken place six months later.

All this Cohen had discovered relatively quickly in the investigation that had begun early one rainy Sunday morning in the early spring of 1974, when the blood pooling out of Masha Karlinksy's body lying on the floor of the small apartment had begun seeping out into the hallway outside the front door. A child riding his tricycle in the corridor had rolled home to the last door on the left, tracing a pattern of blood on the beige stone floor. The child's mother's screams as she traced the blood stains back to the source brought up the hostel manager, who had opened the locked door to the Karlinsky apartment and found the body. He had called the police.

Cohen had arrived on the scene with a troop of investigators and a pair of translators who had sat in on almost all the interviews. Within an hour of his arrival at the hostel, Cohen had learned of the routine shouting and screaming that had gone on behind the closed doors of the famed activist-doctors' room. And when his crews, sent to find the husband at Hadassah Hospital, had called in to report that Yevet was nowhere to be found, the suspicion had fallen heavily on the missing husband.

However, as so often happens in an investigation, as the evidence—witness testimony, forensics, and motive—poured in during the day, the weather vane of suspicion had begun to shift.

That very first day, with Yevet still missing, the two-man crew that couldn't find him at Hadassah did find a second-year medical student whose aghast reaction on the spot when learning of the murder had led to a quick confession of having been one of Masha's sex partners—and of knowing that there was at least one other. But the student had had a strong alibi—he had been in attendance at an all-night surgery on a man mangled in a car accident the previous night. And Masha had definitely last been seen alive at nine-thirty, at the end of the TV news playing in the lobby. So the student's alibi held—on the spot they confirmed it—but it took a while for the pair of investigators to believe that the student really didn't know the name of another sex partner Masha had taunted him about. All the student knew was that the second lover was an Englishman.

A second Cohen crew found the English lover in the ulpan Hebrew school run in the basement floor of the hostel. He was actually a new immigrant from Wales, who hadn't seemed surprised that Masha had ended the way she did, "considering her behavior," he had told Cohen when brought to the temporary HQ set up in the hostel manager's office. "Ask Lerner," added the Welshman, shifting suspicion once again. "Ask how she betrayed Lev Lerner."

Mrs. Lerner, who lived with her husband Lev two floors down from the Karlinskys in the hostel, was slightly built, with a firm handshake and a slight limp from a shortened right leg. But despite those apparent weaknesses, she had defended her husband with all her might.

"He is on a photographic expedition," the woman had told Cohen. Their tiny apartment's walls were a small gallery of desert scenes in black and white. Their bathroom doubled as a darkroom. To make money, she told him—just as the hotel manager had said—Lerner sold prints to tourists.

Cohen asked about how they had met. Both orphaned in the Great War against fascism, he learned, they both had been believers in communism until the 1967 Six Day War, when the Soviets backed the Arabs against Israel. Doubts had begun creeping into their pure Communist souls. Lev was a career officer who was sent as a young major to Czechoslovakia. She had been proud of him, but after the invasion, when he had reported back in letters on how the Czechs hated the Soviet presence, she had begun to become outspoken. By 1972 they had both become unemployed, fired, outcast pariahs because they had asked for permission to emigrate. And they arrived in the last week of November 1973, right after the Yom Kippur War.

Her Hebrew was very good, Cohen had complimented her. She had wanted to become a ballerina, she had admitted, but a tractor accident in a *kolhoz* during the great wheat harvest of 1959 had put an end to that ambition. But she had discovered a proclivity for language while learning French for her dance lessons, and after some more studies ended up teaching languages—French and English—in a Moscow high school until she had been spotted attending human rights rallies. Learning Hebrew had become an obsession during those long months of waiting for permission to leave.

When Cohen commented that they had been in the hostel a year and a half, the longest-term residents in the place, she had said they had taken a government mortgage for an

apartment, but there had been some delays in the construction.

"We move in two months," she said. Meanwhile, Lev
made a little money from the photography—only enough
to pay for itself plus a little left over for groceries—and she
was occasionally working as a substitute French-language
private tutor. Yes, they owned a car.

"Lev has it. He went to the Dead Sea. Early, to be there
for dawn. Masha? We were not close."

Cohen had put an APB out for their turquoise blue Peugeot 404, especially in the Jordan Rift Valley region, and
before he had left Natasha Lerner—and a squad outside
keeping an eye on the hostel in case Lev returned—he had
apologized first for the question and than asked if she was
pregnant. Yes, she had said. Four months to go, she had
added.

A few hours later, around the same time Lerner's blue
Peugeot was stopped by a police roadblock at the road up
to Jerusalem from the Dead Sea, Yevet Karlinsky had shown
up at the hostel, pleading innocence, indeed total ignorance of the murder of his wife until he had awoken that
afternoon at a friend's house and heard the news on the
radio. Yes, they had quarreled often, the husband had told
Cohen. About her affairs, he had admitted. But if I didn't
kill her in the past, he had said, why would I do so now?

"The pressure?" Cohen had asked. "Life is difficult for
you now. Frustration? She at least has her job. You," he had
pointed out to Yevet, "have become a drunk."

Indeed, that had been Yevet's alibi. They had quarreled
and Yevet had gone to a friend to commiserate with a bottle. He had provided a name and address.

Just then, there had been a knock on the door. One of the
investigators assigned to question Lerner—across the hallway in a second interrogation room—had handed a piece of

paper to Cohen. It said, "Please come in here, now," and was signed by the district commander, Cohen's boss.

And for the first time, by virtue of his new job as CID chief in Jerusalem, Cohen would be privy to a decision by one of the country's two senior intelligence agencies to step on the toes of the police.

Lerner, it turned out, had been a colonel in the Red Army, a specialist in logistics, who had seen the anti-Zionism and anti-Semitism of the Soviet bureaucracy in the late 1960s and early 1970s stymie any chance for further promotion in the army. Like thousands of other Jews when détente opened the doors a crack, he had applied for permission to emigrate to Israel. Immediately thrown out of the army, Lerner had lost everything, but he either gambled well or managed to keep some friends in high places, for only a year after his request for emigration was submitted to his commanding general he had arrived in Israel. Like all men arriving from ostensibly enemy countries in those years, new immigrant or not, he had been questioned at the airport about his military background. A Red Army colonel was quite a prize to the Mossad, or at least that's what they thought, when he freely admitted that had been his last position. They whisked him away to a safe house in Tel Aviv. But his expertise in logistics was long-range delivery via railroad of troops, equipment, and provisions. It was hardly an expertise required in tiny Israel, where at most sometimes the railroad was used to move tanks from the Negev to the Galilee in three hours.

Nor was his encyclopedic knowledge of the Soviet rail system of much interest to the Americans, who were emphasizing electronic intelligence, particularly satellite imaging for that kind of information by the seventies. And since he was already in his late forties when he had arrived in Israel, close to the official retirement age for Israeli officers, he wasn't going to pick up a new army career where he left off. So he spent two weeks in a Mossad safe house, questioned by an Israeli team. The Americans sent over an observer, at the invitation of the Mossad, and because the American raised the possibility that Lerner might be a plant by the Soviets, the Shabak, the counterintelligence agency, had also gotten involved.

But after two more weeks of questioning, even the Shabak had had to admit that the former colonel was just that, a *former* colonel, and let him into the civilian world with his two suitcases, an absorption ministry stipend worth a few hundred dollars a month, and a then-coveted place in the hostel, considered at the time the best in the country for new immigrants.

"That was eighteen months ago," said the small baby-faced man with the premature bald spot sitting in the district commander's office, who had been introduced to Cohen only as Moshe from the Mossad. "But things change," said the Shabak officer. "We need him now."

"His wife said nothing."

"She doesn't know."

"He is a suspect in a murder," Cohen said bluntly.

"He didn't do it," said the senior officer. "Trust us, we know. It is a matter of state security."

Cohen gritted his teeth. By virtue of his job as CID chief, he was, as the British say, seconded to the Shabak as an associate, working often hand in hand with the counter-intelligence and counterterrorism secret service. He was part of the system that protected state security, but the Shabak outranked him. But Cohen did not like to leave loose ends. And Lerner was about to become a loose end.

"A few questions. That's all I want," Cohen had said. "You can sit in."

"He'll only confirm what you already know. He was not in Jerusalem," said the general.

"Let him tell me. I need it for the record."

The big brother thought for a moment and then conceded Cohen some time with Lerner.

A tall slender man with a thick scar from the corner of his mouth to just below his left ear, missing the last joint of his middle finger on his left hand, and with eyes not dissimilar to Cohen's—so light as to be silver-gray, set into heavy brows and surrounded by a complex of crow's feet—Lerner had not denied having the affair with Masha. Sticking to his alibi, he mocked Yevet Karlinsky, the husband, as a drunk, a loser, "and as I'm sure you'll decide, a murderer." He had spoken with the self-confidence of an absolute cynic unsurprised by the murder of what he called in a Hebrew much poorer than his wife's, "my part-time woman." He had a witness to his alibi, he pointed out, "on the film in my camera." A Bedouin man, on a camel. "Very authentic," the new immigrant said smugly.

And with that, the big brother cut short the interview, and Lerner was whisked out of Cohen's life.

The film indeed showed a Bedouin on a camel, profiled against the seamless blue of sea and sky at the lowest spot on earth. Lerner was reduced to a single-line mention as having an alibi, in the summation report that the CID chief eventually provided the state prosecutor for the trial of Yevet Karlinsky, for the murder of his wife, Masha. Yevet had claimed innocence all along, until the third time Cohen won a remand order from a magistrate judge for the suspect to be held without bail for fifteen more days of investigation. But soon afterward, and then throughout the trial, Yevet reverted to his claims of innocence. Sentenced to life, he would get out after twelve years with good behavior, only to be killed by a speeding taxi a few weeks later.

All this Cohen knew. It all rushed through his mind in a

sweep of memory when Sonia showed him the video of a boss of bosses grimacing with pleasure as her head bobbed up and down, up and down, in the lap of the man she called Vlad Zagorsky, the man Cohen know as Lev Lerner.

· 28 ·

It was improbable, impossible, crazy, Cohen thought. But he listened to her until nearly four in the morning, as she answered all his questions.

She knew nothing about any Lerner. But of Zagorksy she knew much, starting with the fact he called her one of his favorites, making use of her special talents, as he called them she said, on special occasions. For his business associates, she called them. Proudly, she declared it granted her some immunity from the fear she made clear he could easily impose. "And with this," she added, pulling the pile of cash toward her on the bed, "I can make some changes in my life."

Privately, Cohen doubted it, but he said nothing, not wanting to dam any information she had to offer.

"He owns banks," she said bluntly at first, as if that was enough.

"Where?" Cohen asked.

"Russia," she said, as if it was obvious. "And Cyprus. This I know. He made me an account. And he owns land. Much land. Buildings."

"Where?"

"Europe."

"Where?" Cohen pressed.

"Germany."

"Here?"

She shrugged, a gesture that implied that all she had implied earlier about being her own boss was only partly true.

"Brothels?" he asked.

"It is a business," she said, and suddenly turned on Cohen, rejecting what he assumed was his begrudging moral judgment. "It is work," she said, "like any other."

"Drugs?"

She pursed her lips but remained silent, confirming what he wanted to know, but not daring to say it aloud.

"He has a son," she suddenly added, like an afterthought. "He brought the boy to me in the summer."

Cohen waited for her to fill in the pause she left in her sentence.

"There was nothing to teach that boy. Girls, boys. He knew everything. He could teach *me*. What's happening to the kids nowadays?" she asked, almost making him laugh. But most important, he learned, important enough to pay her another ten thousand, was that Vladimir Zagorksy had been in Israel for the last three weeks.

· 29 ·

Could he be certain that Sonia's Zagorsky was his Lerner? The mere question made him ask himself, for the first time in years, if Karlinksy, the cuckolded husband, had indeed been as innocent as he had claimed, and Zagorksy or Lerner, whatever his name, the guilty one.

Cohen thought about it hard coming out of the Exotica just before dawn. It was not a common name, even in Russia. But unable to think of a reason why Lerner would want him dead or injured, Cohen scratched at his head, mumbling to himself in frustration as he drove out of Tel Aviv, until finally, on the highway just past the airport, he pulled the car over. While the blue light that precedes dawn began to rise in the east over the Judean mountains, he used the cellular phone.

"What?" Shmulik's gruff voice demanded before the end of the second ring.

Cohen laughed.

"Avram? That you?" Shmulik asked. "What are you laughing about?" he asked angrily.

"You. Still getting up before dawn. 'What?' Still answering the phone the same way. 'What?' " he repeated, imitating his old friend, colleague, and occasional nemesis, formerly—to the extent that is ever possible in an intelligence service—of the Shabak. "Old habits hard to shake," Cohen kidded.

Like Cohen, Shmulik was no longer in his force, leaving a few years after Cohen, who still didn't know why Shmulik had suddenly dropped out of the race to becoming the head of the service. Only once did Cohen ask, and since Cohen, despite everything, had officially only been a policeman and not a direct employee of the secret service, Shmulik only gave him a glance that said "I can't tell you, so don't make it difficult on both of us by asking." Cohen didn't. And now he couldn't be sure that Shmulik would be absolutely honest. But they had worked together long enough for Cohen to be able to tell when Shmulik was lying—or hiding something.

Shmulik sighed. "What do you want?"

"It's not for the phone. I'll be outside your house in twenty minutes," Cohen said.

They had worked together as counterparts, sometimes in competing roles, often interchangeable, sharing case files, sometimes sources, and with the clear legal distinction that when issues came to court, it was the police, not the secret service, which brings the arrest. Secret servicemen testified as witnesses, not as arresting officers. Cohen hated to bring *Shabakniks* into court unless it was absolutely necessary. Not because the judges would see through the lies and wink, but because the judges preferred to believe that while in the name of security there had to be a certain leeway in case of a ticking bomb somewhere, they also wanted to believe that nobody would lie to them in the name of security. And no matter how much Cohen wanted to put the wrongdoers away, he didn't want it done with lies. Trickery was a lot more effective than force in any investigation, he taught his juniors.

He waited for a semitrailer speeding in the left lane to pass before he slipped the car into gear and got back on the road. A few minutes later he passed the truck. And fifteen minutes after he called Shmulik, he was at the Kastel peak, where he got off the highway and slipped into the little village of Motza, the sun now in full bloom over the forest-covered mountainside.

Shmulik and his wife, Dvora, had been building their house for years. First it was to change the two-room house into three rooms, to accommodate a first-born. Then, when the couple's second pregnancy turned into twins, one boy and one girl, they eventually added two more rooms. But even after the kids began leaving home, Shmulik and Dvora kept improving the house, up to and including a whole second house built on the foundations of a one-cow stable that had come with the property.

Cohen turned into the tiny street and wasn't surprised to see Shmulik waiting for him in the quiet street.

Cohen rolled down the passenger door window. Shmulik leaned in. "What couldn't you ask me on the phone?" asked the former Shabak officer.

"Zagorsky. Vladimir Zagorksy," Cohen said, not so much impatient as efficient in his tone. He left the engine running. "Did I know him as Lev Lerner?

Shmulik was silent for a second too long.

"Don't tell me stories," Cohen protested.

"You weren't supposed to know then, why should you know now?"

"Why would he have something against me?" Cohen asked.

"I don't know."

"What *do* you know?" Cohen demanded.

"Not very much," Shmulik admitted. "It just happened. His name came up for something the big brothers needed." It was a phrase used by the police and Shabak to refer to the Mossad. "I don't know what."

"But you can find out," said Cohen.

"To hell with you, Avram. I'm retired. I'm out. And I'm not like you. I don't regret it."

"There's a man named Vladimir Zagorksy," Cohen repeated sternly, turning off the car engine. "Deeply involved in the Russian Mafia. He might be connected to Nissim Levy's murder. I think he tried to kill me in Frankfurt. I need to know for certain. Is he Lerner?"

"What makes you think so?"

"I saw a picture. Older, but him. You know me. I remember these things. Is he the same? Is he with them?" Cohen asked, meaning the Mossad.

Shmulik sighed, then bowed his head. "I'll see what I can find out," he promised. He noticed the cellular phone on Cohen's car seat, and smiled. "You, too," he laughed. "What's your number?"

Cohen told him. "Fast, Shmulik. Fast. Today. This morning. Call me." Shmulik's Great Dane came bouncing out through the front gate, slapping his front paws on the side of Cohen's car to see what was so interesting to his master. The dog recognized Cohen and began howling with happiness. Shmulik grabbed the beast by the collar and pulled it off the car, letting Cohen drive away.

It was another fifteen minutes into Jerusalem, just ahead of the morning rush-hour traffic from the coastal plain trying to get into the capital through the three lanes at the entrance to the city. On the way, the Army Radio morning news magazine reported that the police would ask a magistrate's court that morning for a fifteen-day remand of Itzik Alper, Kobi's little brother, a prime suspect in the murder of Nissim Levy.

Again, Cohen couldn't help but wonder if they were right and he was wrong. He never expected to find the answer on his doorstep, nor that it would bring tears to his eyes.

· 30 ·

Cohen waited for them all to leave—the bomb squad, the detectives (including a new CID commander who had come up from Tel Aviv only three months earlier), and the reporters—before he buried Suspect in the back of his garden. The tears came to his eyes when he found the cat. As he buried it, he finally let a few fall.

The cat had been with him nearly fifteen years, and though never pampered was still healthy; old enough to be wise enough not to take every fleeting bird through the garden as a personal challenge, clever enough to manage on his own when Cohen was out of town, clean enough for Cohen to tolerate as a roommate. Not a dog that would have raised a ruckus to scare away an intruder, therefore justifying in the killer's mind the murder, the cat was killed out of spite, the work of someone who wanted to hurt Cohen's feelings before the bomb inside would kill him.

Whoever it was got in through the same window that the cat ordinarily used when Cohen was away, an acrobatic climb but one that even Cohen, heavy and never nimble, had on occasion made when forgetting his keys on his desk at the office after too long a week of on-the-job sleeplessness. The cat wasn't killed on the floor mat before the front door. It was put there. Luckily. For whoever did it left a partial print made of Suspect's blood, which had drained from the lone bullet's exit wound, a massive tear of the fur and skin and skull and brain of the animal.

His sigh made his lungs echo with a rattle of breathless pain. Inside, the phone kept ringing. The inspector general himself had called while the District CID commander was still there, overseeing his dozen men and women on the case, wanting a firsthand look at the famous Avram Cohen, the High Priest gone to hermitage who everyone still said was the best boss to ever hold the office.

Cohen was now convinced, though exactly of what, he couldn't be sure. The bomb—not unlike the one in Frankfurt—was professional. But there was nothing professional about killing the cat. That was personal. And he knew he had nothing personal with any of the Russians— and that the Alper brothers were not in any position to arrange a bombing attempt on anyone, let alone him.

The IG did help Cohen with the press, which clamored for a press conference, if not a series of interviews. Nobody outside of the IG, the new CID commander, and one old investigator Cohen knew well, who showed up on the scene and could tell Cohen was disturbed by something more than the bomb he found under his desk, knew about what had happened to the cat. The National Police spokesman's office issued a statement that the investigation was being taken very seriously. Part of his statement included a quote that Cohen formulated with the spokesman's help: "Retired Deputy Commander Avram Cohen is helping the police in any way they see fit, with their inquiries. Due to the sensitive nature of the investigation, no interviews of any kind will be given until the matter is resolved."

It didn't drive all the reporters away. But using the excuse of a neighborhood canvas, the police did manage to finally push the reporters off the street outside Cohen's house, to the end of it, where by noon only one remained, and by two o'clock he was also gone.

Finally alone, he put on a kettle, took a hot shower, and gave a longing look at the bed. But instead, he changed into clean clothes and stirred at the thick mud coffee, sitting at his desk, thinking. Finally, he stopped stirring and while the coffee powder settled at the bottom of the tall glass, he turned on the computer, took a clean sheet of paper for notes, and like a card player testing a deck, he riffled the little stack of yellow notebooks he had filled during the two months of searching through the archives.

He turned on the computer to download his mail—a digest of messages about cooking, a newsletter about new jazz recordings, an invitation to visit a Web site devoted to counterterrorism—and then, on a hunch, ran a World Wide Web search for Vladimir NEAR Zagorksy.

Seventeen pages came up. Three were by a medical student of that name, living in California. Six were about a German-Jewish underground activist hung early by the Nazis for subversion. The remaining eight pages were all from a large Web site devoted to bee keeping, with one partner named Vladimir and the other Zagorksy. Cohen shook his head in disappointment. He tried Lev Lerner. Nothing. He tried Alexander Witkoff. That name came up in a three-page Web site about Witkoff's chemicals trading company. He tried Yuhewitz. *Gornisht*, he moaned, using the Yiddish word to complain. He had called Ahuva even before he called the Emergency 100 Number, not telling her about the cat, but saying quite bluntly that he feared her life might be in danger. "You were right, I'm afraid," he had said. "The bomber from Frankfurt, he might be here."

"In Israel?" she had asked, not incautiously.

"Yes."

"In Tel Aviv?"

"The country's small," he pointed out.

"I have to be in court most of the day," she said.

"You'll be safe there," he agreed, hoping it was true. He checked his watch. It was just before seven in the morning. It had taken him twelve minutes between the time he found the cat on the doorstep at 6:30 in the morning to find the bomb under his desk. "I'll call you later at your office," he promised. "But it looks like you might be staying at a hotel tonight."

"Will you be there?"

"I hope so," he admitted.

"Then I'll await your call," she pronounced, promising that she would leave for her office within the hour.

He called Laskoff's office after the last detective, the old one with two ex-wives, four kids, and twelve grandchildren (because one of his sons had turned religious and with his arranged-marriage wife was making kids at the rate of one a year for the last seven years) had finally left his apartment. Rose said the banker would not be in the for the rest of the day. One of his clients had died suddenly in the night and Laskoff, as executor, had to step in to help the widow through the coming few days. "But Mr. Laskoff did leave you a message, in case you called."

"Yes, please." Cohen sighed.

"Alexander Witkoff was in a consortium that offered to buy Bank Leumi. The Bank of Israel turned down the bid."

"Did he say why?"

"No."

"Here's another name for him, when he calls in. Zagorksy, Vladimir."

She repeated the name, to be sure she had it right, then added, "Mr. Laskoff also asks if you have any message for him about the house."

Cohen felt like laughing. But he just told her that no, he

had not decided yet, but expected to have an answer soon. "But first tell him to find out what he can about Zagorksy."

Hanging up, he looked at the phone for a second, thinking. He was about to call Shvilli when Jacki called.

"I heard about the bomb," she said.

"How's Hagit?" he answered.

"Much better. They've decided to let her go home tomorrow. With the baby."

"To her parents?"

"No, she's going home to their place. Hers and Nissim's. What about this bombing attempt?"

Cohen ignored the question. "Shvilli's not answering his phone. He was supposed to find out about a girl Nissim saw, Saturday night."

"At the Crown, I know," said Jacki. "Pinny knows about it."

"Can you get through to personnel records?" Cohen asked.

"Don't see why not."

"Pinhas Shlomi, Shimoni, something like that. Maybe even Shlomzion, served at least ten years in Jerusalem. I need his details. A phone number for him."

"I'll have to use the terminal downstairs," she said.

"Now," he ordered. "And call me back. I'll be waiting. Use my home number."

"Fifteen minutes, I promise," she said.

He used the time to unroll the long fax Jacki had sent him, starting with the last month in the log Nissim had kept of his own intelligence gathering.

The Crown Hotel was mentioned twice in three weeks. The second time was a week ago. And in the notes Nissim made, at the bottom of a list that began with Yuhewitz, included Yudelstein and Witkoff, appeared the name "Zagrusky" with two question marks beside it. "Zagorksy,

Zagrusky," Cohen muttered under his breath. "Who are you?" he asked the paper between sips of the cooling coffee. The telephone shattered the quiet, startling him and making him splash a few drops of the drink across the papers on his desk. He was cursing to himself as he answered the phone.

It was Shvilli. "I'm in Eilat. With Pinny. You want to talk to him?"

"Put him on."

"Sir," Pinny said happily, "how are you?"

"Okay, Pinny, fine," said Cohen, impatiently.

"Your health?" the former subordinate asked with unctuous respect.

Cohen ignored the question. "You saw Nissim on Saturday night. In the lobby. With a girl. Was she working?"

"I'll tell you the truth. I never saw her before. She might have been working. Maybe. Very sexy. But she looked too rich to be working. So, after Misha asked, I checked it out with reception."

"And?"

"A guest."

"Name?"

"Maya Bernstein."

Cohen jammed the phone between his shoulder and ear and reached with two hands for the little yellow notebooks that he had filled during the search through his memories in the archives. The Bernstein twins. The girl. What was her name? It was twenty years old, but it was something. Perhaps.

"Tell me about her," he demanded.

"She came in with a big spender. A Russian."

"Name?"

"Zagrusi or something."

"Is she Russian?"

"She has a German passport."

"Did you get her details from the passport? Birth date? Birthplace? Anything?"

There was a pause.

"Check," Cohen ordered, without any anger in his voice.

"Of course."

"She still there?"

"No. They left yesterday."

"To where?"

"I'll have to check."

The call waiting kicked in on the phone but he was clenching the phone, tightly considering the implications, leaving a pause in the conversation. The call waiting buzzed him again. He ignored it. "Are you checking?"

"You mean now?" asked Pinny.

"Now," Cohen demanded. "Give me Misha."

Shvilli was defensive, getting on the phone. "I mentioned Zagorksy, no? At the party on Yuhewitz's boat. When Nissim lost it . . ."

"No, you didn't mention him," complained Cohen. "Tell me about him."

"He's Russian. Lives in Germany. We know he deals women. Possibly drugs."

"Does he have a son?"

"Not that I know of."

"And the girl? This Maya Bernstein?"

"She's a toy for him. A show-off toy. A *tyolki*," said Shvilli, using Russian slang. "As far as I could tell."

"Did you ever talk with her?"

"He kept her close. And he had muscle to make sure she wasn't available to anyone else."

"What would Nissim want with her?"

"I don't know. I don't even understand how Nissim got close to her."

The cellular phone rang. "Hold on," he told Shvilli,

answering the second phone. It was Jacki. "I have Pinny Shimoni's telephone number," she said.

"That's okay, I have him on the other line," he told her. He could hear her disappointment that she hadn't provided some missing information as she said good-bye.

"Shvilli, what's Zagorksy's relationship with Witkoff?"

"Close. Very close. At least as far as we're able to tell."

"And Yuhewitz?"

"Yuhewitz is big in Eilat, but he's small compared to Witkoff. Zagorksy doesn't exactly work *for* Witkoff, at least as far as we know. But they're friends, that's for sure. They eat out together when Zagorksy's in the country."

"Okay. Back to Maya Bernstein?"

"I knew nothing about her, until Pinny made the connection and I realized it was her."

"Tell me more."

"She's very sexy. Very."

"And you're sure he doesn't have a son?"

"Not that I know of."

"That's strange."

"Boss, I can't know everything. I try . . ."

"No, I'm not blaming you. But another source tells me Zagorsky has a son."

There was silence for a long minute, while he thought.

"Boss?" Shvilli asked. "You there?"

"Describe her," Cohen said.

"Like a model, tall. A great figure."

"Blonde, black hair? Long, short?"

"Tall, real tall."

"A mole? On her jaw? A beauty mark?"

"I don't remember."

"Close your eyes. Think. Try to remember."

"I don't know," Shvilli admitted with disappointment.

"You ever shake hands with her?"

"What do you mean?"

"Just what I asked. Were you introduced? Shake her hand? Talk to her?"

"Not really. She belongs to Zagorksy. I'm a good customer for Yuhewitz, but I'm not big money. Zagorksy is big money."

"Are you sure she's a girl?" Cohen pressed forward.

"What?"

"Just what I said. Maybe transsexual? Transvestite, even?"

"A *coccinel?*"

"Yes."

"I don't know what you're talking about. She was very impressive. Wore this high-fashion dress, on the boat, you stood in the right place, you could see everything. Great tits. I can tell you this: She was a she, as far as every guy on the boat could tell."

"And according to Pinny, they're in Jerusalem now. Is he getting what I asked for?"

"Here he comes now."

"Put him on."

"Yes. But before that, boss, please, what makes her so important?"

"It's Zagorksy who's important. And as you said, she's his toy."

· 31 ·

But Cohen wasn't sure if he was hunting the businessman spy or the girl on Zagorksy's arm. According to Pinny, they had gone to the King David Hotel, just up the street from Cohen's apartment, the day before.

He stared at the phone and then punched in the number to ask for the Russian. But before the operator began to put him through, he hung up with a second thought and he re-dialed the hotel's number, tried slightly to adjust the tone in his voice and asked for Rafi Peri. Right after his departure from the force, Cohen had been offered the job of chief of security at the King David. Ahuva thought he should take the job, but after serving as chief of CID, Cohen was not enchanted by the idea of playing baby-sitter for rich tourists, nor gofer to every visiting VIP security crew.

So Rafi Peri had gotten the job. He had briefly reached Tel Aviv chief of CID, a year after Cohen left the force, but unlike Cohen, who had no ambition beyond his job as CID chief, Peri wanted more. When it became clear to him that he had reached the pinnacle of his police career, he opted out of the force and took the high-paying hotel job.

"I was just thinking of you," said Peri after Cohen iden-tified himself.

"Why?" asked Cohen suspiciously.

"The radio is saying someone tried to kill you again. A bomb. Like . . ."

"I'm not calling about that," Cohen lied.

"Really?" Peri asked, but it was uncertainty not disbelief that colored his tone.

"Is there a guest named Zagorksy, Vladimir Zagorksy in the hotel?"

"You're kidding," Peri said.

"I don't usually make jokes," Cohen said.

"I heard Shuki Caspi picked up the Alpers," Peri tried. "Your Nissim made quite an enemy when he went after the big Alper."

"They're wrong," said Cohen confidently, though he wasn't really.

"You sound sure."

"I am," Cohen lied again.

"You're not on the job anymore."

"Nissim was my assistant for a long time."

"So, it *is* personal."

"You can say that."

Peri didn't say anything.

"Zagorksy," said Cohen, and waited.

"You didn't get any of this from me," Peri finally said.

"Of course not," Cohen said truthfully.

"He took three suites with eastern views of the Old City, the most expensive on the floor," said Peri.

"Why does he need three?"

"There's him, a girl, and half a dozen associates. I'd call at least three of them muscle, but it's impolite and I'm in the polite business nowadays."

"The rest?"

"Fancy clerks," said Peri.

"Are they there now?"

"I don't know."

Cohen sighed. "Pick up the other phone and ask," he ordered.

"I don't know . . ."

"Rafi, please. I'll leave you out of it. Nobody will know. You can trust me." He waited for Peri's response. "Please," he repeated. He was using that word more often nowadays, he thought, usually requesting something he didn't want but did need.

"Hold on." Peri finally complied.

While he waited on the line, Cohen doodled, drawing a box around the name Maya Bernstein, thinking about what Pinny said, underlining it, adding a row of question marks and finally, circling the word *twins*. With a question mark. The ideas swirled through his head like dervishes whirling swords. With the sound of the receiver at Peri's end knocking around on the desk before the security officer finally was back on the phone, the swords stopped turning.

"He's here," said Peri.

"All of them?"

"Yes."

"Thanks, Rafi."

"Just leave me out of it," Peri asked.

"Exactly," Cohen promised.

But before he even packed up his wallet and notebook, let alone gathered his keys and his jacket, the phone rang.

"I heard about the bomb," said Shmulik.

"Yes?" asked Cohen.

"Well?"

"What?"

"Are you going to tell me?"

"First you have something to tell me," Cohen said.

"That thing you asked about," said Shmulik.

"Yes."

"The answer is yes, the same. And the word is, stay away. You don't know what's at stake."

"There's a bomb at stake."

"You can't be sure of that. And believe me, your man is covered. He couldn't do anything like that without half a dozen interventions."

"Half a dozen?"

"He's a share."

"With?"

"The Americans."

"And the Germans?"

"Could be," said Shmulik. "But Avram, I don't see how he could be involved."

"Maybe he blames me."

"For what?"

"Picking him up. Back then."

"Believe me, he's never complained about you."

"How do you know?"

"I just do. I know."

"Do you know where I can find him now?"

"No, of course not."

"They were in Jerusalem, at the King David, ten minutes ago," Cohen said angrily. When angered, Cohen usually lowered his voice instead of raising it. "There since yesterday. That's five minutes by foot from my place. Where I found a bomb this morning. A second bomb in less than a year." By the word *year* his voice had begun to rise and he had to grip the receiver tightly to lower his tone.

"I know where you live."

"And so does he, apparently."

"I'm telling you, he had nothing to do with it. He couldn't have."

"And how the hell can you be so sure?" Cohen demanded.

"I told you, he's being watched. Around the clock."

"We'll see," said Cohen, hanging up without saying good-bye. As he did, he could hear Shmulik shouting at him, "leave it be, Avram, leave it."

I can't, Cohen said to himself. I don't have a choice, I have to find out.

Two minutes after he pulled the Sierra onto Emek Refaim, taking a right to the King David, he regretted taking the car. Somewhere further up the road, something was halting traffic. He waited one minute, then two, then five. The driver of the taxi in front of him got out of his car to see past the bus blocking the view ahead. Cohen opened his door.

"I think it's a suspicious object at the Liberty Bell Park," the taxi driver announced not only to Cohen, standing one foot out of the car, but also to the driver behind Cohen. He was stuck in the lane, Cohen directly beside a set of bars that blocked any driver from entering one of the alleys into the oldest part of the German Colony, behind the train station.

Cohen slammed the steering wheel, frustrated. There was no place to pull over and leave his car on the sidewalk to quickly walk five minutes to the hotel. He cursed the bomber—or the fool—who left the package behind, wherever it was at the three-road intersection around the old train station opposite the southern end of Liberty Bell Park. Now, even if he could pull over, the sappers at the intersection wouldn't let him past the object.

So he sat in the car under a slightly warmer midday sun, thinking about the Bernstein family. The sister, who had spoken up too late in the pregnancy for an abortion, had turned in one of her rapist brothers for killing the other out of jealousy. Like Cohen, her parents were survivors. Unlike Cohen, they were weakened, not strengthened by the experience. Shattered, they were helpless in the face of the scandal. There would be no life for the girl if she stayed in Jerusalem. That was for sure. The town was too small for such a scandal. Cohen had no choice because she had no choice. Nobody had a choice. In a tearful session in Cohen's office, the father had said he had a relative abroad, a cousin in Hamburg. The daughter of his uncle.

Cohen had called the woman, who immediately agreed to take the girl, promising a good life for the child. Late one afternoon, Cohen had driven her to the airport, taking her all the way to the tarmac, handing her a passport, promising her that the auntie would be waiting at the other side.

The girl had taken it all passively, accepting her fate like she took the passport, with a limp hand and a look in her eye that said she deserved no better, deserved even worse. She had already decided she was doomed, and even if Cohen did manage with a stupid joke or two to get a hint of a smile to cross her face, nothing was going to halt the girl's march to hell. Not even the child growing in her belly, hidden in fear so it was too late now for an abortion, gave her happiness.

If that child had turned out healthy, he calculated in the car, he—or she—would now be in their early twenties. The cousin, whom he had called aunt from the start, using the term generically to describe the older woman to a young girl, had said that she would take care of the girl and the baby. But it was all so long ago, and Cohen was a cop, not a social worker. He felt like he was grasping water, trying to understand what had happened back then, trying to make it fit now into the events that mocked him with an inner logic he couldn't decipher.

The bus ahead snorted a gray cloud of exhaust and lurched forward. The long cord of traffic ahead unraveled its knots. A few minutes later, he found a place to park on Lincoln, a side street outside the YMCA's old football field. Skirting the field, he came out onto King David Street, directly in front of the hotel. Some VIP was leaving—the concierge coming out into the street to halt traffic to let a small convoy depart. Two gleaming black Mercedes limousines screeched tires as they turned into the sun-dappled street and headed toward the city center. In a block or two, he thought, they'd be stuck in traffic unless they got a police escort.

The hotel loomed ahead, its front shaded by a small grove of trees that shaded the pedestrian entrance, which bisected the curving driveway. He crossed the street and was about to enter the shaded pathway when a tall bald man, tieless, wearing sunglasses, a khaki jacket, and a blue shirt and black trousers stopped him.

"He's not here," the man said, blocking Cohen's way.

"Who?" Cohen pretended, but already knew it was to no avail.

"Your man."

Cohen reached into his jacket pocket for the cellular phone. Its battery had died. He smacked his forehead with self-accusation for his stupidity. He should have recharged the phone.

"They call me Amos," said the man, flipping open his wallet. Cohen didn't need his glasses to recognize the card. He looked back at the Mossad officer. His eyes were hidden by the sunglasses, and his smile barely a twitch of his mouth. With no wrinkles in a clean-shaven leathery face it was difficult to tell the man's age. Anywhere from forty to fifty. It made a difference. In the service, longevity was critical, but few lasted active after fifty-five. It was Cohen's turn to smile, though he didn't show it. Amos's hardcover attaché case was nicked, scratched, and dented, at least a decade old. A *jemzbond,* the Israelis called them, because VIP protection squads used the briefcases to carry their equipment. But a *jemzbond* could also just carry a sandwich.

In Amos's case, Cohen guessed, there were papers. The spy's jacket was tailored to hide a holster. Cohen was wearing his own nine-millimeter Beretta in the small of his back, tucked into the waistband of his trousers hidden by his jacket. He had made sure to take a full clip when leaving the flat. It was a precaution made from intuition.

"He's my responsibility," said Amos. "And he's not here."

"Who?" Cohen tried.

Amos remained stoic. "You know."

"I don't know," said Cohen, not really lying. Zagorksy, Lerner, the girl. Or was she a boy? Again, he had the sensation of trying to grasp water.

"He's my brief," Amos repeated. "And apparently, now you are, too."

"Where did he go?" Cohen asked.

Nothing in the man's face revealed any answer.

"Where?" Cohen insisted.

Amos remained stoic.

"What can you tell me?"

"You have to ask."

"The girl?" Cohen tried.

"Nobody. A toy."

The expression grated on Cohen's ear, and unlike Amos, he let his emotions show on his face. "How long has he had her?" he asked.

"Little less than a year."

"What do you have on her?"

"She's nobody. He found her in a club."

"Where?"

"Hamburg."

"That's all you know about her?"

"We know what we have to know."

"Her parents?"

"An orphan. Nobody. No harm to anyone."

"How long have you had him?" he tried.

"I inherited the case three months ago."

"Inherited?"

"My boss died."

"On the job?" Cohen asked.

"Heart attack," said Amos. "He was out running his morning jog. It was a real shock. He stayed fit."

Cohen couldn't admit as much. He lost his breath too easily nowadays, efforts that he had made in the past were tiring in ways he wished could be repaired. But he was alert, always alert. They were still in the shade of the hotel, in the driveway, looking away from each other, keeping an eye on the surroundings, watching out for others who might be watching. Across the street, a tourist was taking a photo of the hotel. Cohen turned, so that his face wouldn't be in the picture. So did Amos. They both acted instinctively.

Cohen tried a more friendly tone. "The last time I saw him he was selling photos to tourists while his wife brought in an education ministry subsidy. Until you people stepped in."

"That's what they say," said Amos, for the first time confirming what they both knew, that Lerner had turned into Zagorksy.

"Why?"

"There are some things I can't tell you."

"I believe the man might be trying to kill me. Are you aware of that?"

"We know about your bomb," Amos admitted. "To be honest, there are some who wonder why the Germans didn't hold you."

"Because I didn't have the time to do it," Cohen spat back, stating the obvious. "Does Zagorksy have an alibi?"

"He wasn't in Frankfurt."

"But he was here. In Jerusalem last night. I wasn't. This morning, I found a bomb in my flat."

"And your cat," said the spy.

"Yes. And my cat," Cohen nearly spat the word back at Amos. "That made it personal."

"Because of the cat?"

"Because of the motive," said Cohen, adding, "what do you know about the girl?"

Cohen could tell in the way the crow's feet wrinkles at the spy's temples narrowed slightly that the question caught Amos off guard.

"What about her?"

"Was she in Frankfurt? And for that matter, are you sure she's a she?" And now, for the first time, Cohen could tell that Amos was looking at him directly.

The sunglasses hid the younger man's eyes, but his face—a slight twitch at the corner of the mouth, a narrowing of the crow lines extending form the hidden eyes to his temples—gave away more than he intended, even though it was less than what Cohen wanted.

"She's a toy, that's all. A toy," Amos insisted.

"Absurd," Cohen muttered, to himself, to the spy, to the breeze. "Absurd," he repeated, almost stumbled away, blinded by frustration, trying to hide his own confusion, hating the term *a toy*, that even he had used.

Maybe he was wrong, maybe Sonia had lied to him, maybe she was wrong. But he had seen the face and remembered Lerner. It didn't surprise him that the Mossad would have its own man inside the Russian Mafia. But so high? So vulnerable? And for what? He didn't believe they would let Zagorksy run wild, but they couldn't believe what Cohen's instinct told him, that he had become a target for someone in Zagorksy's circle, whether Yuhewitz, Witkoff, or yes, Cohen had to admit to himself, not knowing what to do with the instinct that had no real evidence, the girl.

All through his life he had taken bits and pieces of information, putting them together to fit his purpose at the time—to survive, to succeed, to find the truth that made sense enough to give him purpose. But now, the precision of his information was only as reliable as his own memory—not of the events of the past few days, but of a time nearly thirty years earlier, almost half a life ago. In the past when he was stymied, he'd press on. Now, it made him tired. He wanted to lie down, he wanted to sleep, no, he needed sleep.

But the questions would keep him awake. Could Maya be related to the pregnant Bernstein girl—what was her name? Where was Zagorksy's son in all this, the boy Sonia talked about? Did he pay for lies? What did he get wrong? Misunderstand? How far back did the mistake go, and was it his? Worst of all, most frightening of all, he wondered if the Mossad itself might have had a hand in stopping Nissim's investigation?

But all he got from gnawing at his brain was a headache, realizing what was happening. As long as Zagorksy was in the country, he was protected from Cohen. Amos made that clear, leaving the old detective too proud to ask who would protect him.

"Where are you going?" asked the spy as Cohen started stalking away.

"Home," Cohen admitted, not saying that he wasn't sure any longer where that was. Suspect's newly dug grave in the backyard had turned the garden into a cemetery. It was no place for a Cohen to live.

· 32 ·

When he parked behind the old YMCA football stadium—
two wheels on the sidewalk—there had been room in front
and back. Now an old station wagon plastered with SAVE
THE GOLAN and HEBRON FOREVER stickers was bumper to
bumper behind his Ford Sierra, and a new Japanese car was
bumper to bumper in front.

Inside the car, he plugged in the cellular phone through
the cigarette lighter. It immediately rang to tell him he had
four voice mail messages. He pulled out his little pad and
started to make notes as the phone spilled its stories.

Hagit had called, just to report that she was finally at
home with the baby, and that she had decided to agree with
Bendor's plan for a ceremony at Negev headquarters in
Beersheba. The damage to Nissim's body, however, made
it useless to the medical school for the students, so she had
decided on a funeral at the tiny cemetery in Yeroham.

"Cohen, it's Raoul," came the next message, the pathologist calling to report the same about Nissim's body—and
that yes, the riddle of the cause of death was where Nissim
took the bullets, not where his car, carrying the already
dead body, was pushed into the wadi. "But I hear your case
goes back a long way," said the doctor, already three years
past official retirement and holding out for another two, so
counting his twenty years in Argentina, he'd have thirty-
five years saved in *pensia*.

"They're already gossiping," said Cohen, his paranoia growing. The situation was maddening, twisted, unreal. We're all innocent until proven guilty, he reminded himself.

The fourth message was from Rafi Peri in the hotel. "You wanted to know if they were leaving. They are. Two cars. Seven-seaters. Black unmarked Mercedes. From what I understand, they're heading down to Tel Aviv."

Cohen worked up an angry sweat in the few minutes it took for him to get out of the tight parking spot. Driving down the narrow street, he passed the tourist who had been photographing the hotel and the Y. He was getting into a rented car.

The tourist turned his head as Cohen passed and Cohen's paranoia shifted gears once again, convincing him that the tourist had turned his own face away from Cohen with the same instinct that Cohen had followed when he had become aware of the camera lens pointing at the hotel—with him and Amos in the frame—only a little while ago.

Still, the murder of the cat was madness, not professionalism. The mad make mistakes. That was his only comfort as he cursed his way through the claustrophobic clog of traffic in the heart of town until finally he was on the highway speeding west toward Tel Aviv, hoping without much reason to believe he'd succeed, to catch up with the two black Mercedes.

· 33 ·

Bernstein, for sure. But what was the aunt's first name? It
was a Jewish name, he remembered. Sarah. Rachel. What?
He reached into his memory, trying to see in his mind's
eye the flimsy white paper with its faded purple lines and
his Hebrew handwriting. The name, the address, a phone
number. Hannah. That was it, Hannah Bernstein.

She was ready, willing, even eager to get the girl. "I never
understood why Irwin stayed in Jerusalem. Such a pathetic
little town. Yes. Send me the girl. I will take care of her."

Why did he send her, why did he trust her? He asked her
a few questions. The woman had money from reparations.
No, she didn't mind living among Germans. Yes, she
would be able to handle all the expenses. Including the
hospitalization and psychiatric care. No, she had no plans
to visit Israel. "Once was enough, thank you. It is not a
place for me." She was in her fifties and in her own way
(which she never mentioned) she had survived the war.
Irwin, her cousin, the father broken in Jerusalem, was
already broken by the war. Not her, she didn't have to say.
Irwin went to Palestine. She stayed in Germany. In Hamburg, "where I was born," she had said.

Yes, Hannah, that was her name.

Coming down the mountain from Jerusalem, the cellular phone found and lost its connection as he tried calling
overseas.

"Kristina Scheller's office," answered a secretary in the publishing house in Munich.

"Is Miss Scheller there?" he asked in German, realizing only after he did so that he had been pushed so far that he was now breaking one of the most basic rules of his life.

"Who is calling?"

"An author, Avram Cohen."

· A moment later, his German editor was on the line. "Avram, how are you?" Kristina fluttered. "How wonderful of you to call. It has been so long. We worry so much for you. We . . ." She was speaking in English.

He answered in German, admitting to himself that he was becoming desperate, surprising her. "Kristina, I need a favor."

"Please, what? Anything I can do."

"I need a phone number. From Hamburg. A woman named Hannah Bernstein. I know she was living in Hamburg in 1975."

"You were in Hamburg in 1975?" the editor asked with surprise.

"No, she was. Please. See if you can find her telephone number. And then call me back. Any time of day or night. Here's my new number." He recited the digits twice, to make sure she had it right, and then asked her to recite it back once to him. "I must speak with her," he said.

"May I ask what it's about?"

"I'd rather you didn't. I'd rather not explain right now."

"Is it for a book?" asked the editor.

"No, nothing like that," he protested.

"About your bombing?"

He had to pause before answering, disbelieving that she would know about what had happened that morning, but not at all sure that some quick CNN or wire service reporter might not have picked up the story already from the Voice of Israel. He decided not to mention it. "Just get back to me with the number," said Cohen. "She lived alone. Unmarried. So the phone number will be under her name."

"I have an author from Hamburg. A mystery writer who knows the police. Maybe he can help," Kristina started to explain, but Cohen felt like he was running out of time.

"Whatever," he answered. "Just see if you can find out for me a number for Hannah Bernstein."

Next he tried Ahuva at the office. She would help him straighten it all out in his head; Lerner, Zagorksy, a boy, a girl, she at least would know the right questions to ask. But a clerk said that the judge was in session and could not be disturbed for anything. "Have her call me at this number please, as soon as she can," Cohen asked, leaving the cell phone number. At least she was safe, he decided. And she knew enough so that if she didn't hear from him, she'd check into a hotel or stay with a friend.

He was following his instincts and they were frayed with fear. The unpredictable rhythm of chilly wind blowing through the open window kept him alert, as his mind raced with less control than the routine of his driving. Passing cars and trucks, he pushed the car faster, hoping that just ahead of the next barreling bus he'd spot the convoy of two black seven-seater Mercedes. All he got for his effort was a near accident, and more self-recrimination. It was burning up inside him, the fear he was totally mistaken, that paranoia, not reason, was driving him forward. He tried calling Shmulik, but there, too, only a machine answered. He left no message.

He struggled with the feeling all the way to the city, until finally, trapped in the mundane traffic of red lights and green when he got off the highway at the Tel Aviv Railway station, the wind ceased and his own thoughts settled. He drove the rest of the way to Ahuva's place with a sense of serenity that if not for the peace it provided would have frightened him with the implications of its resignation to fate. Lerner or Zagorksy, boy or girl, he knew he would encounter them. For just as he realized that no matter what happened he could never know the whole truth, he also recognized for the simplicity of the truth that it was not he who was hunting the Russian—or the boy, or the girl—but it was one of them, or both, hunting him.

Thus, the paranoia took over completely even while it felt as if it had passed. He parked in the basement lot, rode the elevator to Ahuva's floor, and used his key to get in.

He made himself some coffee and carried it to the porch beyond the sliding glass doors, pulled one of the plastic outdoor chairs close to the railing so he could put his feet up, and waited. With the sun at midday directly above, the soothing blue of the clean winter sky was changing into a glaring white. Waves were choppy on the distant surface of the sea.

Again he called her office, and again the secretary said she was in court until three and then had the rest of the day free. Again he left a message reminding her to call him on the cellular as soon as she was free.

He leaned backward, with a peripheral view that included the front door to the flat and the beach scene below. And all the while, beside his coffee cup and the ash-tray for his precious cigarettes on the little wrought-iron and marble-topped table, the matte metal handgun, its clip full and its barrel clean, waited with him. But it was neither Zagorsky nor Maya Bernstein, not even Ahuva, who surprised Cohen. His cellular phone rang. It was Shvilli.

"I've got something, boss, I've got something. It's big. Real big. Where are you?"

"Tel Aviv."

"Excellent. So am I."

"What do you have?"

"It's not for the phone. We have to meet."

Cohen decided on the cafe downstairs from Ahuva's apartment. Shvilli promised to be there "as soon as possible."

Downstairs, under a broad yellow umbrella protecting him from the harsh light of the sun swamping the city, he drank a double espresso at a table with a view of the street in one direction and the beach in the other, waiting for Shvilli. He felt exposed but alert, and, in a way, he was almost eager for them to find him, to confront him and get it over, one way or the other.

The Georgian showed up a few minutes later, taking the shallow steps up from the sidewalk three at a time, almost running to Cohen.

"Listen to this," he began, with the same breathless excitement that always accompanied his first telling of a breakthrough. "Remember Yudelstein? At that nightclub in Beersheba?"

"The fat man. The judge." Cohen remembered.

"Yes. He called me, an hour ago. Asked me if I knew how to let the police know something, without it getting back to him."

"Why you?" Cohen nearly spat the question. "See, I told you it's dangerous for you. He knows you're police. The others know."

"Maybe he knows. But I trust him."

Cohen sighed. "Nissim," he said paternally, and for a second they both froze, realizing how Freudian the slip was. "Misha," Cohen corrected himself, then repeated what he said. "You've been doing this too long. If he knows, they know."

"It doesn't matter. *They* didn't order Nissim killed. It wasn't Witkoff or Yuhewitz or even your man Zagrosky."

"Zagorsky," Cohen corrected Shvilli.

"The point is that it wasn't the bosses who ordered Nissim killed. It was a couple of their punks. I know them both. Yosef and Gregory. Dumb. Like only real muscle can be dumb. But Yosef is ambitious. Real ambitious."

"A bad combination."

"Very bad," Shvilli agreed.

"So?"

"He's the one who ambushed Nissim. Stupid, stupid, stupid," Shvilli moaned. "Just some stupid muscle trying to think for their bosses. They saw how angry Nissim made Yuhewitz, and they wanted to make a move. Decided they'd give the boss what he wanted."

"Yuhewitz didn't order it?"

Shvilli shook his head. There was disappointment in his eyes.

"Yudelstein is certain?"

Shvilli nodded. "But listen to this. Yudelstein says it has something to do with the girl."

"What about her?" Cohen demanded.

"He didn't know for sure. Something about her being seen with Nissim that night in the hotel. Jealousy, maybe?"

"I don't believe it."

"That Yudelstein told me this?"

"No, that it had to do with jealousy. You questioned Pinny more?"

"Yes."

"And?"

"That he saw them talking in the lobby. That was all."

"I know that," Cohen said softly, coldly. "Did he say anything about the muscle, these two—what are their names?"

"Yosef and Gregory."

"Yosef and Gregory. Were they in the lobby? Did Zagorsky, or for that matter, Witkoff or Yuhewitz, see Nissim with the girl?"

"Pinny didn't say anything about that."

"Did you ask him?" Cohen demanded, and immediately cut himself off. He had only himself to blame for not asking Pinny.

"No," Shvilli admitted weakly.

"Find out," Cohen ordered.

Shvilli pulled his cellular phone out of his holster.

"Wait," Cohen instructed. "Did you tell Caspi about any of this?"

"Not yet."

"Is there any evidence? Aside from Yudelstein?"

Shvilli grimaced.

"The radio this morning said Caspi brought in the Alper mother," Cohen pointed out. "He's trying to put pressure on the boys." He paused for a second, then made a decision. "You have to tell Caspi," Cohen ordered. "Now."

It was an instinctual command, but it did little to clear his own mind of all the confusion. The girl. Why should she hate him so much? Could she have manipulated the two thugs into helping her? Were they in Frankfurt that night? That helpless feeling of grasping water came back to him.

While Shvilli called first Caspi and then Pinny, Cohen got up and went to the railing overlooking the little park and the path down to the beach. Maybe the assassination of Nissim Levy had nothing to do with him. Zagorsky wasn't after him. But that left the "toy," as all the men so far had referred to the girl—or was it the boy? Cohen was not even sure anymore of that instinct that he had followed.

As if timed to give him the answer, his phone rang. Krista Scheller was on the line. "I did what you asked for, Avram," she said. "But this woman, Hannah Bernstein? She's dead. Has been for years."

It made him gasp slightly and he rubbed his chest.

The pause made her ask, "Avram? Are you there?"

"How? When?" he asked. "Are you sure?"

"My author in Hamburg, a mystery writer with connections to the police. He tells me that there was a fire in the apartment building. The poor woman didn't get out."

"There was a young girl staying with the woman then," Cohen said. "She either just had a baby or was about to have a baby. Did he say anything about her?"

"No-o," said the editor. "You should have said something, I could have asked."

"Please," he requested, "and call me back if you learn anything."

Shvilli came back to the table and sat down, grumbling to himself.

"Caspi's an asshole. He wants to know my source."

"Did you give it?"

"How could I? Caspi will go barging after Yudelstein and everything I've worked for, Nissim worked for, will go down the drain."

Cohen just nodded with sympathy. He was thinking. "What happened to the idiots. Yosef and Gregory?"

"They're being taken care of."

"Executions?"

Shvilli shrugged.

"There's something wrong in that. Wouldn't it be smarter for them to turn in the two? Loosen the pressure."

"There is no pressure. Not as far as I can tell. Nobody's going to move on Witkoff, not without direct orders from the minister."

"Unless there's proof they were involved in murder," Cohen pointed out.

"Which we don't have," Shvilli added.

They sat silently for a minute. Suddenly, Cohen realized what Shvilli forgot to tell him. "Why are you in Tel Aviv?"

"Yuhewitz is here," Shvilli said. "I should have told you

right away. Sorry. I came up with him. On the flight from Eilat."

"And you didn't get anything from him?"

Shvilli scowled at Cohen. "I didn't think this was the time to press."

"So where is he?"

Shvilli covered his eyes. "I lost him. I was stupid. He said he was being picked up for a business meeting, so couldn't offer me a ride. Someone picked him up."

"Get a license number?"

Shvilli pulled a folded piece of paper from his shirt pocket and read out the number. Cohen reached into his windbreaker jacket, which he had taken off in the surprising Tel Aviv heat of winter, when there are no clouds and the sun has time to warm the city. He pulled out his little yellow notebook and thumbed through it until he asked, "What's the number again?"

Shvilli gave it to him.

"That's one of Witkoff's cars," Cohen said with a tone of satisfaction. Finally, something logical was happening. "You think Zagorksy's with them?"

"Could be."

"With the girl?"

"He takes her everywhere."

"What more do you know about Yosef and Gregory?" Cohen asked.

"Gregory was in the Russian army. Some kind of paratrooper unit. Yosef was a boxer. And I only heard that because of some gossip. Neither is much of a talker."

"Paratrooper. That means he knows demolitions."

"You think he had something to do with the bombs?"

"Maybe," he said. But he doubted that either of the bodyguards would have had a reason to kill Suspect. "The girl?" he asked Shvilli. "She's very sexy?"

"Absolutely."

"Is she smart?"

"I don't know."

"What kind of sexy? Hot? Cold? Does she flirt? Hard to get? What?

"Well, she never flirted with me," Shvilli said.

"You sound disappointed."

"You would be, too. I watched her. She could make sure that any man who she talked to wondered if she wanted to do it with him."

"Did she have any power over Yosef and Gregory?"

"They were Yuhewitz's boys. He had the power, not her."

"But could she have used them? Influenced them?"

"I told you, she could wrap a man around her finger."

"Get back to Yudelstein. See if you can find out where Yuhewitz would meet Witkoff in Tel Aviv."

"You just told me to stay away from them, get out."

"Yes," Cohen admitted, realizing that once again he had cornered himself into an untenable position, letting Shvilli make the decision. "But we need to know."

Shvilli looked at his watch. "I need a drink," he suddenly said, waving to the waiter behind the glass windows overlooking the patio. They waited in silence for the waiter to return with a shot of frozen vodka for Shvilli, a balloon of cognac for Cohen.

"To Nissim," Shvilli said grimly, then tossed the drink down in one gulp. Cohen took a first sip to prepare his throat for the long swallow of the liquid heat, then tilted back his head for the rest.

It was Cohen who broke the silence. "It's up to you."

"We need to know what happened," Shvilli admitted. "For Nissim's sake."

"It's not for Nissim. It's for us. To get the system to confront them, once and for all."

"They'll never do it. The politicians will never let them go after them. There's too much money involved."

"If there's evidence, the police will have to act. You know that."

"Only if it's hard evidence," Shvilli said, knocking on the surface of the little table, as if to prove what's hard. "Yuhewitz is careful. Witkoff much more so. What about your Zagorksy?"

"Is protected," Cohen admitted, without explaining why. "Yuhewitz is the weakest link. Witkoff must be furious. I would be. The muscle were Yuhewitz's responsibility. His soldiers. And they screwed up. Witkoff knows that." Once again, Witkoff became a key. Cohen picked up his cellular phone, beginning to enjoy its immediacy. He punched in Ephraim Laskoff's number, then got up and went to the railing to look down on the beach, not needing Shvilli to hear the conversation.

Rose answered. Laskoff had just come in.

"Avram," Laskoff began, "I think I can close the house deal today."

"Forget the house, that's not why I'm calling. I need to know what you have on those names I gave you. Alexander Witkoff . . ."

"The banker. Or at least wants to own a bank. There's no way he's going to get one, not after what I heard this morning."

"What? What?"

"That the Russian police want to question him about the top three officers at the bank he owns in Moscow getting murdered just before he arrived here as a new immigrant."

"When did you hear that?"

"You asked me to ask around. I did."

"Why is he a suspect?"

"According to my sources, he wanted to cover his

money trail. The managers knew the truth. He didn't want the truth known."

"I hear he makes contributions. Lots of contributions."

"He can afford it. According to my sources, he's sitting on at least half a billion dollars in his own investments. Not counting money he's raised for his finance company. Can you believe it? They wouldn't give him a license to open a bank, but they let him open a financing house. For foreign investors."

"What does that mean?"

"That he can take foreign currency, invest it locally, and pay out in foreign currency. No questions asked."

"That's what you do."

"No, officially I'm a consultant. Remember, you signed powers of attorney. But I don't guarantee you interest from an account. I just make professional decisions for you to keep your money. He guarantees interest and can lend, as well as invest."

"So he can run a laundry."

"Yes."

"What about Yuhewitz?"

"Now there's something interesting."

"What?"

"Three weeks ago, bids were opened for a coastland project just south of the Eilat port. Bids ranged from seven to fourteen million. Yuhewitz was signed to a twenty-five-million bid. They had to accept. Says he's planning a hotel and entertainment center. The Tourism minister's in love with the man. We're talking about a hundred-million-dollar investment on his part. God knows how much the ministry will shovel him in subsidies."

"South of the port?"

"Just north of the border."

"You're sure?"

"Avram? Have I ever told you anything about which I was not certain?"

For the first time that morning, Cohen smiled, barely. "Thanks, Ephraim."

"No, wait, wait a minute. What did you mean, 'forget about the house'? What are you talking about?"

"Before that, what about Zagorsky?"

"Nothing on him. Nothing. Nobody heard of him. Nobody in the city. He's neither a buyer nor a seller. Not here, at least. Not through the banks here."

"Makes sense," Cohen muttered to himself.

"What? What did you say?"

"Nothing."

"Are we done on these names?"

"Yes," Cohen said.

"Good. Now, tell me about what you meant."

Cohen took a deep breath, knowing what would follow. "I changed my mind," he said.

There was a long pause, then Laskoff said, "You're joking, no?"

"Ephraim? Have you ever known me to make jokes?"

"Why? Why? After all we went through on this?"

"I changed my mind. People change. Places change. Life changes." Cohen stated it bluntly, in a matter-of-fact tone. "There's nothing wrong with that. Nothing that can be done about it."

"Just a few weeks ago, you were ready to pay a fortune—"

"You need an explanation?" Cohen demanded, almost angrily. But he trusted Laskoff and valued the man's friendship, so he quickly added, "I promise I'll explain. But not now. There are some things I have to take care of. Next week maybe," he promised. "Lunch."

"What do I tell the heirs?" Laskoff moaned.

"That they taught me something about greed," said Cohen with the same simplicity that he used earlier. "And I appreciated the lesson."

Laskoff knew Cohen well enough not to be astounded, but he had to ask, "That's all?"

"What else do I have to tell them?"

"They might sue. We signed some memorandums of understanding."

"Settle it."

"How do I know you won't change your mind again?"

"You'll have to trust me," said Cohen. He turned to look at Shvilli, who was finishing his own phone call. "I have to go. I'll be in touch."

"That's what you always say. And whenever you get in touch, it's a crisis," Laskoff complained.

But Cohen knew that Laskoff loved the occasional excitement that he brought into the private banker's life. "Good-bye, Ephraim," he said gently, cutting off the conversation and closing the phone. Shvilli was doing the same. Cohen went back to the table.

"You still think that bombing in Frankfurt, and what happened this morning, are connected to what happened to Nissim?" asked the undercover man.

Cohen pulled at an earlobe. "No, and yes."

"Usually it's yes and no."

"It's an unusual situation," admitted Cohen.

"You haven't explained it to me."

"I'm not certain myself."

"You have to trust me," said Shvilli.

"I do trust you."

"You're not telling me something."

Cohen nodded, almost sadly. "It has nothing to do with Nissim, or you. And I'm not even sure if it's true. It's my gut talking to me, not my mind. And you know how much I hate that."

"Yes."

Again silence fell between them.

"You were right," said Shvilli. "I talked to Yudelstein again. He says that Witkoff went crazy when he heard that Yuhewitz's boys did Nissim."

"Did he tell you where we can find them?"

Shvilli's smile grew until the row of gold teeth on his lower left jaw twinkled in the sun.

"They're at Witkoff's," he said.

· 34 ·

They weren't surprised to find a pair of black Mercedes parked in the beating sunlight outside the tall apartment building, the two drivers doubling as guards in the shade of the building's entrance. Cohen rolled slowly past the building. "You know them?" he asked Shvilli, then quickly added, "more important, do they know you?"

Shvilli shook his head. "No. Who are they?"

"Zagorksy's drivers."

"So he's here, too."

Cohen nodded.

"How are we going to do this?" Shvilli asked, as Cohen parked.

Cohen thought. "Casually and cautiously," he finally said. "Pass me the cane on the floor in the back," he instructed Shvilli.

"What's this for?" asked the Georgian.

"I twisted my ankle a couple of months ago, needed it for a few days," said Cohen, taking the short staff. "You're accompanying me to the orthopedic surgeon's, for a consultation," he told Shvilli.

Cohen hobbled up the path to the building, leaning heavily on the cane. Shvilli walked slowly beside him. As they approached the guards, Cohen said in a whining voice to Shvilli, "The doctor better give me some better painkillers." Shvilli just nodded.

One of the guards flicked away a cigarette and watched the old man on the cane approaching. He said something in Russian to the other guard and neither challenged Cohen and Shvilli.

With the elevator doors closed, Cohen dropped the cane and pulled out his Beretta, pulling back the barrel to cock it. Shvilli did the same with his Desert Eagle .457, a much larger gun than Cohen's, which the undercover man kept in an armpit holster under his brown suede leather jacket.

They rode silently, as if they had done so hundreds of times before, though only once many years before had Cohen and Shvilli been together so close to the edge. But just before the elevator doors opened, Shvilli smiled and said, "You know what that asshole downstairs said?"

"No."

"That he pitied me for having such a whining father."

Cohen grimaced, and then the elevator started to slow down at the sixteenth floor. They stood facing the elevator doors, waiting for the ride to end and the doors to slide open, their guns already pointed toward whatever lay beyond those doors.

The elevator stopped. Cohen's finger moved from the trigger guard to the trigger. Shvilli did the same. The door slid open. A guard was waiting, but stupidly, too casually for his profession, his mini-Uzi was slung over his shoulder, not pointing back at them.

Cohen's gun, already drawn waist high as the doors opened, moved quickly upward to aim between the guard's eyes as he stepped into the landing area, shoving the guard backward up against the wall. Shvilli unslung the Uzi, held his own gun barrel to pursed lips and hissed "Shh . . ."

Nothing else was spoken, but it was clear what the guard was thinking. How far did his loyalty to his boss go? Cohen's eyes asked the guard the same question as he pointed with his free hand to the penthouse door, his Beretta rock-still and aimed at the guard's face, his smile more menacing than ever.

For a flicker of a second, the guard's eyes seemed to calculate his chances. Cohen shook his head, still silent, still smiling, still pointing with his left hand at the apartment door, still keeping his eyes locked on the guard's.

Shvilli added a jab with the Uzi into the guard's kidneys. It made the guard stand straighter for a second of pain, but then like air let out of a balloon whatever remained of his self-confidence drained away. His shoulders slumped.

Keeping his gun trained on the hair ridge over the guard's nose, Cohen backed the guard toward the apartment door.

Just then, the muffled sounds of a voice rising into a shout could be heard behind the brass and fake-wood door. The guard looked back with worry at Cohen, who just nodded his command. Shvilli rang the bell, but not before he had the Uzi slung over his shoulder, his finger on the trigger, the safety set to automatic.

The three-tone melody instantly silenced the shouting inside. An instant later the door opened, held by yet another broad-muscled guard, the angry question on his face turning into surprise at the sight of the old man wielding the Beretta and Shvilli with the Uzi.

A man's voice from inside the apartment called out something in Russian.

"He wants to know who we are," Shvilli whispered to Cohen.

For a moment, riding up the elevator, Cohen had thought they could both die when the elevator doors opened. The thought flashed through his mind without fear or regret, but merely a recognition of the odds that should have been against him except for one thing and one

thing alone. The very self-confidence and sense of immunity with which the bodyguards and their bosses exuded
their control prevented them from imagining a threat from
an old man, indeed from anyone other than their known
competitors. It was his gamble, and luck, as he knew so
well, could only be created by taking chances, controlling
time itself.

"They're about to find out," Cohen said.

· 35 ·

Everyone in the room froze at the sight of Cohen and Shvilli's entrance, the two guards with their hands held high pushed forward weaponless in front of the invaders.

Cohen scanned the room. Witkoff was in the rocking chair, at the head of the meeting; Zagorksy to the host's right, Yuhewitz to his left. The girl was nowhere to be seen. Nor was Witkoff's blonde. Cohen stole a glance into the kitchen. It was empty.

Three other men were in the room. Two were probably bookkeepers or lawyers, thought Cohen. The third was the tourist Cohen had seen with the camera outside the King David. His eyes narrowed on seeing Cohen, but he said nothing.

Cohen motioned with his head for the two guards they had taken captive to move across the room. They obeyed, hands high in the air. Witkoff started to rise from his chair. Shvilli waved the mini-Uzi to indicate the host should sit down.

Yuhewitz snarled something in Russian at Shvilli.

Cohen let off a shot into the ceiling, surprising even Shvilli. Witkoff threw his hands over his head, Yuhewitz fell to the ground. "Silence," Cohen added softly. "Get up," he said to the Eilat boss. Zagorksy only smiled slightly. It was the same smile that made the scar across the Russian's face grow, which Cohen had recognized from twenty years before when watching the video in the brothel.

"Misha?" Witkoff asked, indicating he meant Shvilli, the tone of the question neither rhetorical nor curious. His eyes went to Yuhewitz, who was trying not to shake in his seat. Witkoff said something in Russian.

Cohen swung his gun to aim at Witkoff. "Silence, I said." Witkoff fell silent.

"What did he say?" Cohen asked Shvilli.

"That Yuhewitz is an idiot."

"Mr. Cohen," Witkoff suddenly said in a friendly tone. "I am so glad to meet you. Your book was wonderful." He spoke a simple Hebrew with a strained attempt not to let the Russian accent through, which of course only made it stronger.

"This is Cohen?" Yuhewitz asked, his voice trembling.

Everyone ignored him. In the distance, beyond the open window to the sea, the sound of a propeller plane taking off from Sde Dov Airport was the only sound in the room—except for Cohen's heart, pounding away inside his chest, the pulse beating under his skull.

"The girl," Cohen finally said, breaking the silence, then snapped, "Higher!" at one of the bodyguards, whose arms appeared to be slowly lowering. There was the sound of cloth tearing as the guard's jacket tore at the armpit. Nobody smiled.

"The girl," said Witkoff, calmly. He looked at Zagorsky. So did Cohen.

"She had nothing to do with it," said Zagorksy, but the conviction in his tone was hollow.

"Enough of that," Witkoff reprimanded Zagorksy, and his eyes went back to Cohen. "Yes, the girl. How stupid, no? Love is stupid, no?"

"Stop it," Zagorksy demanded.

"I know what happened," Cohen said.

"So you know I had nothing to do with it," Yuhewitz piped up. "It was all her fault."

"No," said Witkoff, nodding toward Zagorksy. "It was actually his."

"Where is she?" Cohen demanded. "Here? In the apartment? Where?" His cellular phone suddenly rang from inside his jacket pocket. He ignored it.

The sudden trill of a woman's laugh answered Cohen's question.

Strange, he thought, as she came into the room from a side door to Cohen's left, followed by the buxom blonde who had opened the door for him only a few days earlier. The mole was smaller than he remembered. All those artist sketches were misleading. He wondered how he could have made such a mistake.

But there was no time for wondering now. The girl, tall, tightly wrapped in a pair of jeans and a white T-shirt, paused as she came into the living room, and scanned all the faces until she settled on Cohen. Her green eyes were as cold as her father's, as cold as her uncle's.

They seemed almost amused, those eyes, with none of the fear—nor surprise—that he could see in the expressions of all the other people in the room. If anything, there was a slight measure of disappointment, as if she were hoping for a more worthy adversary.

There was no doubt now, as far as he was concerned. Her hands were casually jammed into her rear pockets, and if not for the circumstances she could have been a model posing for a provocative advertisement for the T-shirt, or perhaps the jeans, or even a perfume. Behind her was Witkoff's desk, a gleaming wooden surface unmarred by papers. They were all staring at her now, except the blonde, whose eyes worriedly shifted between Cohen and her boss Witkoff.

"The Jerusalem policeman," the girl finally said, in German. Her voice was soft and had a natural hoarseness that made it sound like a whisper. "Avram Cohen." There was no disguising the hatred.

He nodded. "Raise your hands."

She held them out to show she held nothing. Her eyes glittered with expectation.

Witkoff asked Zagorksy something in Russian. Again Cohen fired a bullet from the pistol into the ceiling over Witkoff's head.

Both Russians blanched, the bookkeeper and the tourist—Cohen still wanted to know what *he* was all about—threw themselves to the floor, hands over their heads.

"Quiet," Cohen said softly, his voice a deep rumble. "Hebrew. English. German. No Russian," he ordered, with a cold half-grin on his face. "But first, quiet." He turned to the girl. "Why?" he asked her in German.

She only smiled. Her black hair was cut in a bob, her lipstick a bloody red. There was another lipstick smudge on her cheek and Cohen realized it was the same dark orange on the blonde's lips.

"Why?" Cohen repeated. "The bombs? The murders? What was it all for?"

Zagorksy answered for her. "She is obsessed," he said sadly.

"And you knew this?" Witkoff asked. "And let her come here?"

Cohen fired a third time. He could only assume that somewhere in the neighborhood someone would hear the shots and call the police. It was going to be their only way out. But he needed something solid from someone—the girl, Zagorksy, Yuhewitz, someone—if the plan were to work.

He looked at the girl. There was nothing masculine about her. He had no doubt that she was the young woman he had seen in the corridor in the hotel. He had been wrong.

"Do you have a son?" he suddenly asked Zagorksy, surprising them all, except the girl, whose laugh trilled again, softer, slighter, but no less provocatively than her stance. Zagorsky nodded.

"Is he here?"

Zagorksy shook his head.

The blonde started to whimper in fear. Witkoff told her to be quiet.

The bigger guard, the one who opened the door to them, suddenly took a step forward. Without warning, Cohen fired the Beretta, knowing his aim. The heavy man dropped to the floor, gasping, not screaming, clutching a shattered knee.

Witkoff didn't move. Yuhewitz moaned. Zagorksy shook his head with dismay. The girl smiled. And still, Cohen's expression didn't change.

"There are sixteen more bullets in this," Cohen said softly. "And plenty more in that," he pointed to the Uzi in Shvilli's hands.

"I must get out of here—" one of the bookkeepers spluttered.

"Quiet!" both Witkoff and Zagorsky snapped at him simultaneously.

"Now tell me," Cohen demanded of the girl, "why. Why do you hate me so much? To kill? Why?"

The girl spat.

"Why?" Cohen asked the girl again with a patience that belied the pounding in his veins, the thudding in his head.

An executive jet at the airport runway far beyond the open sliding window made a distant roar as it took off. The girl turned to look over her shoulder out the window, ignoring Cohen for a second.

Then she turned back. "My mother hated you," the girl finally said in a simple voice. "She hated you and I hate you. It is simple, no?"

"I helped her," Cohen protested.

"You sent her to hell," the girl shot back. "And me with her," she added bluntly.

"This is hell?" Zagorksy broke in. "You said you loved me."

"You bought me," she shot back at him. "I sold you what you wanted."

"I helped her," Cohen protested again to the girl.

The girl laughed at that. "Helped her? You sent her to that witch."

"Her aunt?"

"Ha!" the girl cried.

"You were a baby. How could you know?"

"She told me everything. Everything."

"That your uncle is your father?"

"They're both dead."

"Yes," Cohen admitted. The jailed twin had been murdered in his bed in Ramle prison two years after his arrival in the jail. "But I had nothing to do with that."

"You sent her away. To the witch. So I'd end up like this. Here."

"Idiot," Witkoff shouted at Zagorsky, adding something more in Russian.

"Quiet!" Cohen shouted, then asked Shvilli to translate.

" 'You brought her here,' " the Georgian quoted Witkoff. " 'You knew this and brought her here.' "

"She didn't tell me this. She told me he had arrested her mother. Sent her to the gutter in Germany. That's what she told me."

"And did you tell him," Cohen asked Zagorksy, pointing toward Witkoff, "that you knew me, too?"

"You know him?" Witkoff asked, astounded.

Zagorksy shook his head with dismay, not denial.

At the far end of the room, the tourist from outside the King David was suddenly leaning forward tensely. But Cohen needed to know more from the girl.

"Who made the bomb?" Cohen tried asking her.

She laughed. "It is so difficult? Only men can do this?"

"Who taught you?"

"A man," she said, in a matter-of-fact manner that made it clear she could get any man to do anything for her, if she decided.

"Yosef," Yuhewitz said. "She fucked him and he did anything she asked."

"He did not," she protested. "The devices were mine. Mine."

"Why Nissim? Why have him killed?"

She shrugged. "You sent my mother to die, why shouldn't I send your loved ones to die?"

"What are they talking about?" Witkoff demanded again from Zagorksy.

But Zagorksy was staring at the girl, ignoring the question. "You used me," he finally realized.

She laughed at him. "And you didn't use me? That's the way the world works. I use you, you use me. We all use each other, no? And those who don't know how to do it, well, they lose."

"Please, no . . ." Zagorksy said softly, staring at her.

The girl mocked him. "Please . . . please . . . you're surprised?" she answered him with a question. "Such a big man you are, so important. You have killed, no? Arranged killing, no? And you, too, Alex, you too have done such things," she added to Witkoff. "But not me? Why not me? He killed," she added, pointing at Cohen. "This, this, saint . . ." she snarled the word. "He says so in the book."

"I saved your mother," Cohen protested. "I didn't kill her."

"You sent her to hell. And that's where I was born," the girl said in a matter-of-fact voice. The grin, a scowl really, grew slowly across her face. Her eyes narrowed as her hands moved back to her hips. She leaned backward against the broad desk behind her.

The thumping inside his skull had been growing stronger all morning. Maybe that's why he remembered too late the switchblade letter opener on the desk.

"And that's where I'm going to send you!" she cried out, reaching behind her and then throwing, with no little expertise, the pointed knife straight at him.

He dodged too late, and the knife struck deep into his lower chest. He gasped, and knew from the pain that the knife had lodged in his lower lung. He fired nonetheless, yet knowing he would miss, watching as the girl acrobatically rolled over the desk to hide.

Shvilli swung to fire. "No," Cohen gasped, wondering absurdly what other tricks she knew. Shvilli halted.

"Maya!" Zagorksy cried out, as the girl reappeared from behind the desk, a gun held with two hands, aiming at Cohen.

He dropped to the floor as she fired, landing on his side, aware of the knife lodged in his ribs digging deeper into his lung. He didn't have the breath to shout at Shvilli this time. The Uzi burst and Cohen looked up.

The girl was looking down at her perfect breasts, with disbelief that turned into a strange look of satisfaction as she looked up at Cohen. Her cold green eyes rolled back, and she dropped.

He grunted as he pulled the knife out of his side and again as he rose to his feet, the pounding in his head echoing the submachine gun bullets that had rocked the penthouse living room.

Blood drained from his wound, a growing rivulet that he tried stemming with one hand, the Beretta still aimed with the other.

"Boss," Shvilli cried out, "I've got it, you can rest. Sit down. Lie down, boss . . ."

"I'll wait," he gasped. He looked around the room. Zagorksy was sitting forward in his chair, a hand over his eyes. Witkoff was watching Cohen carefully. The blonde was in shock, too frightened to speak, let alone whimper. Yuhewitz was sweating profusely, his teeth chattering. The two bookkeepers were silent. So were the two guards, one wounded, the other tense but frozen. But the mysterious tourist was smiling at Cohen and suddenly he realized that no matter what happened next, there would always remain that man's presence in the meeting as a mystery for which he doubted he'd ever have an answer. In the distance, he could hear sirens. A neighbor must have called, Cohen thought. He looked down at his shirt. Blood was trickling between his fingers down his shirt.

Suddenly, the roar of beating helicopter blades swerved close to the building and then backed away. The unit, Cohen figured. Gunshots would mean terrorists. They sent the unit. He looked at the blood on his fingers and suddenly thought foolishly, I'm too old for this. A strong wave of exhaustion swept over his body with a thrashing warmth. But still, he remained standing. The phone rang in the apartment. Shvilli looked at him. Cohen shook his head. "I'll get it. Keep them covered." His voice came out as a raspy whisper, the breath painful and short.

He went to the desk, each step painful, slowly stepping around the table to the body of the dead girl. He looked down at her lifeless eyes, still open. Only then did he pick up the receiver, the splattered blood sticky on the plastic. He said hello, and then listened to the voice at the other end, aware that everyone—except Shvilli—was staring at him.

"It is safe now," he said to the negotiating officer on the end of the line. There was a pause and then he said, "I am retired Deputy Commander Avram Cohen. We will need ambulances." Then he hung up, too tired to talk anymore.

Nonetheless, even after the medics ripped away his shirt and put the first bandage on him before strapping him into the stretcher for the ride down the elevator, out into the bright sun and then into the cool shade of the ambulance, he forced himself to stay awake.

Only in the ambulance carrying him to the hospital did he dare close his eyes. When he awoke, he thought, as the siren began its whoop, he'd tell Ahuva that he was moving to Tel Aviv. Maybe she'd let him move in. "Maybe," he murmured out loud, before dropping into the welcoming darkness.

ABOUT THE AUTHOR

Born and raised in Boston, and living in Israel since 1973, Robert Rosenberg has been writing professionally since 1976, in a career that has spanned daily, weekly, and monthly journalism, as well as the Avram Cohen mysteries.

In 1995 he founded Ariga, an online web 'zine publishing for business, pleasure and peace in the Middle East at http://www.ariga.com

He lives in Tel Aviv with his wife, the artist Silvia Cherbakoff, and their daughter, Amber.

Printed in the United States
1087200002B/1-18

9 780743 244169